Vowed

Farseen Chronicles Book 6

N. R. Tucker

ISBN- 13 978-0-9907163-6-5

Chapter 1

The incoming portal alarm glowed as it pulsated red and orange. With a growl, Ryan closed his laptop and hurried down the hallway. Was it too much to ask to have a quiet shift? His first day as the senior shifter liaison at PAC HQ and someone created an unauthorized gate event inside the facility. Why didn't they open a gate out in the woods and walk through the checkpoint without setting off the alarms?

Unless it's an attack. Ryan picked up the pace and ran.

The portal alarm had been established to notify everyone in headquarters that someone had opened a gate event at the portal, the only place inside the facility where a gate event could be opened. All arrivals were color-coded, with a pulse for the color-blind, for authorized events. For unauthorized gate events, the sound and color code were obnoxious by design. Any gate that opened inside headquarters would not fully open for two minutes, allowing security to arrive before the visitor.

Ryan arrived at the same time as Liron, a representative from the Northern Realm. The other fae representatives were already in place, as were the wizards and vampires.

"Anyone know anything?" Ryan waved toward the portal.

"No." Sam, the shifter currently responsible for portal activities, narrowed his eyes on the portal. "Orders?"

Ryan glared at the portal. "Prepare to fire."

At Ryan's words, the four guards standing around the portal brought their weapons to bear on the platform. Those in the

1

gallery saw the movement and everyone, human or preternatural, who could be somewhere else, left.

"Is that our only option?" Liron asked. He was at heart a bard and a peacemaker. He hated to see a life wasted. "I don't know who it is, or what their purpose is, but allow them to explain."

"No," Ryan moved between Sam and Liron. The shifters were responsible for headquarters security this shift. There had been clashes between shifter, wizard, vampire, and fae security teams worked together, so security duties now rotated each shift. "There are no do-overs. If they don't have authorization, they die."

"Wait," Willow ran up to Ryan. Breathing hard to catch her breath she faced him. "The arrival is authorized. Temp... er, Lady Tempest just called it in."

Ryan barely prevented the eye roll at Willow's slip. The shifters used fae titles at PAC Headquarters just to make sure no one felt slighted. It had been hard for some to adjust their thinking.

Sam pegged Willow with a hard stare, "You sure? The authorizations are valid?"

She pursed her lips at the questions. Willow was no longer a child of their clan. She served as one of the Sovereign's Personal Assistants. "Yes, I'm sure. Yes, I validated the authorization."

Liron and Ryan both breathed a sigh of relief. No life would be wasted today, and no one would fire the first shot in the next preternatural war.

Before Willow could say more, the gate congealed on the portal platform. A tall woman exited and placed her hands on her hips. Her braided white blonde hair wrapped around her head and still the loose end of the braid reached her waist. Her voice carried throughout the gallery. "Where is my brother's eldest?"

All movement at the main entrance of PAC Headquarters stopped. The humans and preternaturals from the Seen looked over in confusion. The fae from the Farseen bowed. They bowed low.

Liron welcomed the unexpected visitor, pitching his voice so that Ryan would hear her name and title. "Lady Z, daughter of Queen Niamh and sister to Lord Ellwood, welcome to the Seen and the Preternatural Alliance for Communication Headquarters, PAC HQ if you prefer.

Willow bowed as the shifters had been taught to do with high-ranking fae. "Welcome to the Seen, Lady Zylina. Lady Tempest will be here momentarily."

"Call me Lady Z or Z, and we'll get along just fine. Call me by that horrendous name again, and I shall blast you into one of the less friendly dimensions." Lady Z's tone was matter of fact as if sending someone to another dimension wasn't a big deal.

Ryan recognized the name but had foolishly assumed her long dead. He moved to stand in front of Lady Z with Willow at his back. If Lady Z were to start slinging powers, he would protect Willow as best he could. It was then he noticed Lady Z was eye level with him and wasn't wearing heels. She was six feet, three inches tall and just as muscular as Tempe.

Lady Z raked him with a glare before a wicked smile spread across her face. "You must be Ryan, the young alpha everyone compares to Val. I don't see the resemblance myself, but perhaps it will become plain when you do something foolish. Do you plan to be a fool today?"

Ryan didn't know if he should laugh or be insulted. He noticed the fae representatives, except for Liron, inched away from him, and Ryan conceded that perhaps he should be worried. Liron, who had become a friend of sorts, remained by Ryan's side. Ryan appreciated the show of support. Before he could think up a suitable reply, another voice reverberated throughout the gallery.

"Lady Z, if you try to provoke Ryan the way you did Val, you will quickly find Ryan is ruled by his brain and his compassion, not his heart, nor his arrogance." Tempe approached the portal with Lady Sierra.

"You left out avarice," Sierra muttered softly. Tempe leveled a hard stare at her, and Sierra tilted her head in acknowledgment of her inappropriate comment.

Walking past the throng of fae who bowed so low they might as well have kissed the floor while they were down there, Tempe waved a dismissive hand. "Go about your business. Lady Z is here to see me."

The fae scattered.

"Where is this shifter of yours, and the quads? I have gifts to bestow." Lady Z breezed past the guards and headed for the main door.

At ease! In addition to the mental order, Tempe sent a quick hand signal to Ryan before he tried to stop Lady Z, who left the portal without permission. *No reason to prove to everyone in the gallery that Lady Z is the apex predator in the room.*

Ryan hated receiving orders directly into his head. He glared at her, but she didn't notice. Tempe rushed to catch up, and Ryan bit back a grin. It was nice to see someone knock Tempe off balance.

"Liron, remind the Northern Realm that prior notice of visitors is expected."

Liron shrugged. "Strictly speaking, Lady Z is not a member of the Northern Realm. She lives as an unaligned fae, moving about as she sees fit.

Ryan nodded his understanding and left. Lady Z was more powerful than he assumed. Only the strongest ruling fae chose to live unaligned. It was a title customarily bestowed on fae who had been kicked out of their realm. They had no safe harbor and no realm backing. He had believed only Father Aldous made that choice freely.

*****

"I will gladly introduce you to both, but gifts are not necessary." Tempe followed her aunt out past the guards and into Bide Park. As they walked, every fae bowed low as soon as they recognized Lady Tempest's companion. Tempe smothered a smile. For once, they were more afraid of someone other than her. She had forgotten how much she enjoyed that.

"Gifts are never necessary, but I will do no less for the quads than I did for the shifter triplets and the human child."

"The triplets? The human? You never met them." Tempe had not seen Lady Z in a thousand years. The possibility her adventurous aunt had finally found a dimension where she wasn't adored by the elementals had been in her mind recently. Tempe knew a gift had been given to Layton, but as he was mostly fae, it was to be expected. Not necessarily desired but expected nonetheless. It would help if the fae witch bestowing a gift on the child warned the family what the talent was, but that rarely happened. A gift was between the witch and the recipient.

"Not in the strictest sense, but I did come to the Seen to bestow on each a gift. The elementals tell me when something big

4

happens in the family. This time I thought to visit with you while presenting the quads their gifts. I came years ago to present the triplets their gifts. I also gave that lovely human male a gift that has passed down to your great-grandson." Lady Z found a flat rock and patted it as she sat down. Pleased to be outside, she took a deep breath and coughed. Once the burn in her lungs eased, Lady Z sent out feelers to the elementals. Just as she feared, the people of the Seen were not taking care of their planet.

Tempe sighed and sat as instructed. No wonder her offspring were so powerful. The most powerful fae witch to ever walk the dimensions snuck into the Seen and gave out gifts. "You should have told me you had been so generous. I would have known to train them."

Lady Z huffed, "Why ever for? You wanted normal. You didn't want your children to be pawns of your father. I'm afraid my foolish brother nearly ruined you. I find myself pleased you stood against him."

"You're pleased? Well, that makes it all right, doesn't it?" Tempe stood, her eyes turning black as night as she fell into the same argument they had any time they met. "If you had stayed Val would still be alive." You could have protected him. You could have protected all of us." Lady Z returned to the Farseen for visits, but she was forever traveling and would be gone for centuries at a time.

"No. Had I stayed I would have been forced to kill Ellwood and take his place as the Forrest Lord of the Northern Realm. I didn't want my brother dead, and I had no desire to rule the realm. We both know I'm selfish enough to refuse to take-one-for-the-team, as the humans say." Lady Z patted the stone again.

Tempe took a deep breath and struggled to reign in her temper. Her eyes returned to their normal jade green as she sat back down. Tempe didn't speak but continued to glare at her aunt.

Lady Z raised both eyebrows, "Child, you are my brother's daughter. You know we're a selfish species. We put ourselves first."

Tempe snorted. That was true. The easiest way to get help from a fae was to prove the action would not impact them at all. The fae rarely helped if it would cause them discomfort unless the cost was worth what they would gain.

"I was saddened by the death of your mother. She was a proper lady, and I remember fondly the chats we had over the centuries." Lady Z's face sobered. "What a disreputable way to end a good life. I would be pleased to assist you in removing from this dimension the fools who caused her death."

And that was the reason Tempe respected her aunt. Lady Z was as self-centered as Lord Ellwood, but she didn't tolerate injustice of any kind. She could also be kind upon occasion.

Tempe inclined her head. "Rayna's children avenged her death in the same way her life was taken, publicly."

"Excellent." Lady Z stood. "Do you prefer to open the way or shall I? Oh, wait. I believe it's called a gate event now. How amusing. Shall I open the gate event?"

Tempe hesitated, "Could we discuss the gifts before you bestow them?"

"Of course not. Once I meet them, I will be able to determine which gift will serve the quads best." Lady Z smiled happily.

Tempe pinched the bridge of her nose and told her head to stop pounding. She opened the gate to Beryl Lane and walked through. Her feet kept time to the throbbing of her head.

Chapter 2

Next time she wouldn't have her phone on speaker. The vow played like a mantra in Sage's head. Ryan called to warn them about Tempe's visitor, and Kyan moved into protector mode and tried to stow Sage back in Calabozo for safekeeping. The two of them had been in Tempe's office when the call came in, and Sage had put her phone on speaker. It frequently saved time when receiving reports from the alphas as Sage included Kyan in most discussions anyway. His knowledge and experience were invaluable to her. This time it worked against her.

As Sage and Kyan entered the room, he glanced out the window and commented, "They're here. Lady Tempest is bringing Lady Z to meet the quads. Let's reduce the number of shifters in this room."

"Who's Lady Z?" Lucas asked from the kitchen where he was washing dishes.

"Lord Ellwood's twin sister," Star replied. She and Joey entered from the room that accessed Calabozo. They each held one of their twins, Lexus and Xander. She glanced over at Kyan, "Lady Tempest told me to bring the twins to meet their great aunt."

None of the shifters in the room moved. Most were shocked to learn that Lord Ellwood had a sister and stared at Star.

Bryce huffed, "If you're not related to Tempe, disappear. Lady Z is described as the strongest witch ever to be born in the Farseen. She makes a mockery of Crystal's powers."

Eyebrows rose at that announcement, with many of the shifters mimicking Tempe's trademark facial expression. Crystal was credited with creating most of the spells and enchantments referenced in the stories of The Brothers Grimm. She had been a powerhouse, and it had taken a task force to kill her.

"Does that make her a wicked scary fae?" Lucas asked with a grin.

Some humans, mostly the AIB and IGI had dusted off the fairy tales and used them as proof of the evil intentions of the fae. The phrase 'wicked scary fae' had become common, even on some of the mainstream news stations and websites.

"Wicked scary fae witch," Logan amended with a matching grin.

Fred, cousin to the twins and another PA for the sovereign, stood up and placed a firm hand on Logan's shoulder, pegging Lucas with a hard stare.

Since their cousin was nearly six and a half feet of well-maintained muscle, both teenagers quelled noticeably. Fred headed for the entrance to the shifter underground headquarters. He didn't release Logan, forcing the teenager to scramble to keep up. "Sage, with your permission, I'll take anyone not needed here to Calabozo."

Sage inclined her head. "Excellent idea." At least Fred asked. Whenever there was a slim chance of danger, Kyan became a tyrant. She knew who Lady Z was and wanted to meet the powerful fae. Tempe spoke of her aunt with respect, and there were few in the Farseen, or Seen for that matter, who elicited that response from her.

Bryce opened the door in time for everyone in the house to hear Lady Z. "We've stood out here, admiring the mountains, long enough. Your shifter sent as many of his clan away as he could. I'm ready to give the quads their gifts."

"Lady Z, welcome to our home. No gifts are required." Bryce donned his expressionless lawyer face. He wasn't sure what gifts she meant, but fae gifts were not to be taken lightly. Gifts from fae witches were rarely benign and frequently dangerous.

"So say you, and Tempe for that matter, but I disagree." Z stopped before Bryce and looked him over, "Nice choice."

"I think so," Tempe gave her husband a what-did-you-expect shrug. "Bryce meet Lady Z."

Bryce bowed, "Lady Z."

8

Lady Z barked a laugh. "You may all call me Z or Lady Z, as you wish. I'm not much for protocol." Her eyes fell on Sage, and she bowed. "Then again, sometimes protocol is compulsory for the good of all. Sovereign, songs of your bravery reached even my ears, and I like what I have been told of your actions. Well met."

"Well met, Lady Z." She tried to keep the surprise out of her voice but failed. Songs? Plural? There was more than one song about her? She knew about Sage's Lullaby. Everyone did. Battle a realm lord and a bard writes it up, but she didn't think she had accomplished anything else song worthy.

Lady Z looked around the room and focused on the twins. "Lex and Xan." She walked over and took Lex from Star and turned to take Xan from Joey. He glared at her and tightened his hold on his son. Lady Z grinned at Star, "I like your consort. He is wise not to trust too willingly. Fear not, Joey. I shall not harm the children. I am here to bestow gifts." With Lex on one hip, she held out her other arm for Xan.

Sage breathed a sigh of relief that Joey remained in one piece. The songs of Lady Z indicated that you could never be sure if she would take offense or be amused when someone stood up to her.

Tempe indicated that Joey should hand over Xan. He balked.

Star explained softly, "Lady Z does not need to hold the children to give them gifts. I suspect they received them as soon as she laid eyes on them."

Lady Z grinned and nodded her agreement.

Joey sighed and handed over his son.

"Fear not, consort. Each boy received a gift suitable to their temperament." She sat down in one of the oversized chairs to coo at the babies.

"Perhaps you could tell Lady Star and her consort what gifts the boys received," Tempe suggested.

"Why ever for? Gifts are given to the child, and the child will show their talents at an appropriate time." Lady Z replied without taking her eyes off the twins. "Lady Star, the boys are lovely. I look forward to watching them grow and learn."

"Are you staying?" Star asked.

"What? By the five realms, no. The elementals keep tabs on my family and inform me of major milestones. I have watched over you since the day you were born."

"You have?" Star asked in surprise.

"Indeed."

The question tumbled out of her mouth before she could think better of it. "Lady Z, did you..."

"Yes, I bestowed upon you a small gift at your birth. I always give the descendants of Ellwood a way to deal with him."

"Well, that didn't work so well with Valiant, did it?" Tempe snarled.

Bryce moved to Tempe's side. She once commented that he could calm her by merely standing next to her. He wasn't sure he believed it, but if ever there was a time to calm her, it was now.

Z huffed, "You know as well as I, that Valiant corrupted his talents and his gifts, and that caused his death. Moral liberty trumps everything."

Tempe nodded her head in unhappy acceptance. Moral liberty, the fae term for free will, frequently caused havoc.

Bryce cleared his throat, "Would you like to meet the quads?" It was the last thing he wanted, but obviously, it would happen. Might as well get it over with.

Lady Z nodded, handed Joey both boys and walked to the quad's bedroom. Joey held his sons tightly.

Bryce looked over at Tempe and mouthed, how did she know?

Tempe responded directly into his brain, *elementals*.

Great. Wicked scary fae witch with spies everywhere. Bryce took a deep breath and followed Lady Z and Tempe into the nursery. The quads would be two in less than a month, and they would move into new rooms.

Willow's grandparents had taken one of the mobile homes they purchased for Eli's property. Most of the couples with young children moved into the remaining mobiles with one being reserved as the schoolhouse. The ranked teenagers had moved into Calabozo, and now there was breathing room in the house. Instead of the twenty-seven people that had been living at Beryl Lane, there were now a comfortable ten, four being the quads. The office, gym, and media rooms, as well as the tree house, had been returned to their original purpose and everyone felt more relaxed.

Likewise, Vitvarg, Eli's home territory, decreased from forty-four residents to nine and his office, gym, and media room returned to normal functions. There was still a lot of visiting back and forth between Vitvarg, Calabozo, and Beryl Lane. Everyone enjoyed the additional freedom that comes from having breathing room.

Lady Z smiled at the toddlers. "Tempest, you do make good looking babies."

"I had some help, you know."

Waving her hand dismissively at her niece, Z focused on one of the quads and laughed. "Tavian is going to be a handful. He will bring back to you all the mischievousness that you and Val unleashed on Lord Ellwood."

Kyan laughed, while everyone else looked at Tempe in surprise.

Sage smacked Kyan on the shoulder, leaned on the doorway, and asked, "What about Lady Temperance?"

"Lady Temperance, even as a child, was the most proper daughter to ever grace a realm, any realm. I don't think she caused Lady Rayna or Lord Ellwood one moment of discomfort. She was the yin to Lady Tempest and Valiant's yang." Lady Z twirled Julian around and looked over at Star. "Thank goodness she finally outgrew that. I'm just amazed it took her so long.

A blush crept up Star's face, but she remained silent.

Lady Z put down Julian and picked up Adrian. "I hope he prevents Adrian from being serious all the time. Julian will be self-sufficient and fun. Vivian will need some specialized training. I may have to visit more often."

"What special training?" Bryce asked sharply. What type of gifts did she give the kids?

"Worry not, shifter. The quads' predispositions were set long before I arrived, and that specific talent is not one I have the ability to bestow. Vivian was born with it."

Wicked scary fae witch with spies everywhere said not to worry. Definitely time to worry. Bryce looked over at Tempe. She shrugged again.

The blast shook the house.

"What in the five realms is that?" Lady Z exclaimed. She handed Adrian to Bryce and headed for the door.

"It's just another barrage of cold iron hitting the shield," Sage explained.

Lady Z looked back in surprise. "Why would they catapult iron at your shield? You're not fae."

"The humans believe cold iron weakens all preternaturals." Kyan looked at the security cameras as more iron hit Sage's shield and ricocheted back toward the ones who threw it. They dove to escape the projectiles. He looked over his shoulder and smirked, "Oops. I guess we failed to explain that properly."

Chapter 3

It worked! Beyond her wildest expectations, it worked.

For months Victoria pulled data from the satellites trained on PAC HQ. Among other things, she had watched changes in barometric pressure, air pressure, and temperature. The last was tricky. The point of departure or arrival could raise or lower the temp significantly or not at all. But she found the answer. Victoria could see a gate event, dimensional or earth side, open outside of PAC HQ and identify both points on a map. She still had some work to do to differentiate between departure and arrival, but she was closing in on a solution.

Victoria still needed points of reference within the Farseen. A gate to or from the Farseen simply identified the portal as connected to that dimension. She didn't have enough data to identify Farseen specific locations and no preternatural would provide the information. She couldn't track gate events within PAC HQ either. The shield over the facility, or something else, blocked those events from her. For those who had to walk through the checkpoint, gate events were opened out in the trees. Those gates could be tracked.

"Eureka, I've found it!" she shouted and leaned back in her chair. A few of her fellow lab rats looked up and chuckled at her comment. She grinned, "I've always wanted to say that."

"Found what, Dr. Nelson? Hopefully, it was worth disturbing your coworkers." Geoffrey Watson, department head, walked over to her workstation. The others hastily returned to their work.

"I found the indicator, frequency if you will, that broadcasts where both dimensional gate events and earth side gate events are opened and closed."

Geoffrey looked over the data before loading it to a flash drive. "Excellent, this is just what we need. Perhaps it was worth the shout out, but don't make a habit of it." He hurried off with the flash drive.

Victoria grinned. Finally, her efforts would help keep preternaturals safe. If gate events could be tracked, governments would know when a preternatural entered their country. Preternaturals with the ability to move freely from country to country had made many humans nervous. Once preternaturals could be observed and carry passports like humans, everyone would be safer. Tracking a gate was the first step. Once all magical energy could be detected, like serial numbers on a gun, there would be no reason for the hate groups. Life could return to normal. Full disclosure, that's what would keep everyone safe.

Her aunt married a shifter, and he ran one of the Harmony bars, leading the family to discover they had a shifter in the family. The bars are owned and operated by shape shifters, and only preternaturals are hired to work there. When the big reveal happened during the dual full moons, it was explained that the Harmony bars were places where the preternatural community could meet under the Treaty of Harmony. The Treaty of Harmony served as a preternatural code of conduct, decreeing that anyone who met under the banner of the treaty could not be harmed, and all written or verbal agreements were binding.

Victoria smiled and packed it in for the day. The only blemish on this moment of success occurred as she was leaving. Her backpack wouldn't zip. She tugged hard, and the zipper broke, sending the contents tumbling to the ground. At least she managed to catch the laptop.

Chapter 4

Now, this was a secure facility, even better than PAC HQ, mostly because PAC HQ and its location was public information. The existence of Calabozo remained a closely guarded secret. Rafael looked around in awe, as did the other invited prifs. The prifs knew Rayna built a new facility, but none saw it before her death. In fact, their first view of the command center had been via teleconference when the humans killed Rayna. Yesterday, each invited prif had been picked up by alphas capable of opening ways, or gates as they were now called, and brought into the underground facility.

Impressive living quarters with a medical wing and multiple conference rooms were available. The sovereign's office contained numerous monitors for teleconferences and a relaxed, but somehow commanding, vibe. The offices of the sovereign's squire and PAs were functional, but the command center stole the show. An elevated captain's chair resided in the center of the room, with a full view of everything, and always an alpha in the chair. Rafael wanted that chair and the power it represented. As did a couple of other prifs, Rafael observed. It was hard for many of the older prifs to accept the newly ranked sovereign. If Tempest weren't around, a revolt would have already happened. He glanced over at the sovereign's second, currently sitting in the command chair. She looked up and winked at him.

He winked back. No reason to tip his hand, as if the alphas didn't already know his view. He had been too vocal and well he knew it. He and Tempest had never been friends. His eyes fell on

Bryce and Phoenix, both men had their heads buried in a monitor. How did Bryce deal with such a powerful companion? Rafael had never had a lover who was his superior by rank. His late wife, who had died after the birth of his twins, had been his superior in every other way. She had been kind, intelligent and happiness followed wherever she went, but it was the job of the man to protect the woman, not the other way around. A lot of people seemed to have forgotten that. Even though the alpha males had been outed, it was obvious the alpha females still ran things.

"Prifs, if you'll follow me into the main conference room, we'll begin." Serenity beckoned them to follow her and smiled in welcome.

Rafael smiled and followed Serenity. Perhaps there was one alpha female he could work with. He took his seat, pleased Tempest remained in the command center. Tempest gave Rafael the impression that she somehow knew his thoughts, and he found it disconcerting.

*****

"Do you believe?"

Rafael looked up as Dimitriy, prif of the Saint Petersburg Clan, sat down with his tray. The empty cafeteria wouldn't remain that way for long. He took a swig of beer but said nothing.

"Well, do you?"

"Believe what?" Rafael glanced around to make sure no one could overhear. He had no desire to be caught up in one of Dimitriy's schemes. That man plotted, but never actually did anything. Dimitriy goaded others to action but always slithered off before he was caught doing anything suspect.

"The new sovereign. Does she believe the happiness and joy she's spouting?" Dimitriy took a bite and muttered, "At least the food is good."

"Possibly, she is young after all," Stanislav, prif of Ukraine, sat down.

Rafael looked warily at the new arrival. Stanislav might be opposed to Sage, or he might be a supporter. Stanislav would do what was best for Stanislav.

Dimitriy gave Stanislav the same look Rafael had. "If Tempest were the new sovereign there would be no question, I would follow. But Sage, she is young. What if she orders Tempest to do something foolish?"

"You're right, the food is good," Stanislav took another bite, savoring the flavors. "Sage seems to listen to her elder siblings, all of them. Rayna certainly had a large brood."

"Yes, for now, but think of your own children." Dimitriy waved his fork in the air, "Who amongst us would want our teenager leading our clan, much less all clans?"

Rafael leaned back and nodded to some other prifs as they placed their food orders. While he agreed with Dimitriy, he did not intend to have this conversation with so many alphas and alpha supporters around.

"You are too silent, my friend," Dimitriy glared at Rafael. "I can't believe you are satisfied with our new sovereign."

"It remains to be seen if Sage is up to the task. Meanwhile, her brothers and sisters support her, and no non-alpha has ever won a challenge against any member of the Alpha Clan. If you wished to challenge Sage, you should have done so right after Rayna's execution. Sage made the offer then. Unless she instigates a direct challenge, you will have to challenge to a duel every member of the Alpha Clan to get to the sovereign, including Tempest." Rafael stood and picked up his tray. "And there's a reason no shifter has challenged Tempest in centuries. Fighting one-on-one, she is unequaled." Rafael left the group, disposed of his tray, and turned to leave, nearly running into Estevan.

"This is the first time I've heard you praise Tempest, no?" Estevan grinned as he disposed of his tray.

"Only a fool discount her fighting skills." Rafael smirked, "I am many things, but fool I am not."

*****

By the end of the three-day meeting, Rafael was not a happy prif. It appeared the new sovereign did not trust her prifs. The Alpha Clan withheld information. He glanced over at Tempest. In response, she looked up and raised an eyebrow, as if to ask him what he wanted. He huffed and shook his head.

After the meetings, the prifs cued up to hitch a ride through a gate. Three days and only the Alpha Clan had been allowed to leave the facility. Serenity said the object was to safeguard the prifs, but in reality, the prifs remained inside so they wouldn't

17

know where they were. That was a bust. Calabozo resided somewhere in the southeastern United States. No other setting made sense. Most of the alphas, and all of their cyn, lived in the area. The real question, the exact site, could not be answered. Was it in East Tennessee near Tempest and where the sovereign currently lived, or Western North Carolina where the former sovereign had lived? Granted, they were adjacent, with only the Smoky Mountains separating them, but it still left a lot of land to search if someone wanted to find the facility.

Rafael tried to hide his boredom, but no one called him a patient man under the best of circumstances. Waiting in line was not even an okay circumstance. He felt eyes on him and turned. Serenity smiled and waved him over. He grinned, at least boredom was gone. He walked over, and Serenity placed her arm through his and led him into one of the small conference rooms.

"I'm glad I caught you before you left. I wanted to thank you."

"I'm happy to be thanked, but what have I done to earn such thanks?" Rafael's eyes softened, and he placed his hand over hers, still hooked through his arm.

"I heard you defended Sage."

"And I'm sure I know who told you," he shrugged her off and stalked over to the video screen that showed the outside in an attempt to get his anger under control. He had been fascinated that they were broadcasting security camera feeds giving the feel of views from windows, and yet they managed to hide all landmarks from sight. That was an impressive use of camera angles.

Serenity followed him and laid a hand on his shoulder, "Actually, Joey heard the entire conversation. He had not intended to eavesdrop. He was helping the techs run more cable and had crawled underneath the cafeteria at the time."

"The Sovereign's Squire running cable? How democratic of him." Rafael snarled.

"Don't take that attitude with me. Joey was part of the sovereign's tech team when Rayna was sovereign. He's run more cable in this facility than anyone." Serenity glared at Rafael with her hands on her hips.

Rafael bit back a grin she wouldn't appreciate, but she was adorable when annoyed. "Forgive me. I have no right to complain.

18

To be honest, if I were running this facility, I would have bugged every room in the place."

She looked at him, appalled, "You wouldn't?"

"Oh, yes, I would. And for that reason, I recommend you take everything heard with a grain of salt. I'm not the only one who assumed the place was bugged, some would parrot what they think you want to hear."

Serenity laughed.

"You're amused?" Rafael cocked his head to one side.

"Tempe said the same thing. The two of you are in agreement."

Rafael leaned his head back and laughed. The smile remained until he said goodbye to Serenity and walked into the gate event.

*****

A week later, back home in Brazil, Rafael's lip curled. He longed for the days a letter could be wadded up and thrown in the trash or set on fire. Now letters came via email. More efficient, but the delete button was not nearly as satisfying as physically tossing it in the trash or watching it burn.

Another parent wanted assurance that her child remained safe in the presence of shifters. The clan's teenagers, including his own twins, were still attending Ensino Medio, upper secondary education. They were allowed to remain in school because the clan ran the private school they attended. Only three of the teachers were not clan members, and they were witches. Rafael himself was the principal and taught a couple of classes. His exposure had resulted in a few parents pulling their kids out of the school, but most remained. After all, graduates from his school traditionally scored in the top two percent of the vestibular (entrance exam) for any public university. Most parents decided lessons with shifters were acceptable for test results of that nature. But it didn't stop the emails from concerned parents.

He had exposed himself and his children during the dual full moons. By association, the Brazilian government identified most of his clan. He had two clan members and one unranked teenage shifter who could set a weak shield. Layered together, they had been able to protect his clan from attack for a short period. After his reveal, the entire clan took refuge in his home. A few hours later, alphas Ben and Serenity had arrived with a couple of local wizards. They created a more robust shield, and now only the strongest of his clan members lived away from his home. It was safer for most to remain at his house. The wizards made weekly trips to his estate to reinforce the shield. They did so in exchange for reduced tuition for their own children. So far, it had been well worth the lost revenue. Security was a beautiful thing.

Rafael looked out the window and growled at the birds playing tag. After a minute he opened the window and whistled, waving the birds into his office. As the birds flew past he glared, "Why didn't you call?" He didn't need an answer. If Sage had called, he might have prepared for her arrival, and the alphas were sure he wished the sovereign ill. Rafael wasn't so sure. He most definitely wanted Sage replaced, but she was young, and he felt no ill will toward her as a person. He had never harmed a child before, and regardless of her legal standing as an adult, she remained a child in his eyes.

Sage, Raven, Ryan, and Kyan shifted as they landed. Kyan and Ryan took up defensive positions on either side of their sovereign. Ignoring the overprotectiveness, Sage turned to Rafael, "I wanted to make sure your clan is alright after their exposure."

Sarcasm coated his response. "How considerate. We are as well as can be expected. The wizards keep the shield stable. For that I am grateful."

"Is there anything I can do to help?" Sage asked

Rafael glared at the young sovereign and started to make a snide remark about being too late but stopped himself. She hadn't ignored him, as Tempest would. Nor did she order him, as Rayna had. She waited for his answer. Sage was either naïve or working an angle he didn't understand. Only time would tell.

"Your concern is appreciated but unnecessary, as are your guards."

Ryan crossed his arms in front of his chest and stared at Rafael, "The sovereign does not travel unescorted. Not with the current situation."

"What situation?"

"They're still working out the bugs, but humans can track earth side and dimensional gates." Sage shrugged, "We knew it would happen sooner or later."

20

Rafael raised his eyebrows. That was a game changer. It was well known that Tempest traveled by gates frequently since the preternatural exposure. If she could be tracked, her effectiveness would be severely curtailed, and not just with humans. Now he needed to decide if that was a good thing or a bad thing. "Why are you here?"

"I'm making quick trips to visit certain prifs, one-on-one. Sometimes the teleconference screen warps my perception of the real issues." Sage looked over at her guards, "Please wait in the hall. I wish a private word with Rafael."

Ryan bunched his muscles to the point Rafael braced for an attack from the young man, but it didn't happen. Ryan turned and opened the door. Raven walked out, followed by Kyan. Ryan joined the others in the hallway, glaring at Rafael before closing the door.

"You surprise me," Rafael stared into the eyes of the young sovereign. She maintained eye contact offering him the chance for a dominance push, one that could change the shifter world. He didn't bother. He could feel her power. She would win a dominance push. No. The only way anyone would replace the current sovereign would be to destroy the entire Alpha Clan. He dropped his eyes, "I mean you no harm sovereign, but this is a mistake."

Sage tilted her head, surprised he hadn't even tried the dominance push. All other prifs she had visited, Dimitriy included, had tried and failed when she offered them the opportunity. "How so?"

"You're purposefully offering a prif the chance to challenge you for the position of sovereign, without other alphas in the room. That could be dangerous. While I have no doubt you are the dominant shifter, Tempest is your second after all, in hand to hand you are still young and inexperienced. Someone might kill you before your guards could return to protect you."

Hands on her hips, Sage faced off with Rafael, "If you think I need guards to protect me, you should kill me now."

"Defeating one realm lord does not make you blood proven. You incapacitated him, you didn't kill him. You have no confirmed kills to your name," Rafael explained. In truth, it was the reason he doubted her ability to lead. She might not have the stomach to kill. The Alpha Clan had attributed a few kills to Sage, but no one outside their clan had witnessed those kills.

Sage didn't bother to correct his assumption that she hadn't killed. Her assurances would not change his mind. "My negotiation skills have not yet failed me, however, if they do I shall kill. I was trained by Tempest, and I think we can agree that, regardless of my age, I'm well trained."

"Well trained, but unproven," Rafael replied, surprised that his voice held a tint of regret. He was beginning to like this young sovereign.'

"Unfortunately, with the current unrest between humans and preternaturals, I'll be blood proven sooner than anyone would wish. If your clan needs any assistance dealing with your government, please contact me." She inclined her head before raising her voice, "We're done."

Her bodyguards returned to the room. They shifted and flew out the window that had been left open, following their sovereign.

Rafael closed the window and watched them fly high in the sky. He remained in that position long after he could no longer see them. His respect for Sage jumped up a few notches. Rayna had never spoken to him alone. Never.

Chapter 5

"Don't do this! Not today," Ryan muttered. He managed to pull his truck to the side of the road before it sputtered, coughed, and surrendered to whatever ailed it. Ryan sighed and pulled out his phone. No power. He dropped the useless thing back in his pocket.

He looked around. Of course, his car dies on the day he decides to take a back road. After leaving the interstate, as expected, he hadn't passed a single vehicle. Ryan had planned a pleasant country drive as the sun came up. Followed by another three-day shift at PAC HQ. It had been decided that opening a gate was only for emergencies now and he had driven up from North Carolina.

Ryan grabbed his duffel and decided to open a gate. If he didn't, he would be seriously late, and Serenity would not appreciate having to stay late to cover. He could open a gate to a field of trees in the park outside PAC HQ and walk the last half-mile or so into the office. Risky? Yes, since it could be tracked, but much better than being shot for opening a gate inside the facility without authorization.

He exited the gate and immediately felt a pinch to his neck. He dropped his bag and touched his neck. Ryan pulled a dart from his neck. He looked at it, before falling to the ground, unconscious.

Sometime later, Ryan woke to a blade of grass tickling his nose. He didn't hear breathing or movement, so he opened his eyes, and found himself on the ground where he had fallen. Amazed that whoever drugged him didn't move him, Ryan rolled over to one knee and stood up, promptly lost his balance, and fell back down onto the same knee. After his head quit spinning, Ryan tried again, pleased he achieved a standing position with only minimum swaying. He reached down to pick up his duffel, only to feel stiffness in his shoulder while his head resumed spinning. Ryan took another moment to be still, so his head could clear. As he left the clearing, Ryan passed a squad of armed wizards, presumably going to guard the tree-lined clearing. Too bad they hadn't arrived a few minutes earlier.

At the checkpoint, Ryan signaled the need for an escort. The protocols for notifying the preternatural guards that a preternatural needed assistance, pretending the telepaths who scanned everyone wouldn't already know, were well documented. After clearing the checkpoint, he smiled with relief at the person who waited on the other side of the door.

"You're late," Tempe slapped Ryan on the back, "And you have grass stains on your khakis."

Ryan nodded and rubbed his shoulder. "Yeah, car trouble."

They walked into the shifter wing and back to medical. Two shifter guards followed them.

As soon as they closed the door, Tempe moved him toward a gurney as the medical personnel closed in. Ryan hopped up on it and said, "My car broke down. My phone was dead. So, I opened a gate to the trees just outside PAC HQ. As soon as I arrived, I was shot in the neck with a dart. They didn't move me, so I suspect they've implanted a tracker or something."

One of the med techs looked up from the scan he was performing, "Oh yeah, you've been tagged. The device is embedded in the left shoulder where you can't reach it. Delivered by injection, just like the others."

"Others?" Ryan asked in confusion.

"Yes, today's the day humans made use of their ability to track gates."

A short time later, Ryan lay face down on the gurney, listening to an argument. Jeff Long, shifter, doctor, and father, argued procedure with Lea, alpha shifter, healer, and aunt.

"Do you guys ever not argue? Dad, remove the tracker and let Lea heal the area. It's not brain surgery."

"No, it's not," Jeff responded wryly, "But that solution has already been tried this morning. When fresh air touches the tracker, it releases a toxin that will leave you brain dead. We would like to remove the tracker and keep your brain functioning at its current level."

"Okay," Ryan drew out the word. "Tempe can create a shield around the tracker. Then you, Dad, can remove the tracker and Lea can heal the area quickly.

"A wizard died following a similar plan. Wizards think they have an answer. We're waiting for them to finish testing." Lea explained.

"We're done," Murdoch, wizard of the high coven, walked in the room with Tempe.

Ryan relaxed a little. Murdoch was a trusted friend. Or he was until Ryan turned his head and saw five other wizards crowding into the room. "What's the plan?"

Murdoch grinned, "Relax. We don't think it will take this many to keep the device in the spelled shield, but why take chances? Congrats, you've been promoted to lab rat."

Ryan would have rolled his eyes, but it made sense. Many of the preternaturals at PAC HQ were civilians. He might be in his early twenties, young by shifter standards, but he was also a soldier, and a member of the Alpha Clan cyn. He was the one who should take the risk. He relaxed his shoulders as best he could. "Okay, let's do this."

Tempe leaned down to look him in the eye. "Concentrate on keeping your personal shield down. The natural reflex will be for the shield to manifest when you feel the spell. For that reason, you have to remain conscious. Unconscious, your shield would manifest." Tempe patted him on the shoulder without the tracker and then gripped his arm.

Ryan sighed. She was preparing to block his shield from forming. He would have been insulted, but he suspected she might need to do that.

"No local either. We're afraid it could interfere with the spell. You will feel it when I slice into your shoulder," Jeff explained.

Surprised that his dad would do the cutting, Ryan almost said something, but then he understood. Even in pain, he would be less likely to hurt his father for cutting into him than anyone else. Ryan never considered it before, but as powerful as he was, regardless of his intent, Ryan could injure a lot of people.

He felt his shoulder tingle as the spell formed under his skin, assumingly around the tracker. As usual, Tempe was right. It took all of his concentration to keep his shield down. Like anyone with the ability to create a personal shield, Ryan had been trained to use it if he felt magic near him. Fighting that training was hard.

"Cutting now." Jeff's voice was calm.

Ryan felt his dad cut into his shoulder and had another realization. He could ignore a knife cut in the heat of battle. Cut while lying on a medical table was completely different. Nothing to focus on, except keeping his freaking shield down. He gritted his teeth and focused on the no shield thing while trying to block the pain. Later he would ask Tempe for hints. Somehow, he suspected this wouldn't be the last time he would have to deal with something of this nature.

After what seemed like an hour, Ryan, covered in sweat, felt his father stitch up his shoulder. Stitches he understood, and the pain was manageable.

Finally, Jeff stepped back. "All done. We can give you something for the pain now if you wish."

Ryan moved his shoulder and shrugged. "Should be fine now. Just a dull ache."

"If you change your mind, let me know."

"Thanks, guys." Ryan waved to the wizards as they left.

"No prob," Murdoch said. Turning to Tempe, he added, "The instructions for this casting will be sent to you but call for wizards if you need numbers. It took all six of us to keep the shield steady around the device. That's a lot of manpower considering how easy it is for the humans to embed the device."

*****

"Non-preternaturals can do more than track gates." Destin presented his findings to the Alpha Clan cyn and their tech advisors in the sovereign's office in Calabozo. Some were in the conference room. Others were on the monitors. "The electrical impulses are easy to track once you know what to look for. The kicker is they can track from the point of origin to destination. Anyone tracking will know where you leave from and where you end up. The gates, regardless of species, send the same frequency range so at present they can't identify who opened the way, just point of origin and destination. It took them a while to track without watching a specific location, but they can do it now."

After Kenley died, Destin had somehow become the go-to guy for the shifter's tech research division. As a mostly human member of Tempe's family, unable to shift but with the ability to set an active shield, Destin tried to hand off all the projects he had worked with Kenley, but the shifters decided he was one of their own and let him stay. Magic was just science with a kick and Destin excelled at finding patterns where others couldn't. The things he had learned in under a year made a mockery of what he had learned in the previous thirty.

"How can we mask it?" Gerbold, prif of a German clan, son of Bliss from the Alpha Cyn, asked from one of the teleconference screens.

"That's the point," Destin ran his fingers through his hair. "You can't, at least not yet. So far, every shield and spell we've tested to mask the signature has failed. There are still a few options being researched, but right now any preternatural who opens a gate will be tracked."

Gerbold looked down at the data, "Does it track locations outside of the Seen? Other dimensions?"

"Yes, but without knowledge of those dimensions, you can't pinpoint details. I can track throughout the Farseen, only because I was given the knowledge of the Farseen to make the comparison. So yes, eventually others will be able to do so."

"Are you saying you can track a dimensional gate if I open it from here to the Northern Realm, and you'll know I'm in the Northern Realm?" Tempe leaned forward.

"I'm saying if you open a gate to Saffron's herb garden in the Northern Realm, or Lord Layton's receiving room in the Western Realm, or the sand dunes of the Southern Realm, or anyplace else, I will be able to pinpoint to that level of detail." Destin shrugged.

"By the five realms, no one has ever been able to do that." Tempe leaned back in her chair and chewed her bottom lip. A nervous response she had honed over thousands of years. At this point, she doubted she would ever lose it. "The magic could never be traced to that level of detail. Every realm will demand that knowledge. This could start another war between our dimensions."

"It's not magic, it's science, and it's traceable. The good news is humans can't arrive at the destination as fast as the gate transports you. If you don't go to where they are, they won't meet you there. And teleports cannot be tracked, yet."

Ryan leaned back in his chair and absently rubbed the shoulder where the tracker had been embedded. "Isn't that special?"

Chapter 6

"Brazil, here we come," Serenity got comfortable in the private jet, surprised that she was looking forward to perhaps seeing Rafael. Still in Alaska, they had flown back as birds to Fairbanks, found a place to shift, and walked back to the hangar. Ryan, under cover of his veil, had shifted to his dragon form and flown back to Tennessee for another assignment. "It's amazing how well Cole and Carl trained themselves without teachers."

"Not really," Tempe opened up a granola bar and took a bite. "Cole was reading everyone's mind when they still lived with the Alpha Clan. He learned to control his telepathy by reading my mind and yours. He didn't think he should try to read Rayna's mind."

"When did he tell you that?"

Tempe smirked. "He didn't. I read his mind. I figured turnabout was fair play."

"Apparently, our entire family needs to work on communication skills. He must be strong to read us without our knowing it. He should be on the hook for telepathy duty at PAC HQ." Serenity leaned back and closed her eyes.

"I already made a note in the report," Tempe murmured. Anyone who could reduce the load of the telepaths verifying everyone who entered PAC HQ would be used. The work was grueling, and many telepaths left with a headache after a twelve-hour shift.

Serenity woke as the plane made its final descent. "Same plan as before?"

"Nope. New plan. I'm tired of playing nice."

The sisters exited the plane and proceeded through customs. As soon as they were cleared, they disappeared, leaving a lot of unhappy officials behind.

Under Tempe's spell of invisibility, they shifted to birds and flew out the main doors of the building as a family entered the electronic entrance to the airport. Once outside of the city proper, she dropped the spell, and the two birds continued on to their niece's home. They landed in the trees near Teirra's temporary quarters on Raf's property, shifted, and headed for her front door.

"You've angered my government," Rafael Soto, prif of the Serra Dourada Clan, stood in at the entrance to Teirra's home, hand on hips.

Tempe sneered, "You couldn't care less about the human government. You're angry I arrived in your territory without contacting you first."

"Si. This is my territory. Two alphas, especially the sovereign's assassin, should not be here without warning." Rafael's face flushed with anger.

"Family business," Tempe replied. "We needed to talk to Charity's daughter. This has nothing to do with your clan."

"Teirra is in my clan. That makes it my business."

"Raf, if I didn't know better, I would think you're challenging Tempest." Serenity smiled, slid her arm through his, and guided him into the house. "We should have called you, of course, but we're making quick trips to the family to pass on small bequests from Rayna to her grandchildren. Since gates are trackable, we're using airplanes. The trip to Alaska irritated my sister. Obviously, we should have taken a break before coming here. Her famous temper, the one the fae bards depict in song, is showing."

Rafael relaxed under Serenity's touch. "Well, I suspect the restrictions would be irritating to one accustomed to traveling by gates, but you should have called."

"Yes, and I'll make sure we do so going forward." Serenity pulled Rafael down beside her on the love seat, "Surely you'll forgive us."

"Of course, you're forgiven," he smiled, his focus entirely on Serenity.

She smiled and changed the subject. "It's fortunate you're here. I wanted to talk to you about your kids. I'm setting up a retreat at Chimera Farms for the teenagers who have been exposed. Most feel stifled under the rules we have now. I want your twins, Roya and Faron, to attend. It would be good to give them some breathing room. Chaz will be there, as well."

"That's a generous offer, and timely too. Faron's been unhappy of late. Teenage boys do not like restrictions."

"Neither do teenage girls," Teirra said.

Rafael inclined his head toward Teirra before turning back to Serenity as he stood. "Let me know the date, and the twins will be there. I'll leave you to your family business." He walked out the door, calling over his shoulder, "Tempest, following protocol in the future will save us both some irritation."

Tempe inclined her head and wisely kept her mouth shut, allowing Serenity's efforts to keep the peace stand. Serenity breathed a silent sigh of relief.

Teirra spoke softly to her prif before closing the door and turning to face her aunts with her hands on her hips, mimicking Rafael's earlier stance. "Why didn't you call him first? Of all the prifs to blindside, you pick the one most likely to start a shifter war."

"I'm not in the mood to worry about his petty schemes," Tempe joined Serenity on the love seat.

"Well, get in the mood. Raf's petty schemes are not so petty." Teirra sat on the couch, "He's not happy about Sage, and he's not happy to the point where the clan may have to choose sides, his or the sovereign's."

Tempe sat forward, "You safe here?"

"You planning to ride in and save my family? There's no need," Carlos walked into the house and kissed Teirra. "Tempest, you made the news. Don't force my prif to make a bad decision because he's angry. He's been more accepting since Sage visited him, but you shouldn't rile him."

Tempe bit back her response. She had not wanted Sage to make the rounds, especially when she found out her young sister spoke with the prifs privately. "You think my playing nice will prevent his plans. I don't."

"No, but it might give me time to talk him down. He's a good prif, but he doesn't trust Sage's age, and he believes your family holds too much power. He exposed himself, his kids, and his clan to save humans during the dual full moons. He believed you should have come and taken care of it." Carlos kissed his wife again, this time on the cheek. "I'll leave you to your family business."

Teirra saw the look on her aunt's face and sighed, "We know you were injured the same night Raf was exposed and understand you can't be everywhere at once. Especially now that you can't create a gate event without being tracked, but you need to understand how it looks to the masses. All the super-powered alphas live in the southeastern United States. The impression is that you protect yourselves first and everyone else second."

"Actually, I protect everyone – shifters and humans – first, the Alpha Clan and our sovereign second, and my own children third," Tempe said.

"I did say impression, but at this point perceived preferential treatment is the same as real preferential treatment." Teirra tilted her head in acknowledgment. "Okay, why are you here?"

Once the tests completed, Chaz sat down on the bench and looked up at his aunts in disgust, "So no cool superpowers for me." He quirked a smile at his Mom, "Opening a gate event looks like it's pretty cool."

"But only within the Seen and now that they're tracked I suspect it's only for emergencies." Teirra patted her son on the shoulder before turning to her aunts, "You going to see Xiomara next?"

"Yes, as long as we're in the area," Serenity smiled.

"In the area? She lives over four thousand kilometers away. By car, the trip is fifty-eight hours. It might be shorter as the bird flies, but you guys will be flying for a while."

"It's under control." Tempe motioned for Serenity, and they walked back to the woods, shifted, and flew into the sky.

The sisters flew for a while, eventually turning toward the sun, and flying as high as they could. Tempe opened a gate, and they flew out the other side still high in the air but a lot closer to

Xiomara's family. They landed in another set of woods, shifted, and walked up to knock on her door.

Galo, Xiomara's husband, answered the door with his trademark grin. "At least you haven't irritated my prif."

Tempe smirked, "It would be almost impossible for me to irritate Estefan and requires no effort on my part to irritate Rafael."

"If you caused a scene in Bolivia like the one you did in Brazil, I would be most angry," Estefan said from the living room. "Tell me you did that for a reason other than to give Rafael more cause to hate the alphas, because that, mi amigo, is what you did."

Tempe dropped into a chair next to Estefan, "I did. I had to demonstrate why trying to track us is a waste of everyone's time. I will admit I chose Brazil because of some of Rafael's recent activities, to remind him that he, too, should be wary."

Estefan scoffed. "He knows. All shifters know. That's one of the reasons no one ever challenged Rayna, and it's the reason everyone is giving Sage a chance to grow up and prove herself, without a shifter war. You are the driving force that keeps the Alphas in charge. If you were to die, many shifters would turn on each other and try to take more power for themselves."

"Sage is well able to defend herself, and you know it."

"Yes, I do. I also know that if any shifter attacked the sovereign, you would attack with the full force of your powers and extraordinary fighting skills. While Sage would search for a peaceful solution, you would not hesitate to take out entire clans to keep the sovereign safe." Estefan's lips turned up into a grin, "You're just lucky that most of the prifs know that. It saves effort we can use elsewhere. Most of us agree it's better to have someone else dealing with all the politics that go into being the sovereign, especially now that the humans know about us. I wouldn't want Sage's job – or yours for that matter – for all the wealth and prestige in the world." Estefan bowed and left.

Serenity explained why they were there, and they got down to business. Once testing completed, the sisters once again flew into the air, opened a gate, flew out the other side, and proceeded to return to the airport in Rafael's territory.

They reappeared in the airport right where they had disappeared. It was hard to say who was the most upset, the airport guards or the reporters who didn't get a good photo or interview.

In the end, the sisters' cooled their heels for hours in an interrogation room. One fool tried to separate the sisters, and Tempe demonstrated why that was a bad idea. Since no one tried to touch either sister, Tempe reigned in her famous temper and even answered a couple of questions.

At hour fifteen of the interrogation, Tempe stood up. "Enough. We are leaving. If you think you can detain us without our cooperation, by all means, try. If you think you can stop our plane from taking off or shoot us out of the air, do it. If you think you have any control over my actions, prove it. I have wasted days playing nice all over this planet just to give the various human governments the illusion that they can control preternaturals. I'm done."

Serenity tossed the officials an apologetic smile and followed Tempe out of the room and through the facility until they came to their plane. Guards followed the women to their aircraft, but none tried to detain the duo. Their pilot greeted them by clapping as they boarded the plane.

"Not sure what you said to the officials, but I just got clearance to take off. They muttered something about 'the sooner, the better,' but I don't think I was supposed to hear that." Ben returned to the cockpit, laughing.

"At least our baby brother's having fun," Serenity sighed.

Chapter 7

Tempe and Serenity walked into the sovereign's office in Calabozo. Joey finished writing a note, grabbed his laptop, and closed the door behind him as he left.

Alone with the rest of the Alpha Cyn, Serenity provided a report to the sovereign of the new powers discovered in Rayna's grandchildren. Once she finished, Tempe leaned back in her chair, "I don't believe Bliss, Serenity, or Ryan need to be here for the next discussion."

"Perhaps you two need a mediator." Serenity's eyebrow raised in a Tempestesque like manner.

"No," they replied in unison.

"Fine, page someone if you need medical attention or a healer. We'll be in the Command Center." Ryan herded the others out of the room.

Sage sighed after the door closed, "Could you have been more confrontational in South America?"

"You know I could. I did not kill, maim, or inflict the slightest injury on any human. I would say I was restrained."

"Restrained, no. Not the word I had in mind," Sage stood up and paced, something she rarely did. "I know what Rafael is up to, and I almost had a tentative agreement with him. Your actions damaged that. He called to tell me so. You do not need to protect me from everything."

"Yes, I do."

"No, you don't. Tempe, it's an open secret you're spread too thin. Tell me the last time you spent time with Bryce and the quads. Just them? You can't open ways at the drop of a hat now, so you can't take on everything. Delegate."

"I do," Tempe snarled.

"No, you farm out benign tasks, but if there's a chance of danger, you do it yourself." Sage sat down, put her elbows on the desk, and weaved her fingers together, "When I became sovereign, and the humans found out about us, we had to restructure my position for this new worldview. Now we need to restructure your position. You have spent centuries taking all punitive action for shifters. You can't protect your brothers and sisters anymore. You need their help."

Tempe barked a laugh, "Is that what you think? I protect the family? You do remember I killed one of our siblings not that long ago, don't you?"

"Of course, I remember. For centuries you've been the sovereign's assassin, the alpha who killed shifters for breaking our laws. Kyan protected the sovereign and killed for the Tetrad, but you addressed all internal shifter issues. In the year and a half since we were kicked out of the preternatural closet you've killed more shifters for crimes than you have in the last nine hundred years."

Tempe looked up in surprise, and Sage's lip curled up in irritation, "You think no one did the math? I can send you the report if you like. Even though The Three have verified all kills as just, the deaths are beginning to wear on you. How could they not? Fewer people are willing to mentor a shifter who breaks the law now because humans are watching. The result is you kill more often. You need to regroup and regenerate."

"Whom will you send? You, as the sovereign, can't go. Ryan is strong enough but still inexperienced. Raven has enough experience, but she lacks the full range of powers to survive long. Most of the rest simply aren't the killers they have to be to hold the title executioner. And before you say Kyan, he shouldn't be sent to kill, at least not on a regular basis."

"I know about Kyan's issues and... wow, you really think I haven't thought this through." Sage handed Tempe a folder, "Read this, then we'll talk. Have one of the PA's add you to my calendar. I want the entire cyn at that meeting."

Tempe opened the folder and glanced at item one. "Pairs. All alphas will work in pairs from now on?"

"Actually, all alphas will work in teams of at least two," Sage responded with her trademark sweet and innocent smile. "This way there's backup. The issue opening gates make it difficult for help to arrive if the alpha has difficulty."

Sage walked out of the room and shut the door in a dignified, politically correct fashion.

Tempe looked at the closed door and grinned. She would have stormed out. Yet another reason Sage was the better sovereign. She opened the folder again and read.

*****

Once again, Destin presented the findings of his department, but this time the entire Alpha Clan and all senior prifs were in attendance, either in person or on video, with a few on audio only. He faced the sovereign and addressed his comments to her. "There is one type of gate event that can be created without being tracked."

"Excellent." "Great!" "About bloody time." "We're back in business." The comments came from the prifs. The alphas waited.

"But," Destin held up his hands for silence, "only an elemental can open it."

"Crap." "Seriously?" "You've got to be kidding."

Tempe laughed.

Quill's glare filled his screen. "Care to share, Sis? What's so friggin' funny?"

Tempe took a deep breath, but the grin didn't leave her face. "Oh, I don't know. I guess it's the fact that I can't work with elementals, ever. No one born of two dimensions can. And for the most part, elementals don't like males or anyone of an aggressive nature, so that leaves out most preternaturals. It figures that with everything going on we end up with elementals as our best option."

Quill grinned at Serenity. "Looks like you're our new contact for opening ways. Can we get Lady Z to stay? They like her."

"Doubtful," Tempe faced Destin, "How about PAC HQ? What's the deal?"

Destin shrugged, "There's so much magical energy in use that they can't yet separate the electrical impulses of gates opening and closing from anything else. It's only a matter of time. They'll crack that as well. I have."

"And the test we did in South America with a gate at altitude?"

"I could track it. However, since you flew a while before opening it, there was no way to tell your starting point and landing point, just where the gate opened high in the sky. We got the coordinates of the gate but nothing else. You must be careful of your location when you open a gate. The AIB might decide to bomb such an area." Destin closed his folder and waited to be dismissed.

"That's something, at least for those who take a flying form," Estevan commented.

Rafael rubbed his neck. "Only if you can fly and be invisible and open a gate. Just how many alphas can do that?"

"Thank you for the report, Destin." Sage nodded, and Destin left.

Once the door shut, Sage faced the monitors and focused on Rafael. "Not many, not nearly enough, but at least a few will be able to provide quick support again, but caution is still required."

"Why? Tempest and Ryan are out. They could open a gate at her house and exit in the sky wherever they need to be."

"Any gate opened within Beryl Lane, Tempe's home, will be assumed to be Tempe and the humans will think they know where she is. Even if it isn't her, it could cause more problems than it would solve. The authorities get a bit too excited if they think she's around."

Rafael barked a laugh, "Sí, I noticed."

He didn't say anything else, and Sage sighed in relief. Sometimes it seemed that they had fewer problems with Rafael if Tempe didn't speak.

Chapter 8

Ryan, hands on hips and a snarl on his face, pegged Lucas and Logan with a stare as they exited the way. "No clowning around. This is a military base. Some of those guys holding weapons are looking for an excuse to open fire."

He didn't see the need for this trip and wasn't happy. The driver's license wouldn't do the kids much good. They were all outed as preternaturals, and it would be too dangerous for them to drive often. Even now it was dangerous. There was a solid wall of soldiers, weapons drawn, staring at the shifters. Some of those soldiers did not look happy to see them. While waiting for the kids to show up, Ryan had identified a couple of the soldiers. Brian should be in jail, not the military. And he definitely shouldn't be armed.

Ryan turned in response to a loud crack that echoed through the valley. A teenage sorceress appeared with the demon that had transported her. The beast had taken a vaguely human appearance, perhaps in an attempt to put the humans at ease. Epic fail. Most of the soldiers now pointed their weapons at the demon. If they fired, it would only irritate the creature and probably cause him to attack, especially as there wasn't an adult sorceress or sorcerer with the teenager.

In this instance, demon didn't mean demon in a religious sense. Preternatural religious beliefs were as varied as those the humans held, with no more knowledge of God, and the divine, than humans have. Demons in the Seen had more in common with a goblin from the Farseen, except that demons held as much brute casting power as a wizard. Lucky for the Seen, demons didn't perfect their talents unless they were bound to a sorceress or sorcerer. Unbound demons remain deep in the earth, in caves or volcanoes, using brute force in battle.

Approaching the young sorceress and her demon, he said, "I'm Ryan of the Alpha Clan. You must be Lilith. I thought Hadley would accompany you." The wind whipped around Lilith blowing her long midnight blue hair and her cloak. Her cloak was open, so it blew back, revealing a skintight outfit. The wind touched nothing else. The young sorceress was showing off.

"Mother has no need to escort me to such a trivial task," Lilith responded.

A shield of wind arrived a couple of seconds ahead of the wizard and witch teenagers. With them was Murdoch, a member of the wizard high coven. Murdoch looked like he had just left the gym, his normal state. He took in the scene, dropped his shield and motioned his charges toward the hangar. "Lilith, stop the performance. Ryan, let's get this show on the road, shall we?"

Lilith snarled but stopped the wind. She followed Murdoch with her demon guard in tow.

*****

From his hillside post, Airman Brian Collins sneered. "Look at them. They look like normal teenagers, except for the gothic one with the demon. My sister could be dating a preternatural, and she wouldn't even know." What he would never admit is that he had dated a shifter and hadn't known what she was until the Smokey Mountain Clan was exposed.

"Forget that," Airman Chad Raman replied. "Can you imagine dealing with teenagers who have powers? There's no telling what those freaks could do."

"You don't need to worry about what they can or can't do. You better worry about what I will do if you don't cut the chatter. You're on duty, not at a family picnic." Sgt. Chris Hall bellowed.

He glared at Collins and Raman. Those two were trouble. Both had joined the military to get out of jail time, and both were members of the IGI. In theory, their get-out-of-jail-free option required them to give up the IGI and harassing preternaturals. They had found each other within an hour of being assigned to the same unit. Hall purposefully selected them for this security detail to gauge what their reaction to preternaturals would be. Now he knew.

"Mouthpiece," Collins muttered under his breath. Of course, he kept his voice soft. The sergeant had a soft spot for preternaturals, even admitting that he had worked with and admired the courage of some of them. Fool. But fool or not, Sgt. Hall was a huge man with a righteous temper and serious skills on the training mat.

*****

Lady Z took a walk around Beryl Lane listening to the elementals. She had spoken with the four mother elementals and didn't like what she heard. If the humans didn't watch it, they would have an uprising on their hands. The question was, should she stay and help or leave the people of the Seen to fix the problem they were creating.

She normally didn't concern herself with such issues, leaving the cleanup to those who created the problem. This time, if she didn't help it would be her family who was injured. Regardless of what Tempe believed, Z felt terrible for leaving her nieces and nephew to Ellwood's not so gentle parenting.

As she approached the house, an impromptu party kicked into high gear. Steaks and veggies on the grill, side dishes everywhere and a couple of chocolate confections.

"Lady Z, wanna see?" Logan swaggered over, obviously pleased with himself.

"See what?"

"License. I can drive anywhere now." He eyed the powerful fae. "Don't suppose you need anything from the store, do you?"

"Which store?" Lady Z smiled at his enthusiasm although she wasn't sure why he was so happy to be able to drive. It was much easier to open a gate, but then not all shifters could do that.

"Any store. I can drive anywhere!" Logan all but danced around the patio.

Cinnamon rolled her eyes and looked over from the chair she was currently lounging in. "If you want to drive, you have to earn money for gas."

At his sister's words, Logan's face fell. "Aw man. No fair. I can't get a job. No one will hire a known preternatural."

"And it gets better," Nash commented as he plopped down beside Cinnamon. "The local cops are fond of following us around. You will get pulled and given a ticket, not a warning, for any infraction."

"And the cops know you just got your license. The names of the preternaturals that just passed the driver's test, which I'm proud to say was all those who tested, have been posted on the IGI web site," Tempe commented from her chair in the shade.

"Who leaked that?" Ryan growled.

"Probably one of the people giving the test."

"Or that jerk Brian." Lucas popped another veggie in his mouth, waiting for the steaks to get done.

"Brian?" Willow looked over at Ryan in surprise, waiting for an explanation.

Ryan glared at Lucas and then shrugged, "I didn't see any reason to mention it. He must have joined the military to get out of going to prison."

Brian had dated Willow until the preternatural exposure. Once he found out she was other, he dumped her, in email no less. He then went on to join the IGI and got himself in a spot of trouble.

As one, they looked over at Tempe. She kept track of everything.

She sighed. "Yes, he did. Brian, along with a lot of humans who had spotless, or only slightly soiled, records, before we were exposed, were given that option."

"So, the humans are training and arming the people who most hate us. Wonderful." Willow scowled.

Logan sighed at the injustice of life. It would be limited driving for him, but at least he had his license.

"Logan, Lucas, come over here." Both boys ran to see what Bryce wanted. Bryce tossed his keys to Logan. "Tempe wants ice cream with the brownies. Why don't you drive over to Vitvarg and get some vanilla out of the freezer? Logan drives over. Lucas drives back."

"Alone?" Logan asked, not believing his luck.

"Well now, you both have your license, don't you?"

"Yes, sir," Lucas replied in a rush.

"Then why would anyone need to go with you?" Bryce raised an eyebrow.

"Let's go." Logan grabbed his twin, and they ran for the car before anyone objected.

As the boys enjoyed their first solo drive, they didn't notice the Gyrfalcon in the sky or the mountain lion and panther tracking them on the ground. They also didn't know about the avoidance spell that Ryan sent to keep the humans away. They simply enjoyed their first drive without adults. A rite of passage realized.

Chapter 9

Meeting over, Joey grabbed his laptop and headed for the door.

"Wait up Joey," Tempe said.

Joey sighed and closed the door. He turned to face Tempe and Ryan. "I'll work harder. I'll be ready."

Ryan leaned back in his chair, not sure what was going on. He only stayed because Tempe held him back. Tempe had kicked Joey's butt on the mats earlier, but she kicked everyone's butt, so that couldn't be the issue.

"What?" Tempe wrinkled her forehead in confusion for a moment before it cleared. "Oh, don't worry about this morning. Your training is proceeding rather well. No, the problem is Lord Ellwood."

"What now?"

There was a knock on the door and Star entered without waiting for approval. She held up her phone with a text message. "You demanded my presence, urgently, and said to walk right in."

"Good timing," Tempe motioned to a chair, and Star sat. Joey walked over and laid a hand on her shoulder. They faced Tempe and waited.

Ryan watched in envy. Star waited with patience, as expected since she was raised in a realm court. Joey showed significant improvement in the art of waiting. Ryan wished he could say the same of himself.

"Lord Ellwood decided to invite representatives from each realm to visit for the entire two weeks we'll be there, a chance for

44

the younger generation to get acquainted. Those are his words by the way." While Tempe spoke, the others moved forward in their seats.

"What's his plan?" Star asked.

"Unknown," Tempe shrugged, "But I doubt this is a benign proposal."

"Who'll be there?" Joey ground out the words.

Ryan smothered his grin. His friend wouldn't appreciate it, and he understood the frustration of dealing with the Farseen.

"From the Central Realm: Kamden, Beval, and the Ladies Misty and Samma."

"Expected." Star leaned back and sighed. She and Samma were sociable enemies.

Tempe grinned, "Apparently, Ascan is working to fix his interest with Lady Samma, so I doubt you two will have the desire, or time, to engage in verbal sparring now."

Star raised a skeptical eyebrow but didn't respond otherwise.

Joey narrowed his eyes on Star, "Is Kamden the one who chased after you before you shifted?"

"Yes, but only because he wanted to apprentice under Father. He got the apprenticeship, so he's not an issue."

"I doubt that," Joey couldn't stop the growl this time.

Tempe ignored the side conversation, "The Eastern Realm will send Thorn, Varg and the Ladies Varya and Geena."

"Misty will like that." Star smiled. Her sister and Thorn had been friends since they were kids. As they grew, so did their friendship.

"The Western Realm will send Feri, Uxio and the Ladies Kaner and Idell."

"Also expected, and none will cause issues for us." Star nodded.

"The Southern Realm will send Rune, Pagan and Ladies Dawn and Fawn."

"Congrats, Ryan," Joey muttered.

Again, Tempe continued as if she hadn't heard him, "Father Aldous is sending his son, Asphodel, as his representative."

"Great, just perfect." Ryan tried to keep his growl to himself but failed. He and Asp were both interested in the same lady of the Southern Court, and they had little tolerance for each other.

Tempe stretched in her chair, "And just to round out the party, Lord Ellwood has invited the shifters to send four additional guests. Ryan, you were invited specifically."

"I'm going as a guest and not a guard?" A slow grin spread across his face.

"Yes, let the good times roll." Tempe stretched her neck, trying to remove the tension.

*****

"Tempest, I never thought I would say this, but do you know what you're doing? They're all I have left of my wife. I noticed you aren't taking your kids." Ben winced, sorry as soon as he said it. It wasn't fair. Thank goodness the rest of the alphas had dropped from yet another videoconference. He shook his head, "Sorry. I do understand. You need to take adults, unmated males and females, who have the power and training to defend themselves against the creatures of the Farseen. It's not a large pool to pick from. I get it, but you're taking all of my children to the Northern Realm."

"Would you feel better if you came with us? You could be one of Star's guards."

Ben snorted. "We both know I would be too busy watching my kids to pay attention to Star. That would be a disservice to everyone." Ben paced around the room and then laughed bitterly, "You made the offer on purpose, didn't you? To force me to admit I wouldn't be value added on this trip."

Tempe wisely didn't respond.

"Okay, fine, but I expect frequent reports."

"Already taken care of. Dylan will send daily reports to the alpha distro. Talk to him if you want additional statuses."

Tempe finished up with Ben and headed back to Beryl Lane, looking forward to a few minutes of downtime. Being exposed to the humans had upped the paperwork and the irritation. How could the humans think preternaturals would roll over and do what they said? It was no secret that preternaturals were stronger. The humans were lucky the rulers of the preternatural world, the

Tetrad, did not want to rule the humans. There were times throughout history when that wasn't true. Humans still didn't suspect that some of the ancient leaders, and even some of the so-called gods, were preternaturals. Hopefully, humans would never find out just how some preternaturals had ruled.

She took the steps from Calabozo and exited into her home office, ready for some peace and quiet. Tempe pulled up short and raised an eyebrow, "Naomi, has something happened?"

Naomi, the human wife of Theo Clark, was one of the calmest people Tempe had ever met, but today she set aside the book she had been reading and nervously wrung her hands. "I'm afraid so. My niece meant no harm."

Whenever Tempe heard the phrase 'meant no harm' it meant harm had been inflicted, intentional or not. She walked over and sat beside Naomi on the fainting couch. Fainting couches were spread throughout her home, a joke of sorts. "What happened?"

"Victoria, my niece, believed she worked for the good guys. She thought her research would make preternaturals safe." Naomi shook her head, "She hoped to keep me safe. My family knows about Theo. Since he runs a Harmony Bar, they figured it out pretty quick. Anyway, she's young and idealistic. She believed if magic could be traced and licensed, like a gun, humans would quit blaming the preternatural community for everything."

Tempe leaned back and groaned. Save her from the idealistic fools of the world. They believe the world promised safety and friendship for all. "What did she do?"

Naomi sighed, "She's a brilliant scientist."

"And?"

"She's the one who figured out how to track gate events. Once she understood the knowledge was being used to hurt, not protect, she left. She came to me because she wants to make things right."

"She's here?" Tempe didn't bother to hide her surprise. For a human to walk into a known preternatural stronghold was unusual. Either Victoria was too idealistic for her own good, or too brave, probably both.

"She's at the bar waiting to talk to you. Victoria knows she caused huge problems for the preternatural community and you specifically. She wants to help fix it."

Tempe stood and walked out the door. "Let's not keep her waiting."

*****

Victoria watched the entrance to the bar since Naomi left, ignoring her entourage. In retrospect, she shouldn't have told her family the real reason for her visit. Her father and brothers decided they needed to protect her. Like those three could do anything if the powerful shifter became angry. Fact was, she didn't think Tempest would hurt her. She had paid close attention as the preternaturals were exposed and Tempest protected everyone, not just shifters or preternaturals.

The door opened, and most of the room turned toward the entrance. Victoria noticed the preternaturals did that when someone of strong powers entered the building. The scientist in her filed that data away for review at another time.

Tempe and Naomi walked into the Harmony Bar. Tempe nodded to the room, and everyone resumed their varied activities.

Victoria's family took defensive positions around her.

Naomi smiled, and said, "Tempest, this is my brother Olivier, his sons Rhett and Tad, and his daughter Victoria."

"Ma'am," Olivier held out his hand.

Tempe smiled and shook the proffered hand. Most humans backed away from her now, few offered to shake her hand. Apparently, Naomi wasn't the only strong-willed Nelson on the planet.

Victoria pushed past her brothers and extended her hand, "It wasn't my intention, but I've caused you a lot of trouble. I'm..."

One of the wizard waitresses interrupted by laying out sodas and snacks. "Theo said y'all might be hungry." She turned and left without a backward glance.

Tempe grinned. That was Theo's way of reminding her these people were his family. Even though she rarely invoked the rule in the Seen, she was half-fae, and an apology was as good as a favor owed. Tempe grabbed a nacho and sat down. "Let's hear your story."

Victoria started at the beginning. "While completing my doctorate, I received an offer to work on a government funded project. At least, that's how they explained to me. I wasn't the only one. We were all doctoral hopefuls at the beginning and being

48

invited to work on a well-funded grant is the stuff of dreams in my world. Upon completion of our degrees, some of us received full-time positions. The way they explained the work I understood I would be helping preternaturals, making the world safer for good people of all species and identifying the bad." She hung her head, "I was wrong. They took my findings and used them to hurt you and yours. I'm the reason gate events can be tracked now."

A couple of unaligned fae glanced over at that comment, but Tempe stared at them, and they turned away. They didn't stop listening. Tempe waved her hand in dismissal making sure her voice carried. "I'm sure you're intelligent, but if you hadn't discovered it, someone else would have. It was only a matter of time."

Victoria smiled, "I'm glad you feel that way. I didn't turn over all my research. I can track a lot more than just earth side and dimensional gates."

The unaligned fae stopped all pretense of not listening. Tempe stared at them until they turned and left. Tempe sighed. She would need to protect this human and her family from the preternaturals as well as the humans. The fae were much more likely to kidnap someone for their knowledge than to try and work with them. She ate another nacho before saying, "There's someone you need to meet."

*****

Just after midnight Destin looked up from the research and stared at the young woman who had only recently completed her doctorate. It was a good thing she wanted to help the preternaturals, not harm them. "You've found markers to track almost all magic."

Victoria shrugged, "Once I found the first marker the rest sort of fell into place."

"Are you sure you deleted all traces of your research?" Destin wasn't optimistic. IT wasn't her field of study, so she probably missed the backups.

"Not exactly. I deleted everything I found, and I used a virus to go after the rest. I left six hours ago at the end of my shift and didn't tell anyone I wasn't coming back. I doubt they've started looking through my files yet.

Destin grinned, "What's your user ID and password? And where did you get that virus?"

Chapter 10

"I'll miss you," Sage sighed. It was hard to watch everyone go to the Farseen, but as the sovereign, it would be a political nightmare if she showed up in the Northern Realm again without an express invitation. That fact did nothing to stop her from feeling guilty.

Landon pulled her in for a quick kiss, "Right back at you. Please take care of yourself and don't get overloaded."

She smiled. Structure changes within the Alpha Clan had improved her daily life. She felt guilty about that too. The couple walked to the meeting place in silence.

"Hi, Ho, Hi, Ho. It's to the Farseen I go," Ryan sang as he tossed his backpack on his back and followed the others into Tempe's living room.

"You are mighty chipper," Sage said.

"Any reason I shouldn't be?"

The last visit, Kyan had gone to protect Star and Joey's twins, while Ryan behind remained to guard Sage. This trip, Kyan would remain in the Seen with the twins, and Ryan was one of the invited guests. The other shifter guests were Ben's children, Bridget, Shawn, and Sara.

"Nope," Tempe turned to face the team. "Okay, this trip is a little different. It's a party. As we're staying in a realm court, we follow their customs. I would remind all female guests that you must behave like ladies of the court. Since I'm the senior attending representative of the shifters, make no plans with any male without my express approval."

"Yes, Lady Tempest," Sara and Bridget curtsied beautifully.

Tempe's lips curved up in amusement. The sisters had done exceptionally well in their realm training. She gave Ryan and Shawn her best headmistress stare, "Mind your manners, and don't start a war... with any of the realms."

Both males nodded.

"And for goodness sake, don't thank anyone," she muttered.

"As you desire, Lady Tempest," the four invited guests said in unison, the males bowed, and the females curtsied.

Amid chuckles, Tempe opened a gate, thought happy thoughts, and led the others into the Northern Realm.

The portal platform in the Northern Realm was large but still crowded. Star was accompanied by a total of eight guards, not counting Tempe, and the four invited shifter guests. In total, fourteen visitors from the Seen.

"Fairly met and greetings shifters from the Farseen," Lady Saffron opened her arms in a welcoming manner.

Tempe smiled, "Sister mine. I did not expect you to greet us."

"Lord Ellwood is currently attending to his realm. I shall escort your party to the family tree houses. All other visitors will stay in the realm guest quarters."

Tempe took the lead and Ryan the rear. The rest lined up as they had been instructed. Saffron described various points of interest as they walked, making sure to identify landmarks that would help the new visitors navigate the labyrinth that was every realm residence.

*****

Shawn tried to look interested in what Saffron, no, Lady Saffron, said. But dang, how large did a home need to be? The portal platform was in the fortress part of the castle and, according to Tempe, resided in a mountain. However, it still looked like a castle with walls, floors, and ceilings throughout. This place was larger and more ornate than the largest castles in the Seen. They passed some girls – no, ladies of the court – who qualified as eye candy. Time would tell if their intelligence matched their looks.

The lady with brown horizontal stripes in her white blonde hair smiled at him, and Shawn replied in kind. This place might not be so bad, after all. He would have to talk to Ryan and get more information on court rules. Tempe had gone over the basics, but undoubtedly there was a way to meet up with a lady of the court without having to declare intentions. He wouldn't mind a little fun but did not want to end up carving vows or, he glanced at Joey, become someone's consort.

"Careful," Dylan whispered. "Lady Snowbell is Ridge's niece."

Shawn nodded, grateful for the tip. Definitely didn't want to get on the wrong side of Ridge. Come to think of it, Tempe, Lady Tempest, might feel protective of Lady Snowbell as well. Shawn smiled. A name was the first step.

Geez, she was right. Tempe had warned them they should think in the way they would need to speak in the Farseen. If he slipped this much in his thoughts, Shawn would have real issues speaking, assuming he ever got the nerve to speak out loud.

*****

Sara looked around in wonder. Lord Ellwood's home was huge. It also served as the Northern Realm's government offices, but still. She watched Shawn's exchange of smiles with a lady of the court and was jealous. Sara would be seriously irritated if Shawn enjoyed this trip more than she did. It wasn't as hard as she expected to remember the rules. Her time at PAC HQ had helped prepare her, and she felt reasonably comfortable with the rules, although it was odd that Lady Tempest would have to approve all of her activities.

Crossing from the formal court into the family tree houses, Sara imagined growing up in such an enchanted place. She glanced out every window they passed and tried not to slow down and stare. Dragons flew overhead, along with a few birds whose colors matched the vibrant feathers of rainforest birds in the Seen. Unicorns, centaurs, and all manner of hoofed creatures stood in herds in the open fields. River merfolk and such swam in the river, and apparently, jellyfish in the Farseen fly through the air as well as swim in the water. Interesting.

Saffron passed a few tree houses without comment. Finally, she pointed to one, "Ryan, you and Shawn are here." Ryan raised an eyebrow but didn't speak. "Ladies Bridget and Sara will be across the hall. Everyone else will stay where they have before. Itineraries are in each room, and green stars indicate mandatory attendance. Since you reside in the family quarters, know that I shall retain my rooms, but no other guests or Northern Realm residents will stay here. The midday repast is casual." She left the shifters to themselves.

Tempe headed toward her childhood tree house. Due to its size, it doubled as a meeting room. The massively oversized living quarters had been a gift from Lord Ellwood. A present when she attained her majority. Tempe assumed its purpose was to drive a wedge between her, Val, and Temperance, but it hadn't worked. It had become a joke for the siblings. "Settle in and meet back here in thirty minutes. We'll walk back together for the first repast.

Chapter 11

The noon repast consisted of a few members of the Northern Realm and the shifters. It was a gentle introduction for the shifters and concluded without incident. The shifters spent the afternoon touring more of the residence with Saffron, followed by another round of instructions from Tempe on what they were expected to do and, more to the point, not do.

Returning to their quarters, Shawn looked around and took it all in. He couldn't get over being in a tree house.

As they changed clothes, again, Shawn finally asked the question he had wanted to ask since they arrived. "Okay, what's with this tree house? You seem surprised to be here." Dressed for the evening repast, Shawn snarled at his tights and billowy shirt, adjusted his saber, and turned from the mirror. He was a friggin' pirate. He glared at Ryan who looked okay, even though they were wearing the same style of clothes.

"This treehouse was Val's." Ryan shrugged as he tied his bootlaces.

"Val? As in Tempe's brother? That Val?" Shawn forgot about the depressing clothes. Val was the alpha poster child for doing things wrong unless Tempe was around, and then he was the model brother taken from his family too soon. Everyone in the family learned early in life not to mention Val in a negative light around Tempe.

"That's the one," Ryan said.

"Explains the weapons." Shawn looked around again. "Now I'm afraid to touch anything. Wonder if Tempe will inspect the room to make sure it remains pristine."

"You and me both. I thought it was a shrine to Val. I know no one has stayed here in the last three thousand years."

"Wow, there must have been some serious clean up before we arrived." Shawn looked around again, trying to get a sense of Val. He had a heck of a weapons collection, including a few that defied explanation. It's possible that they were created to kill a specific lesser fae. If so, it would be wise to not meet those lesser fae.

"According to Tempe, pixies cleaned all rooms, except the dungeons, so I think it stayed clean." Ryan shrugged.

The door clicked open, and both men turned to face their visitor. Surprised, Ryan asked, "Did you forget to tell us something?"

"No, but I should explain a few things about your quarters. First, no one has stayed here since Val died, either to remind everyone how ruthless Lord Ellwood is or because he felt guilty. This is a subject that has long been privately debated. Second, you should look around the room and make your own impression of Val. Should you find anything of interest, perhaps you should inspect it to determine if it should be shared. Third, I assigned you these rooms, not Father." Saffron walked out before they could respond.

"Did that sound like an invitation to snoop to you?"

Shawn grinned, "Sure did."

"Well, all right. That gives us something to look forward to, but right now it's time to join the others."

"How the heck did you know that?" Shawn looked down at his wrist, where his watch typically resided. Timepieces ran in the Farseen, but since the Farseen day was shorter, and had fewer than sixty minutes in an hour, it was easy to get confused. They had been warned to leave watches behind.

"The position of the sun and the moons," Ryan pointed to the open window.

Shawn tossed Ryan the obligatory you've-got-to-be-kidding eye roll.

56

Ryan laughed and waved toward the top of the door. "Itzal meet Shawn. Shawn, Itzal. He'll pop in to let us know it's time to be somewhere or see if we need anything."

Itzal flew down from his perch above the door and stopped less than five inches from Shawn's face. "Well met, Shawn, shifter of the Seen."

Resisting the urge to swat the small pixie away, Shawn forced a smile, "Well met."

"And Ryan is correct. You're expected in the hall. The others await you." Itzal popped out of the room.

Shawn shook his head and followed Ryan. Walking down the hall, he glanced around looking for pixies.

Landon leaned over and grinned, "Pixies move too fast for you to track. I spent most of my first visit looking for them. You won't see them unless they want you to."

Shawn laughed.

*****

"Ryan, I see you are once again here to guard Lady Star," Asp commented with a smile and a bow.

"Didn't you listen to our advisor? Ryan is a guest, the same as we are," Pagan commented as the Southern Realm approached the shifters to exchange pleasantries.

Asp's lip turned up in a snarl, but he didn't reply. Instead, he turned his attention to Sara, gently taking her hand and kissing it, "How refreshing to see you outside of PAC HQ. Are you enjoying your stay in the Farseen?"

"We only just arrived, but I find the Northern Realm enchanting. I look forward to seeing more."

"I would be pleased to show you around. Perhaps we can set up a day trip to visit Father's holdings in this realm."

Before Shawn could tell Asp to back off, Ryan stepped between them. "Asphodel, when did you meet Lady Sara, my cousin." He emphasized the family relationship.

Sara smiled back at Asp. "We've worked together on a couple of projects at PAC HQ."

Shawn glared at his sister. Was she flirting with this Asphodel? And why wasn't Tempe telling him to move on? She was supposed to be watching the unmated females. He glanced over at Bridget, expecting his eldest sister to maintain a dignified distance from the fae. Nope. Bridget laughed at something Rune, also from the Southern Realm, said as he kissed her hand. Shawn snarled at the sudden realization he wouldn't get much R & R on this trip. He hadn't considered it before, but if the males of the Farseen were going to flirt with his sisters he might need the ceremonial sword attached to his hip, the one Tempe made him practice with regularly after he was selected for this trip. Especially if Sara kept smiling at Asp. He hadn't realized Sara's time at PAC HQ gave her access to unacceptable males. In fact, Shawn was surprised she dated.

"Relax, soon as a male completes the formal introduction or hello he can't talk to your sister again this evening unless Lady Tempest gives permission," Dylan murmured.

Shawn nodded his acknowledgment of the information, but he didn't feel better. The intros took forever. The more introductions, the angrier he got. When did his sisters become flirts? To make matters worse, those nearby smiled and glanced Shawn's way when his stomach growled loud enough to be heard. If this happened at every repast, he would ask Itzal for a snack before every meal. His stomach gurgled its agreement. And seriously, how many sons did Pinus have? After a raised eyebrow from Tempe, Shawn plastered a smile back on his face and greeted yet another son of Pinus.

Finally, the assembled throng of people headed for their seats. The sound of voices could be heard on the landing. Shawn, along with everyone else, looked up to see who had the unfortunate timing to arrive late.

"Lord Ellwood, brother dearest. I knew you wouldn't mind if I dropped in. I claimed Liron's escort just as he was leaving PAC HQ for the repast." Lady Z's voice carried throughout the room. "I'm afraid I'm responsible for his being late."

Shawn wasn't sure what the big deal was, but most of the fae seemed surprised to see her. They also seemed slightly afraid. He had observed Lady Z over the past few weeks and found her to be amusing. Apparently, the fae didn't agree with him.

Lord Ellwood smiled, "Lady Zylina, my dear sister, welcome. Perhaps Liron can entertain us with songs of his recent travels as payment for his tardiness."

Liron paled, and a few of the shifters grinned. Liron had indeed written songs and sung a few for his shifter friends, but according to the bard, they were not yet fit for Farseen ears.

While Ellwood spoke, his table was quickly modified to make room at his table for Lady Z. Liron escorted her to the table and promptly moved from the family reunion, joining Lady Saffron at her table, where she held a place for him. Liron sat down, grateful to be away from Ellwood's table.

*****

Stomach full and happy with the cuisine available in the Farseen, Shawn eyed the band in the final stages of warming up. He had survived his first formal meal without making a fool of himself. He had hoped to get out of dancing since the two female guests from the Seen were his sisters. No joy. Tempe had put the kibosh on that in no uncertain terms. If nothing else, he would dance with his sisters to make sure they did not become wallflowers. Didn't look like that would be a problem. Quite a few males had approached Tempe since they first entered the hall. Regardless, he stood ready to dance, should any in the Farseen think him a worthy dance partner for whatever female they were responsible for. Apparently, saying no would be a serious insult to the fae in question – and their realm – as this was as much a political meet and greet, as it was a social setting.

At least the first dance, with an order of progression onto the dance floor, was reasonably safe. Lord Ellwood escorted Lady Tempest out on the dance floor, followed by Lady Star and the sovereign's page. Thinking of Joey as the sovereign's page still made Shawn, and most of the shifters, smile. Although, thinking of Joey as Star's consort made the male shifters laugh. Lady Saffron, escorted by Salix, also hit the floor, along with the senior representatives from the other realms, including Lady Temperance and Cloud of the Central Realm.

At the appropriate moment in the first song, the invited ladies from other realms and the Seen were led to the dance floor by whoever was approved by their guardians. Ryan escorted Lady Dawn, irritating a few males in the room. Shawn and Dylan exchanged smiles. Shawn's smile immediately turned to a frown as his sisters joined the dance.

"Don't frown," Serenity, one of Star's guards, cautioned.

Shawn schooled his features to a bland expression.

"Better. The males have Lady Tempest's permission, and on the dance floor their actions are watched."

Okay, he could respect that logic, but he still didn't like it. Rune of the Southern Realm twirled Bridget around like a pro. He had seemed friendly and was an acquaintance of Ryan's, but still, there should be a rule about a brother approving any male who wished to dance with his sisters. And Tempe had some explaining to do. He watched Asp lead Sara out on the dance floor. Like him or hate him, Asp and Sara looked good on the dance floor. Shawn took a deep breath and watched them dance for a minute. Yep, still hated him.

The next opening in the first song, when everyone else could join the dance was fast approaching. He looked around, so far so good. No one had presented him with a lady to squire on the dance floor. He started to relax.

"Shawn, son of Benevolence."

He turned to see Ridge approaching with his niece, the one with the brown and white striped hair. Now there's a lady he wouldn't mind dancing with if he could remember the steps. Smiling, Shawn bowed, "Ridge."

"I present my niece, Lady Snowbell."

"It's a pleasure to meet you, Lady Snowbell." Shawn followed protocol with a light kiss to her hand and a bow.

"And you as well, Shawn."

As he expected, she curtsied beautifully.

Ridge handed his niece off to Shawn and watched the young couple join the others on the dance floor.

"I'll bet you never expected to hand one of your nieces off to one of Lady Tempest's shifter nephews for an opening dance." Serenity chuckled.

Ridge smirked and bowed. "I refuse that bet."

Serenity laughed out loud as he walked away.

*****

"I didn't think I would enjoy myself so much." Sara had changed into the shorts and t-shirt she slept in. Her sister wore one of her beautiful, silky nightgowns. Sara had never understood how anyone slept in those things. The straps never stayed put, and the long skirt wrapped around her legs and woke her up. "Did you?"

Bridget smiled at her younger sister's enthusiasm. "Did I what? Enjoy myself, or think you would enjoy yourself?"

"Enjoy yourself, silly. Rune seems nice, and he's rather focused on you. I didn't know you guys were acquainted. He's at PAC HQ a lot."

"I know. Rune travels the Seen in his time off, and he's been to Scotland a few times."

"A few times? The whole of earth to visit and he makes repeated trips to the small country of Scotland. I wonder why." Sara looked at her sister slyly. A nice blush ran up Bridget's face, causing Sara to smile, "Do you two have something going on? Does Tempe know?"

"We're just friends, and of course Tempe knows. When was the last time she didn't know what was going on?"

"True. Did she run down a list of rules for behavior if courted by a male from a realm court?"

Bridget laughed, "Rune isn't courting me. We're friends."

Sara's smile widened. The response was just a bit too firm and spoken too fast. Rune was definitely courting her sister, at least in a playful way. What fun.

Bridget walked over to answer the knock at the door to get her sister off topic. She wasn't sure what was going on with Rune, but she enjoyed his company and wanted to see where it led. She opened the door to Star.

"Hey cousin. Need something?" Sara didn't move off the couch.

Star focused in on the reason for her visit, "Are you seeing Asp on the side?"

"What? No, and I wish. I know he and Ryan have a macho thing going on, but Asp is fun and I've enjoyed spending time with him at PAC HQ."

Star huffed. That was not the answer she wanted. "Asphodel is the son of Father Aldous. Consider carefully before you do anything more than dance with him. Asp has a reputation as a user."

"Are you seriously lecturing me on guys? You got knocked up by the first guy you dated in the Seen."

Bridget's eyed widened, "Sara!"

"Don't Sara me. You know, Asp warned me my family would try to keep us apart, although I thought Ryan and Shawn would be the naysayers. I didn't realize that the entire family would weigh in." She stomped off to her bedroom.

"That did not go as I expected," Star said. "Perhaps I should have told Tempe and let her deal with it."

Bridget silently agreed.

Chapter 12

"Tempe, you're missing the point."

Tempe massaged her neck as if it were stiff. "You want me to order Lady Sara away from Asp? Okay, how about I order you two away from Lady Dawn and Lady Snowbell?"

"That's different," Ryan growled.

"How?" Tempe's eyebrow raised.

"The ladies Dawn and Snowbell are nice," Ryan huffed. Okay, that sounded lame even to his ears.

"That's the best you've got?"

Unfortunately, yes. Ryan looked at Shawn, and they both shrugged.

Tempe glared at her nephews. "All of Asp's time with Sara has been supervised. If I hear you're badgering either of them, I will find a suitable way to address your actions, and I guarantee you won't like it. Sara won't break the rules as long as she's treated fairly. We return to the Seen in thirteen days, where she can date anyone, without supervision or approval from her family. At that time, she will be at PAC HQ – with Asp – and none of us are there full time to watch over her."

Ryan and Shawn looked at each other in horror. Neither of them had considered that possibility.

*****

Shawn looked up from the breakfast spread just in time to choke on the piece of grape-like fruit he popped into his mouth. What the heck were his sisters doing? Sundresses? They weren't at the beach, and they were showing entirely too much… everything.

Ryan slapped Shawn on the back to help with the lodged food and followed Shawn's eyes. He winced in sympathy. Sisters, no female relative, should look that stunning.

Lady Samma joined the sisters. "Your dresses are lovely."

"Sundresses, suitable for a day outing, unless we're doing serious hiking." Bridget looked at the fae. They were all dressed in uniforms of some sort and looked ready for serious physical exertion.

"I love the style, and no, we aren't going to hike. We'll be in open-air carriages for the tour, so we can talk. In court, we mostly wear these uniforms with our realm colors, and formal wear in the evening, although many, like Lady Saffron, wear the flowing day dresses."

"Oh, should we change?" Sara sighed, a bit dejected at the prospect of putting on the peasant dress she had contemplated earlier or jeans.

"By no means," Rune walked up. "You look great."

"Besides," Lady Samma added, "Your aunts are wearing the same type of dress."

They looked past Rune to see Lady Tempest and Lady Saffron decked out in sundresses as well. Tempe looked over at the sisters and winked.

Sara laughed and whispered to Bridget, "She really does know everything."

Breakfast was a casual affair. Food was laid out buffet style, with no assigned seats. Everyone took advantage of the rare opportunity to talk with someone from a different realm. The chaperones sat in a group, watchful, but content to allow the guests freedom.

Lady Fawn sat down beside Sara and asked, "What's the most beautiful natural sight in the Seen? I haven't been yet, and I'm sure the paintings don't do justice to the real beauty."

Sara chewed slowly, at a loss for how to answer. Swallowing, she decided honesty was the best policy. "Of the sights I've seen, I think the northern lights are the most amazing, but there's a lot of the Seen I've yet to visit."

"Travel must be harder now that the humans know about us. Are there restrictions?" Pagan asked.

64

"In the Seen, we use passports to move between countries and must go through checkpoints. That's true for humans and preternaturals. The human governments don't stop us from traveling, but they tend to focus on our travel plans more than they do humans with the same itinerary," Ryan explained.

"That's the truth," Shawn added. "They haven't been happy to find out that they aren't the most powerful creatures on the planet. Some fear us, others want to study us, and, of course, there are those looking for ways to control us and make money off of our gifts."

"Sounds like they're impacting your daily life. Why not teach them a lesson?" Asp asked. The looks sent his way would have concerned a lesser man. He shrugged, "I'm not talking injuring humans but showing them that they can't control what you do?"

"Oh Tem... Lady Tempest did that." Shawn replied. "For the most part, humans consider her armed and dangerous."

Asp laughed, "Who doesn't consider her dangerous? As for armed, we're all armed." He created a small fireball and used water to dissipate it before the chaperones could object.

"Weapons from the Seen are registered and can only be carried within certain confines. Most governments think preternaturals should be registered as well." Joey popped a small pastry in his mouth.

"Good luck with that," Pagan muttered.

"Exactly," Joey agreed. "We won't tell them our specific abilities and what our weaknesses are because they would use that information against us."

"Are the humans that angry?" Lady Dawn frowned.

"Nope," Ryan replied. "They're that frightened."

"Well, it's understandable," Asp commented. "If I didn't have any magic to call, I would want to know what powers everyone else had so I could at least try to protect myself. But at the same time, I can see why you don't disclose everything. It's for the same reason. To protect kith and kin."

"That's it," Ryan nodded, surprised he agreed with Asp. "The humans don't trust preternaturals, and the preternaturals don't trust humans. Both have valid reasons to mistrust, but it makes working together hard."

Lady Samma had no interest in the politics of the Seen. It was hard enough to keep up with politics in the Farseen, but Farseen politics were essential to her personal goals. She leaned forward and changed the subject. "Does anyone know where we're going today? I hoped we might take the path along the Kaveri River east toward Psyche Falls. I've never seen that waterfall, and Moelur Basin is said to be beautiful this time of year."

"You're in luck, Lady Samma," Spruce of the Northern Realm said. "We plan to parallel the Kaveri River until we reach the falls. There we'll have a small snack before continuing on to Moelur Basin. And yes, the basin is in high bloom now. We'll return via a Farseen side gate, I think that's what the humans call it, so we'll be on time for tonight's repast." He grinned at Joey, "No one tracks our ways."

Joey smiled but didn't comment. Tempe wasn't sure how the fae would react when they found out that the humans could track to the Farseen. Joey didn't think it was a big deal, but what did he know? As they headed out to the carriages, Joey whispered to Star, "Why is everyone so polite? Spruce and Asp both seem to be on their best behavior."

"Guesting laws. When all realms meet together, there are specific laws that govern behavior. While Spruce might torment you if just the shifters were visiting, he dares not with all realms in attendance. It would bring shame to the Northern Realm, and that would anger Lord Ellwood."

Joey grinned. This might be an okay visit if Spruce had to behave. He saw Spruce board a carriage and the grin dropped from Joey's face. It was the same carriage he and Star were assigned.

Once everyone was seated, the carriages, pulled by unicorns, not horses, took off at a sedate pace. Lady Star leaned into Joey and whispered, "Grandfather is making a statement of his power. Very few can train unicorns to pull or carry anything. When he was young, he was known for his ability to work with unicorns."

A pod of river merfolk followed the carriages for a while. It was hard to tell who was more excited, the merfolk or Lady Fawn.

"How lovely. The river merfolk never come near the Southern Realm residence. I've never seen them before," Lady

Fawn looked over at Spruce, the only representative of the Northern Realm in their carriage. "Do you think we could stop?"

"No reason to. Two pods reside at Psyche Falls. You'll have ample opportunity to speak with them," Spruce explained, smiling at her enthusiasm. His smile widened when Pagan moved closer to Fawn in an attempt to block Spruce from her view.

"Do they only speak Fae?" Joey asked.

"Some, but many speak the major Seen languages. They learn languages as quickly as any fae."

"That must be nice," Joey groused. Working as the sovereign's squire, he was trying to get up to speed on multiple languages, and he had no fae heritage to fall back on.

"Is it true that humans don't pick up languages as quickly as we do?" Pagan asked. He wanted to visit the Seen but so far hadn't been assigned to PAC HQ. And since the exposure, no fae wishing to remain in court life visited the Seen without prior approval from their realm lord and PAC HQ.

Joey huffed, "Not just humans. The preternaturals of the Seen do not pick up languages as quickly as you do either. We have to study and work to learn a new language. It takes a while."

Spruce cocked his head to one side, "You don't hear the intent of the sounds?"

"No," Joey retorted. "Believe me, I would love to pick up languages fast. I spoke English and Spanish growing up, and now I'm trying to master a couple of other languages, but the learning curve is high."

Spruce's eyes lit up in amusement at the admission he was sure irritated the shifter to make. It was also useful information to have.

Joey looked at Star and smiled, "Milady has been a real help, translating for me when needed."

"If I may ask, what are your duties as the sovereign's squire?" Pagan leaned around Lady Fawn to look at Joey.

Joey blushed, "Probably not as glamorous as it sounds. Meetings, meetings, and more meetings, and I travel for the sovereign frequently. More so now that we can't just open gates in the Seen."

"Is it true the humans can track point of origin to point of arrival?" Spruce asked.

"Oh yes, Lady Tempest is presenting the findings to your High Court this trip," Joey responded, relieved that he had been given permission to tell that if asked. He wasn't sure he had the ability to lie outright and be believed, not even for political reasons. This was especially true as many fae were able to somehow sense an outright lie.

"I heard ways can now be tracked down to the specific location," Spruce commented while he watched jellyfish playing tag with the merfolk, keeping Joey in his peripheral vision of course.

"Yes, coordinates by latitude and longitude," Joey watched the same game of tag with Spruce in his peripheral vision as well. "The humans can't use the information for the Farseen and won't be able to until they acquire the needed knowledge of the Farseen. Currently, humans only know that a dimensional gate has been open. The preternaturals of the Seen are working hard to prevent them from acquiring knowledge of other dimensions."

"I'm sure, but I suspect the humans are working equally hard to gather that knowledge."

Joey nodded his agreement.

Chapter 13

Sara watched the merfolk and jellyfish play tag for a while, mostly to tune out the politely veiled threats Ryan and Asp were exchanging. She leaned back and looked out the other side of the carriage. "What the heck is changing that lagohair?"

Every eye in her carriage followed where her finger was pointing.

"That, Lady Sara, is a werewolf," Asp explained.

Sara winced as the werewolf pounced on the creature the humans called a jackalope. The lagohair was a four-foot tall rabbit looking creature with horns. During the dual full moons, the humans had dubbed them jackalopes, and perhaps lagohairs did create the legend, in the same manner the gorkongs were the cause of the Bigfoot and Yeti legends.

Lady Dawn patted Sara's shoulder in sympathy, "You've never seen a werewolf before?"

"No. I've seen drawings and some blurry video during the dual full moons." Sara shrugged.

"They're one of the more dangerous predators in the Farseen," Asp commented.

"Why?" Sara asked, not taking her eyes off the sight of the werewolf eating its kill. "I've seen larger and more efficient predators from the Farseen."

"Of course, but most predators behave within certain confines. You can protect yourself with knowledge. Werewolves are cursed fae, and they act like something possessed. You have no clue what will provoke them," Kamden of the Central Realm responded.

Asp nodded, "Exactly, better an angry gorkong than a sleeping werewolf."

"Interesting maxim. Is there a story that goes with that?" Ryan asked.

Lady Dawn laughed, "It's one of those sayings taken from a bard's song. In fact, it's the song sung about the first recorded kill made by Lady Tempest."

"Hmm, perhaps one of the bards will sing it while we're here," Ryan grinned.

Asp laughed. "If not, I'm sure Liron knows it."

Sara's forehead wrinkled in confusion. "Do all fae have to battle werewolves as part of some rite of passage?"

"Hardly, many would not survive such an encounter, especially before our powers are fully developed," Asp admitted. "According to the song, Lady Tempest – or Mistress Tempest as she was at the time – was somewhere she shouldn't have been, doing something she shouldn't have been doing. She upset a gorkong and woke a sleeping werewolf."

Ryan laughed. "We have to make sure Phoenix hears that song." Sara was the only one to join him in laughter, so Ryan added, "Phoenix is one of Lady Tempest's younger brothers. As a child he was frequently in the wrong place at the wrong time and once – while still a child – he attempted to singlehandedly defeat a pack of hellhounds. Lady Tempest had to save him, and Phoenix still gets kidded about that. Seems only fair that he be told his eldest sister did something similar as a child."

"Indeed," Asp grinned, glancing up in the skies, trying to remember which of Star's guards was Phoenix. It might be the golden eagle, but it could be the falcon, both were brothers of Lady Tempest. It had been said magic reacted oddly around Phoenix, but Asp didn't know the details. "We're almost to the falls, just around the next bend you should be able to see them."

"How do you know this area so well?" Kamden barely kept the irritation out of his voice. Asp seemed to know a lot about a realm he had never lived in. Since his mother was from the Northern Realm, Kamden expected to be the person to answer questions in this carriage, and he had looked forward to sharing his knowledge.

"I've traveled with Father between his holdings many times." He looked over at Sara and admitted, "I'm just lucky no bards recorded some of my more foolish deeds."

Sara gave Asp a warm smile.

Ryan gritted his teeth. Obviously, Asp was going the good old boy route, or whatever the fae called that persona. Too bad it seemed to be working.

"Our tour guide is right, there's the falls." Kamden pointed off in the distance.

"Pretty, but not as high as I expected," Sara commented.

Kamden smiled. "You see before you the shortest falls in the Farseen. Their highest point is only fifteen feet. Anything shorter is just a rapid. For height, you need to visit the Western Realm."

Sara looked over at Ryan, "Do you think we could run the rest of the way?"

"I don't know…" Ryan looked up in the sky where Tempe flew in her dragon form. Before he could signal his aunt, Sara shifted and jumped out of the carriage. "Sara!"

Shawn looked over, "What the…" Shawn stood to follow his sister.

"Shifters stay in the carriages." Ryan jumped and shifted to his lion and took off after Sara.

Ryan's order stopped Shawn cold. Unsure what was happening, Lady Snowbell placed a hand on his shoulder. Shawn snarled and sat down, never taking his eyes off his foolish sister.

Sara's little fifty-pound dog form had already drawn the attention of a river dragon. She was running full out, but the thin river dragon – which reminded Shawn of a Chinese dragon – was closing in fast. River dragons grew to no more than fifteen feet in length with short, stubby arms and legs, but they were still large enough to eat a fifty-pound dog, maybe even kill an African lion.

Ryan leaped over Sara, shifted to his blue dragon, and caught the river dragon in his jaws. He landed at the edge of the river, pleased that Asp stood between Sara and the river. He was not so pleased when Sara shifted and grabbed hold of Asp for comfort.

"Sir, our companion did not realize the creature was a shifter. He saw only a tasty treat. It has been many years since we have watched for shifters when hunting near our river and he is young."

Ryan turned with the dragon in his jaws. Standing before him, river merfolk, the ones with frog-like digits on their hands and feet, patted the dragon and spoke in a language Ryan didn't understand, but the dragon did. He could feel the dragon relax in his jaws.

"If you release him back into the river he will not trouble you or yours again this day, honored guest of Lord Ellwood."

Excellent suggestion. Let's not upset the river merfolk or river dragons of the Northern Realm. Ryan heard Tempe in his head and agreed. He dropped the dragon into the water and shifted to human form. The dragon bowed, and Ryan inclined his head in return.

"What was the form you took before the blue dragon? Your dragon is impressive, but the other form pleases me," one of the merfolk asked.

"Uh, African lion," Ryan shrugged, keeping Asp in his view. Amusingly enough, Asp had the same look on his face that Ryan had sported a couple of years ago when Lady Dawn had sought the safety of his arms. Asp was terrified of causing a public incident. Good. Ryan looked back at the carriages. None of the adult fae had moved. Not surprising. According to the rules of conduct, they could not interfere or assist without an invitation. To do so would be an indication that they didn't think the shifters could protect their own.

"African lion. It's larger, bulkier, than the cat form Lady Tempest takes. Yes, it is a pleasing form."

Ryan nodded and walked toward Sara. He looked up and saw that Tempe had kept her distance and he preened just a little, realizing the fae would consider her lack of involvement as an indication that she trusted him to take care of the issue. Ryan stopped and bowed to Asp, forcing the words out of his mouth, "Your actions have pleased me this day." Asp nodded with only a slight smirk, handed Sara over to her cousin, and returned to the carriage.

Ryan waited until the carriages moved toward the buffet and whispered, "What were you thinking?"

"That I wanted to run, obviously. Don't start…"

"Do not cop an attitude with me! That river dragon nearly had you for lunch."

"I know," Sara sobbed. "I screwed up, huh? Will Tempe send me back?"

"I doubt it, but you have to think. This isn't the Seen and, while you've got the rules of court down pat, you apparently haven't studied the predators of this dimension adequately." Ryan took her arm, and they walked toward where the others were exiting the carriages and gathering around the buffet.

Sara looked up at her cousin, "Did you see Asp stand between me and the dragon? Wasn't he brave?"

Ryan glared. He took on the dragon, and she praised Asp for giving her a shoulder to lean on. Women!

"The question you should ask is why you put Asp in danger by forcing him to come to your rescue?"

Sara turned to face Tempe, "I didn't! Did I?"

"You think Asp and Ryan ran to challenge a river dragon for fun?" Tempe's trademark eyebrow rose.

"I guess you're right," Sara replied sadly.

"You guess," Shawn stormed over.

Bridget tapped Shawn on the shoulder, "Hush. Sara's antics broke the ice and the others are discussing their own foibles now. Seems to be something of a game, each trying to prove that their mistake was the greatest or the most embarrassing." Bridget hooked her arm in Sara's and herded her toward the food, "But don't do it again. This is the only vacation I get this year. I don't want to spend the rest of it explaining to Father how I failed to keep you safe."

As the sisters approached the group Asp called out, "I've prepared a plate for you, Lady Sara, should you be inclined to eat."

Bridget watched as Sara blushed and joined Asp. He might not be as bad as Ryan had painted him. He was undoubtedly treating Sara well.

"I hope your sister is unharmed." Rune stopped beside Bridget and offered her his arm. "I prepared a plate for you as well."

Bridget beamed at him.

Fed, and after another short carriage ride, they walked a scenic path through a field of flowers toward Moelur Basin. Lady Samma sighed, "It's as beautiful as I expected."

"Oh yes, the flowers and butterflies seem brighter here than in the Seen," Bridget agreed, snapping pictures. "I wonder if it's true or if I'm just noticing the beauty since it's my first trip to the Farseen."

Rune smiled and helped her cross a small stream, using short pillars that had been placed as stepping-stones. "Based on my experience in the Seen, I think it might be a little of both. Every place I go in the Seen seems magical to me, more so than my reactions to similar sights here. I believe your reaction to the Farseen is similar."

"Do the pixies and nymphs dress to blend in with the surroundings? I've noticed the ones in the forests wore mostly brown and dark green, while the ones in this field seem to prefer light green and the colors of these flowers."

"It's not a requirement. Though most dress to blend in with their surroundings, you will find some who dress to stand out."

"We're almost to the Soul River. It runs through the center of the basin. At this point it's wide enough and deep enough that we might catch hippocampi playing with the merfolk," Kamden commented as he passed them.

Bridget's face lit up, "I've only ever seen drawings." She topped the hill and squealed, "How lovely, and so many colors. I had no idea."

Hippocampi were, in fact, swimming and playing with merfolk. The merfolk in the basin were larger than the ones they had seen earlier but still shorter than the fae and shifters, and they had flippers for hands and feet. The hippocampi, with the head and front hooves of a horse and the tail of a fish, came in various colors and markings. Some had recognizable hoofed creature colors like Pinto, Appaloosa, and even zebra. Others had coloring similar to brightly colored fish.

Rune smiled at her enthusiasm. It was contagious. He looked across the river, and his smile turned to concern as he shouted, "Watch the wasteland skies."

Chapter 14

A massive gold dragon flew to greet the flock of red dragons approaching from the west, rendering Rune's warning unnecessary. Lady Tempest, in dragon form, had already flown over to greet the flock of red dragons that headed toward the basin. Lady Tempest, due to her age, was as large as any supreme matriarch. She dwarfed the largest member of the red flock. He turned expecting Ryan to take his blue dragon form and join her. He wasn't the only one.

Ryan smiled but didn't take his eyes off the skies. "You think Lady Tempest needs my assistance?" In truth, he wanted to go to her aid, but her mind speak orders had been clear. This flock was friendly. She didn't want anyone to join her. He watched Tempe stop in front of the prominent red while the others hovered in a V behind their leader.

"Excellent point," Asp commented as he, too, watched the skies.

After a quick conversation, the reds flew off, and Tempe flew back to the carriages where the others waited.

*****

"Nothing," Ryan muttered. "Not one piece of paper. If Val wrote anything down, it's long gone.

Shawn looked up from his Kindle, "You're still looking? I gave up days ago."

"You are wise." Ryan looked at the weapons on the wall again. He had wasted every spare moment trying to find something, anything to explain Val. "I just wanted some insight into Val."

"Why, because everyone compares you to him?" Shawn shrugged.

"No, well maybe," Ryan conceded still staring at the weapons. "I've been able to track down every weapon but that one." He pointed to a wooden handle with a dull, square blade on it. It was at the highest point in the room. It looked similar to an ax, but the stone was larger and thicker. "When I've asked the fae about it they assume I'm making it up."

Shawn looked up at the weapon, "Did Val fly?"

"What? No, not like the Central Realm Air Guard, but he could take a bird form." He looked at the weapon and over at Shawn, "You think?"

"The only way to get to that weapon is to fly or find a three-story ladder, and I haven't seen a ladder in the Farseen."

Ryan shifted to his eagle and flew up to look it over. The weapon didn't look like a fake. He pushed his bird body on the stone, nothing. He tried pushing on the handle, nothing. Staring at the weapon in disgust, he noticed tiny little chips in the stone. If he hadn't been in bird form, he doubted he would have seen the indention. The area looked like it had been tapped with a small nail or a beak. That was it! He pecked at the stone once with his beak. Shawn yelled, and Ryan looked down at the opening in the wall. Ryan swooped down, shifted, and picked up the book. Excited, he opened to the first page.

"What's it say?" Shawn leaned around Ryan to peer at the book. "What language is that?"

Ryan groaned. It was written in fae, ancient fae. Figures!

Chapter 15

Sage narrowed her gaze on the U.N. rep and growled, "We will not become pawns in your petty government battles."

"You're an American citizen. You owe it to your country to help protect our borders." Aubrey Ewing, the U.S. representative to the U.N., commented across the table. She hated coming to PAC HQ, but it was the only place the shifter sovereign and high wizard would agree to meet. Once PAC HQ was up and running, they refused to return to the U.N. building in New York City.

"Preternaturals are only citizens in this country because you want access to our power and financial resources. You hope to use us as spies, assassins, and saboteurs," Nova, high wizard, commented dryly.

"We would never do such a thing," Aubrey replied indignantly, mostly because Nova was right. And that was a fact the U.N. representative would never admit out loud.

"You just asked us to send a telepath to the U.N. That person would be a spy," Sage explained slowly, as if to a child.

"Only to protect us from other telepaths," Aubrey explained again.

Sage took a sip of her tea and breathed in the orange blossom smell. She had chosen that blend to help keep her calm. Epic fail. "No one in the U.N. has a telepath on staff. At least not a telepath with any real power."

"How do you know that?" Aubrey pegged Sage with a hard stare. The child who ruled an entire dangerous species was either a fool or cunning. Aubrey, like most of the human ruling elite, assumed Sage was a figurehead. Tempest was the obvious power and true leader of the shifters.

"I know because true telepaths are rare even amongst preternaturals. All have been notified by their respective leaders that using their talent to aid humans is punishable by death. In fact, any preternatural who sells their unique gifts to the highest bidder forfeits their life, and unlike you, Ms. Ewing, they understand that there will be no trial and no appeal, just death," Sage smiled sweetly.

The intercom chirped on, "High Wizard, Sovereign, with apologies, you are needed in the command center. The issue is urgent." Both leaders ran from the room, leaving Aubrey sitting alone with aids and guards.

*****

Lieutenant Colonel John Anderson walked toward the checkpoint where humans wishing to enter PAC HQ lined up. He no longer had to patrol, with his recent promotion he had other duties, but Anderson found that non-scheduled outings kept his people sharp, and if he enjoyed stretching his legs, well, that was nice too. "Sergeant Hall, how is the day progressing?"

"Not too bad, sir. There's a bit of a line but no issues," Sergeant Hall said.

Sergeant Hall was newly assigned to PAC HQ, but the colonel had been pleased to see the young man again. Both had worked the Salt Lake dual full moon gate events, and he found the sergeant to be an excellent soldier. Anderson looked at a helicopter approaching the landing pad a little too fast, "Who's that?"

"Unknown," Hall tapped his headset, "Incoming. They're passing the chopper pad and heading straight for HQ. The chopper is armed."

"Everyone to the bunkers," Anderson ordered as the troops, human and preternatural, rushed to do just that. According to the preternatural leadership, those in PAC HQ were safe from a bomb, even a nuclear warhead, but everyone outside the shields had no protection. Doubting everyone would fit in the bunkers, Anderson took a second to be proud of the men and women under his command. They sent as many civilians as possible into the hopeful safety of the bunkers. There were few preternaturals outside, and apparently none who could open a gate.

No one tried to enter PAC HQ. Even the visitors knew that, in the event of an attack, those outside would remain outside. Shields stronger than blast doors lowered over the only entry into the building. A tint had been added to the shields so that everyone, even humans, could see it. PAC HQ was locked tight.

When as many as could fit were in the bunkers, those who remained outside closed the heavy doors. Incredibly, only two human soldiers and three preternaturals remained. Everyone else had fit. They turned toward the chopper and watched two bombs drop.

Anderson and Hall nodded to each other, accepting their death as the price paid to save others.

"Gentlemen, my shield awaits," Jarvious, a relative of Tempest, called. As the two soldiers joined the preternaturals, he added, "It won't stand against one of your nuclear devices."

"Better than nothing, Jarvious. We accept your offer," Anderson said. The shield closed, and Anderson looked at his companions.

"Liron of the Northern Realm," the male bowed after he reinforced Jarvious' shield. "You are Anderson and Hall. Lady Tempest honored your contributions during the dual full moons."

Anderson blushed. What did that mean? He nudged Hall, whose mouth hung open. He didn't blame the kid, he barely kept his own mouth closed.

Liron pointed to the female, "Lady Windy of the Central Realm Air Guard."

Anderson smiled. The air guard was touted as the best trained flying force in the Farseen.

"Gentlemen," she didn't take her eyes off the bombs, closing in fast.

Hall could finally identify the bombs with his binoculars, "The first isn't nuclear. The second is."

"Well then, I believe the correct expression is 'it's a good day to die'," Jarvious glared at the bombs.

"Or not," Liron pointed to the shield that formed around the bombs. "But I'm not sure any have the power to contain a nuclear explosion completely."

The bombs exploded casting an odd sort of firework display within the shield.

"It's pretty," Hall commented, surprised that they hadn't died immediately.

*****

Nova glanced at Sage before returning her eyes to the swirling mass of bomb remnants in the shield, "How long can you hold that abomination?"

"If I don't have to do anything else, a few hours. I don't know what to do with the nuclear waste."

"I say we return it to sender," said Lady Trea of the Western Realm.

"While I agree in theory, we don't know where it came from," Nova replied calmly. "And anywhere we place it will contaminate more than just that location, in much the same way that cold iron impacts the Farseen."

"Can you send it to another dimension?" Aubrey Ewing asked.

Sage turned to stare at the U.N. representative who should not be in the PAC HQ war room.

"With apologies, Sovereign, High Wizard." Lady Sierra of the Northern Realm bowed. "The U.N. Secretary-General requested that Ambassador Ewing represent the U.N. in this matter.

Nova gave an unhappy nod. Later she would make sure the fae understood that the U.N. was not to be granted such favors. "We will not send toxic material to another dimension. This was caused by the Seen, it shall remain in the Seen."

"But surely there is a dimension with no intelligent life. This waste could be dumped there without harm." Aubrey ignored Nova's growl.

"You think to transport this mess to another dimension. How shortsighted of you." Lady Z's voice was heard before she was seen. She dropped her veil and glared at Aubrey. "You want to destroy other dimensions with no regard for their environment. I can assure you I have never found a dimension without elementals, and they are all intelligent, apparently more so than humans. Preternaturals, hear me now. If I learn that any waste from the Seen is pushed into another dimension, I will lead the elementals in the war they are already contemplating here in the Seen over what has been done to their planet. Don't make me prove to everyone that I'm the power you have to worry about. If I start a war, I will clean this planet and The One can start afresh.

No one moved as Lady Z simply disappeared.

"Who does she think she is?" Aubrey crossed her arms in front of her and glared where the strange female fae had been.

Nova barked an unhappy laugh, "She thinks she's the one being that is able to communicate with elementals in all dimensions, and she's right."

"If she were to lead an elemental war against humans and preternaturals, we would lose," Sage explained.

"And if she starts that war the fae will leave the Seen with extreme haste. No fae will act against Lady Z." Lady Sierra looked at Aubrey and added, "I feel a strange obligation to warn you that Lady Z might still be in this room. I know of no one who can see her if she wishes to remain unseen, and there is no shield known to the fae that will keep her outside if she wants in."

Aubrey's mouth dropped open, "You mean she can go anywhere, and no one can stop her?"

"Yes."

"How about Tempest? She's powerful."

Sage shook her head. "You could ask Tempest when next you meet, but I wouldn't recommend it. Back to the current problem, I need some place to deposit this nuclear waste, or it's going to drop on the U.N."

"What?" Aubrey turned an interesting shade of red.

"Well, I'm not dropping it on PAC HQ, and since we protected your U.N. from a bomb a while back, I think that's where the waste should fall. I have no clue where it came from, do you? I wasn't joking. I can only hold it for a few hours."

"Then hand it off to someone else."

"No! This ends now. You give me a place to drop this waste that is secure, or I drop it on the U.N. You have one hour to provide a location." Sage turned and walked out of the room knowing full well that the humans would provide access to one of their nuclear containment facilities. She just hoped it was soon. The strain of keeping the waste contained was already wearing on her.

Nova smiled and followed the young shifter. As the door closed, Lady Sierra said, "I think I like this new sovereign."

*****

"Did everyone enjoy themselves?" Tempe asked once the shifters were gathered in Tempe's oversized tree house. It had become their default meeting place.

"Wonderful. You grew up in a magical place," Bridget dropped onto one of the large pillows.

Tempe smiled at her niece, but her expression was pained. "Some days it was magical, other days, not so much. Seen news update, someone dropped a nuclear bomb on PAC HQ. Sage encased it in a shield before it exploded, and the waste was placed in a containment box and sent to a nuclear facility for storage. No injuries, but apparently a U.N. representative made a bad suggestion, and Lady Z has vowed she will lead the elementals in a war against the Seen if they don't clean up their act."

"Do we know who dropped the bomb?" Ryan's voice rose over all other questions and comments.

"No, but we'll find out. Tomorrow I'll be in closed meetings all day. Ryan will approve all activities."

"It's official, these rules are weird. I've got at least sixty years on him," Bridget commented.

"Yes, you do, but you don't outrank him," Tempe replied.

Bridget shook her head. Ryan pressed his lips together to keep from smiling.

"Okay, cousin, Tempe already approved my pre-breakfast walk with Asp. You better not mess with my plans." Sara glared at him. To Tempe she asked, "Anything else?" and left when Tempe shook her head.

Tempe turned to Joey, "You'll be with me for the first hour tomorrow, but then you'll be able to rejoin Star."

"Who will be with milady?" Joey winced at how quickly he reverted to using milady in reference to Star. It got him a lot of ribbing in the Seen when he made the mistake back home.

"I'm quite capable of taking care of myself, thank you very much," Star stood and walked toward the door. "Come, you can apologize while we dress for dinner."

Joey gaped after her.

"She knows to remain with her guards anytime I'm in closed meetings. For goodness sake, go after her," Tempe gently pushed him toward the door.

Joey left, and the others followed.

Ryan waited until the others had left and asked, "Is everyone alright? Should I return?"

"Emergency plans are in place. Kyan will not leave Sage's side for any reason until we return."

He nodded, "Okay, next crisis. What did the reds want?"

Tempe sighed. "I'm to present myself to Ralliner, supreme matriarch of the reds, at sunrise tomorrow."

"Can a dragon summon you like that?" his eyebrow raised.

"The supreme matriarchs can," Tempe said. "If a supreme matriarch summons a ruling fae and they don't attend, the matriarch responds by calling all of their dragon tribe and attacking that fae's realm."

"Want me with you?"

"No, you'll remain with the shifters. Don't worry, I've done this before."

Don't worry, not likely. Ryan needed more information, but her stance indicated she had said all she would say on the subject. As he walked toward the door, he asked, "By the way, was the sleeping werewolf a magical day?"

"The sleeping werewolf? Don't tell me the bards still sing that song?" Tempe laughed.

"Someone alluded to it today," he admitted.

"I was around ten when that incident occurred. I had to explain my bloodied condition to Lord Ellwood in his crowded receiving chambers. That resulted in the first song ever sung about me. The bard who wrote it seemed to think it would be a better song if I were brave and undaunted, not scared to death."

Ryan laughed and walked out. Alone in the hallway, he shook his head. His aunt killed her first werewolf before she could shift or had any shifter powers.

Chapter 16

"What's the catch?" Sara eyed them with distrust.

"No catch." Shawn held his hands up in surrender.

Ryan returned her gaze with an innocent expression. "We decided to run to Koukakala Falls during the full moon. They mark the border between the Northern Realm and the Western Realm. It's the first time we've had a full moon in the Farseen during Star's visit, and apparently, the pull is strong if more than one moon will be full. We thought you might like to invite Asp to join us, is all. We know we haven't been friendly to him. Just trying to make peace," Ryan shrugged.

"Isn't that a long hike?"

"Round trip is just under forty miles. We will run out there and then we'll either run or open a gate back. We'll shift, and the fae will run. The fae are pretty fast on open ground."

"Okay, I'll ask, but this better be on the up and up." Sara still didn't trust those two. She walked away and headed straight for Tempe, only to find Star and Bridget with her.

"What's up?" Tempe looked up from some paperwork.

Not one to beat around the bush, Sara asked, "Did you approve the moon run to Koukakala Falls?"

"Yes, did Ryan do such a bad job of explaining it?"

"No, but he and Shawn have been so anti-Asp I wanted to make sure they weren't cooking something up," Sara admitted.

Tempe smiled, "Father Aldous, Bridge, and I will chaperone, along with Star's guards, Captain Tero's Air Guard

Squadron and a select few of the Northern Realm warriors, so I doubt anyone will start anything on this hike."

"Good, I want to meet Asp's father." Sara turned and left, happy with the arrangement.

Bridget turned to her powerful aunt. "Seriously, you're making it far too easy for them."

"Yes, I am. With so much togetherness, either Sara or Asp will grow bored and end it, or we need to be on speaking terms with Asp. You should just be glad that Father Aldous and I are friendlier than we used to be."

*****

"I expected Ridge to go with us." Star looked around.

Tempe shook her head, "While they can behave in large gatherings where they don't have to interact, Ridge and Father Aldous do not attend the same small functions."

Star's mouth dropped opened. Perhaps the songs she had heard as a child were true. There were various versions of a dispute between Ridge and Father Aldous concerning an unknown lady (though many assumed it was Lady Tempest) of an unspecified court, but no one who saw the exchange would tell the tale. Most fae viewed the songs as fiction. Neither male came out the winner in any of the versions.

"I've heard three versions of the rift between Ridge and Father Aldous. I wonder which is accurate, assuming it's a true tale?" Rune commented to no one after Lady Tempest left, although his eyes cut to Asp.

Asp shrugged, "I've heard five, and Father will not discuss the subject with me. Last time I asked, he released one of his young reds to chase me. I won't ask again."

"Aren't young dragons at least ten feet long?" Shawn looked over in surprise.

Asp nodded.

Shawn grinned, surprised he agreed with Asp. "In that case, I suspect none of us should ask. As his son, you might get a young dragon, but the rest of us would probably get a full grown, hungry dragon."

Asp returned the grin. The casual first meal had been pleasant, and the day was beautiful. He had enjoyed spending time with Sara back at PAC HQ, and that was before he found out she was Ryan's cousin. He had observed the looks that passed between Ryan and Shawn. Neither male was happy with Sara's choice, upping his pleasure.

"Father, 'tis pleasant to see you," Asp bowed as Father Aldous approached. The others joined him in a formal bow.

"I'm sure it is," Father Aldous inclined his head. He nodded to the young and walked over to join the chaperons.

"I shall join the run this day." The younger set looked over in surprise. Lady Saffron wore combat clothes instead of her standard high heels and flowing dress.

A few minutes later Tempe said, "Shifters, two of the three moons are lined up to be full tonight. The pull will be stronger than normal. Enjoy the run, but don't chase anything without approval. As you've already learned, not all is as it seems here."

Everyone nodded. The briefing had been long and detailed earlier in the today. The moons called, and the shifters answered. Ryan took his lion form but was ready to turn into a dragon if needed.

Tempe and Saffron shifted together, Tempe to a jaguar and Saffron to a tiger. Father Aldous, closest to Saffron, eyes widened, but he didn't move otherwise. The rest of the fae gasped as Lady Saffron bounded across the field and led the shifters in their run. It was the first time Saffron had shown her animal self to the fae of any court.

At mile five, Shawn admitted to himself he was impressed. He hadn't believed the fae would keep up with shifters running in their other forms. He was wrong. The fae were apparently built for long distance running. No wonder they didn't use cars and such. In his human form, he could not match the pace Lady Saffron set. Happily, his mastiff had no issues, and he paced Lady Snowbell. The Ladies Snowbell, Dawn, and Misty were as fast as Pagan, Asp, and Rune. Lady Fawn was faster. She practically flew over the ground, however, she didn't fly. She ran even with Saffron who remained at the front, probably to make sure the shifters didn't take a wrong turn. Father Aldous and Bridge kept pace with the ladies, though it was evident that they weren't working all that hard and could pour on speed if needed. Ryan and Tempe moved around in the pack, keeping an eye on everyone.

Most of Star's guards flew overhead. Abbie, a wizard, had stayed behind, but Siri, a wizard fae half-breed, soared through the sky with the Central Realm Air Guard. Sam, Serenity, and Phoenix took their bird forms and flew lazy circles around the runners.

At mile twelve Asp admitted, if only to himself, that he was impressed. The shifters could move. For the second time, Sara took the form of a small white dog she called a Samoyed. He stayed close because she couldn't weigh more than fifty pounds. If anything attacked, she would be so much fodder. Why didn't she choose a more powerful form? Even a bird would be safer than such a small canine predator.

The trail Saffron followed crossed the Kaveri River twice going west toward Koukakala Falls. At the first crossing, near her home, a pod of merfolk swam with jellyfish and a river dragon clutch. They were the same merfolk that had begged for the dragon's life on the first tour of the Northern Realm. The largest dragon reared to its full height. Asp moved between Sara and the dragon at the same time Ryan did.

The dragon smiled and bowed, "Worry not, I have informed the dragons of my flock to be courteous to the visiting shifters, as they were courteous to my youngest son." He turned his eyes to face Saffron and Tempe, still in their large cat forms, "Tis good to see the daughters of Lord Ellwood running together. You have been missed by many, Lady Tempest."

Tempe inclined her head but didn't shift to speak.

"Your understanding and restraint did not go unnoticed."

Ryan turned, still in lion form, expecting to see river merfolk. What he saw surprised him. The male who had spoken had the single tailfin of a sea merman, but he had wings on his back like a nymph. A female with the same appendages flew down to join him.

"I am pleased with the result as well," Ryan replied after he shifted, thinking that Star needed to add this species to her list of Farseen creatures. Were they merfolk or nymphs? Good thing the shifters were in their other forms or someone would probably have said something insulting, or at least inappropriate. Hopefully, he wouldn't.

The merman-nymph turned to Lady Saffron, "I am gratified to see you running in the forest. It has been too long."

Saffron shifted, "Well met, Tehuti. I have little time for such pursuits now." Turning to Ryan, the only shifter in human form, she added, "Tehuti and Kailani are siblings. They moved to the Northern Realm before I reached adulthood, and we have long been friends."

Ryan nodded but didn't speak for fear he would say something wrong. It was rare that lesser fae who didn't conform to standards survived to adulthood, but now that he looked at them, they must have had nymph and merfolk parents, and it appeared Saffron had been their patron. That would explain why they had lived.

Ryan and Saffron shifted, and the run resumed.

To cool down, everyone slowed down to a trot for the final mile to the falls. Shawn topped one last hill and could see the falls he had been able to hear for a while, along with a picnic spread that would please a prince. Excellent, he was starved.

Tempe shifted and drew her Sais, "Was anyone expecting this?"

"No," Bridge pulled his weapon and eyed the spread in distrust. No one ate unattended food in the Farseen. Everyone in human form followed suit. The shifters spread out to better defend the group, even though they were confused by the concern.

Lord Ellwood appeared. He took in the battle-ready condition of the runners and smiled, "I believe the human expression is, 'surprise,'" he spread his arms out. "Lord Layton and I prepared a post run snack."

The runners relaxed, marginally.

In their dragon forms, Lord Layton, and his young twins, landed beside Lord Ellwood and shifted. Delton headed for the food, "Brilliant, I'm starved."

Layton placed a hand on his shoulder, "Greetings first, food second."

Delton rolled his eyes. He hated the trappings of court life. He bowed a single bow to everyone, "Well met," turned back to his father, "Food now?"

Father Aldous grinned, "Delton, you remind me of your Grandmother. Come, let us lead the others to this snack."

Asp frowned, and his eyes narrowed on Delton. "If I had done that Father would have rearranged my reality and not in a good way."

Breton overheard Asp and nodded his agreement. Only Delton could insult the entire party and amuse Father Aldous at the same time. Breton sighed. He would have been grounded for a hundred years.

*****

Shawn finished dressing, ready to get to the final formal repast of the trip. He looked in the mirror and grimaced. He would never get used to looking like a pirate. Shawn headed for the door.

"What's your hurry?" Ryan asked.

Shawn tried for nonchalant, "Just a walk before the last meal."

"Are you walking alone or with someone? Perhaps Lady Snowbell?" Ryan raised an eyebrow in a Tempesque move.

"Just a walk. We didn't plan to meet up," Shawn forced an easy smile.

"Uh huh," Ryan didn't buy that for a second and narrowed his gaze at his cousin. "Did you, perhaps, mention that you might take a walk before the evening repast?"

"Might have mentioned I wanted to stretch my legs. Anything wrong with that?"

"No. Be careful. You cause an incident and Tempe will have both our heads, once the fae finish with you."

Shawn patted Ryan on the shoulder before leaving, "Just a walk, cousin. Promise."

Ryan shook his head, both envious and irritated. Envious because he would love to meet up with Lady Dawn, and irritated because that wasn't going to happen. Any unauthorized meeting between him and Dawn would cause a real incident between the fae and the shifters.

Shawn headed for the hall of battles to view depictions of great battles fought – and won – by the Northern Realm. Oddly enough it was a good meeting place. If you happened to bump into someone there, because you were both admiring the carvings, well, how proper.

He didn't bother to look out the windows. The creatures of the Farseen had become almost normal to him. Besides, the only

Farseen creature Shawn wanted to see was a beautiful Lady of the Northern Realm with black, horizontal stripes in her white blonde hair. He slowed his gait to something resembling a stroll and stopped at the first carving he came to. Looking over the pillar, it was obviously one of Lord Ellwood's more recent battles. Wondering how long he should devote to each column, he continued to stare at the intricate carvings.

"You might want to view the scenes from oldest to newest," Lady Saffron commented as she walked by. "Lady Snowbell is currently viewing the oldest carving in the hall, and she knows the battles, if you have questions."

"Excellent suggestion," Shawn blushed and hurried over to Lady Snowbell.

Saffron didn't bother to hide her smile when Ridge walked over.

"You could have sent the shifter away from my niece and not into her arms," Ridge groused.

"I could have, but the young have met in the hall of battles for over six thousand years. In fact, you and Lady Tempest are credited with starting that tradition."

Ridge didn't dignify the remark with a comment as he walked away. He wasn't worried. Lady Saffron, regardless of flippant remarks, was in the hall specifically to watch the numerous guests who happened to meet up in the hall of battles. In truth, he was surprised it took Snowbell and Shawn until the last night to meet up.

Chapter 17

No more watching every word that came out of his mouth. No more stepping to the tune the fae played. Being home was comforting. After flying in his golden eagle form, Ryan sat on the ledge overlooking the valley. He pulled the book out of his back pocket and paged through it again. Ryan would have to ask someone for help translating it, but who? Tempe was the obvious choice, but he wasn't sure she would interpret it properly. Tempe was still over the top protective of Val's memory. If Ryan asked anyone else they would have to keep the secret from Tempe, and aside from that being a hard task to accomplish, he didn't want anyone to lie for him.

He sensed a presence and dropped the book back in his pocket. Ryan looked down and watched a raven fly toward him. She soared up and landed beside him, shifting in the process.

"Is this a private Zen moment, or can I join you?" Sage asked, even though she had already plopped down on the ledge.

Not wanting to go into the whole thing, Ryan commented, "Just thinking."

"Anything I can help with?" She smiled when he didn't answer and asked another question, "What were Val's quarters like?"

Ryan shot her a suspicious look, "You already know, don't you?"

"You're difficult for me to block." Sage smiled. "Tempe says it's because we're so linked. Of course, I still don't know what that means."

Ryan laughed and leaned back on the cliff. "Yeah, I suspect she'll drop that bomb on us at some point, but I haven't wanted to ask."

"Exactly. I have to return to Calabozo soon. I just wanted you to know you could talk to me. We haven't had much time to just talk with everything that happened."

"True," Ryan watched Sage stand. Before she shifted, he added, "I don't think you can read ancient fae either." He pulled the book out of his back pocket.

Sage turned in surprise, "Did you find that in Val's quarters? Tempe or Star is probably your best bet. I know Tempe doesn't like to talk about Val, but if she agreed to translate it for you, she wouldn't hide anything, but she might take a long time to translate it." She jumped off the ledge and shifted.

"My thought as well," Ryan muttered. He sat for a few more minutes with the book in his hand. A slow smile spread over his face as an idea occurred to him.

*****

Victoria looked around in awe, still amazed after a month at her new job. She had been vetted and allowed into a shifter research facility working for Destin. He spent her first morning showing her around, and she was seriously impressed. The preternaturals, shifters at least, seemed to have money enough for every cutting-edge gadget. Heck, they invented or improved a few of them.

Getting to work every day was interesting. Meeting up with other humans working the same shift at the facility, they rode in the back of a van with no windows and arrived inside the complex in less than a minute. Victoria suspected magic kept her and the other humans from realizing the passage of time, so they couldn't figure out where they were going. Each trip passed without the vehicle speeding up or slowing down, and with no external noise.

The shifters ran their facility like a military installation. Victoria's badge granted her access to her work area, the restrooms, cafeteria, break room, and a first aid station. That was it. The only other door, she assumed it accessed the rest of the facility, was guarded by two uniformed shifters at all times. The only human who ever used that door was Destin. Occasionally, a shifter would enter from there, but that was it. Even with all the cloak and dagger, it was the nicest place she ever worked. The facility was underground, but the break room had screens hooked up to show video cams from all over the world. You could watch street scenes in Italy and Japan, underwater video of a reef, the open plains in Africa and jungles in South America, and even various news stations. It was relaxing.

Victoria finished up her work for the day and left for her vanpool. Once in her car, she ran a few errands. Back home, Victoria hopped out of her vehicle, slung her purse over her shoulder, grabbed two bags of groceries, and grinned. Her bangs didn't fall in her eyes. They were finally long enough to pull back out of her eyes.

At her door, Victoria placed one of the bags on the ground to put her key in the lock. Door open, she picked up the bag, and something pinched in her neck. Geoffrey Watson, her old boss, the one who had corrupted her research, walked toward her. With him was a huge man Victoria didn't know. She fell to the ground, unconscious.

Victoria woke with a hangover. The bed was too firm. She groaned in confusion. She hadn't gotten drunk since that one time in college, freshman year. Who wanted to feel that bad the next day? There was too much to learn to waste time on self-inflicted pain. Oh, no! Her eyes opened wide. She was in a cell, not her bed. Geoffrey stood on the other side of the bars

"Where am I?" She pushed her bangs out of her face, realizing that the band that secured her bangs was no longer in her hair. Did they think she could use it as a weapon? Perhaps someone could, but not her.

"You shouldn't have left like that, Victoria. You shouldn't have deleted your research." He grinned, "But all's well that ends well. Now you'll tell us everything you've learned about the shifters, working in their secret facility."

"I won't betray them." Victoria sat up straight and eyed her former boss.

Geoffrey laughed and walked away.

Victoria sat back down on the bed. Yeah, Geoffrey was right to laugh. She didn't know anything about interrogation but doubted she would present much of a problem for a seasoned interrogator, or a new one for that matter. At least she couldn't tell them anything other than the specific research she was working on. Two guards opened her cell and Victoria looked up. She didn't cause a scene. She simply walked with them. No reason to waste the energy.

Five hours later she was returned to her cell, in handcuffs. Victoria curled up on the bed and breathed deeply, relieved to be alone. She hadn't given anything away, not even about her research, but so far, they just asked questions and threatened, nothing physical, but she was sure it was coming. Geoffrey said something about taking it to the next level. Exhausted, she drifted off to sleep, only to be shaken awake.

"Get up. Let's go." A rough hand pulled her up and pushed her toward the door.

Victoria stumbled down the hallway, fully alert with the realization that they were done playing nice. They took her to a different interrogation room, sparser and much more menacing. Victoria's mouth fell open in surprise. Dave Roberts, former director of the defunct AIB, sat across the table. He smiled.

Victoria sat down but didn't return the smile. She had heard the whispers about the AIB and what they did to humans and preternaturals alike. Victoria even watched the 60 Minutes exposé on the AIB last year. How could she rank a visit from the preternatural boogieman?

"Ms. Nelsen, can I call you Victoria?"

"Call me anything you like. I'm not talking."

A smile spread across Dave's face, "Okay, I'll talk, Victoria."

She rolled her eyes.

"You've been lied to. You think you're helping humanity, but you aren't. If these... creatures... are allowed to move about freely they can destroy the world. Their powers are dangerous."

Victoria huffed, "Of course they're dangerous. Humans aren't the apex predator anymore, never have been really, and it sucks, doesn't it? But the fact is, they've been on this earth with us since the beginning, and for the most part they're more humane than we are. They protect the weak. They haven't made slaves of us all, and it's obvious they could. Only humans are trying to kill that which is different." She held up her cuffed hands, "Seriously, you have armed guards in this room, and I'm in cuffs. I have no special powers and zero military training. I'm a geek."

"But we don't know that, do we?" Dave nodded to someone behind her.

"Know what?" Victoria looked up in surprise.

"If you're human."

The blow to her shoulder connected with such force that she fell out of the chair and hit the floor with a thud. The guard stood over her, poised to strike again.

"Preternaturals heal faster than humans. Consider this your verification that you're human." Dave watched, disinterested.

Gasping for breath, Victoria raised her right arm to block the next hit, forgot she had on cuffs and nearly pulled her left arm out of the socket. The second blow the guard dealt landed on her ribs, and she heard bones break. She hit the ground, once again gasping for breath. This time it hurt. She couldn't get her mouth open to protest as tears fell down her face. A simple blood test would verify that she didn't carry the magic gene, as it was called. This was a statement of some type.

Overhead an alarm pulsated.

"A gate just opened," Geoffrey ran into the room, leaving the door open. The sounds of fighting grew steadily louder. He eyed Victoria's injuries and cringed. "What have you done? You said you just wanted to talk to her."

"And you… you believe him?" Victoria's voice was so soft that she didn't think anyone would hear her.

"Fools believe what they're told," Tempe explained from the doorway. Standing with her was Serenity, Ryan, Bryce, and Phoenix, all well-known public faces of the shifter community.

"You came for me," Victoria sighed in relief.

"Of course, we came. Hold still so I can heal you enough to get you out of here," Ryan said.

She looked at him in surprise. She must have spoken out loud.

Ryan got good and rattled. He couldn't heal her. He didn't have the medical training to do it correctly. A shifter could recover from the damage he would inflict realigning the ribs, but he wasn't sure a human could. Ryan grimaced and then gave her his version of the medical everything-will-be-all-right smile, "You have broken ribs. One punctured your lung. I'm taking you straight to our doctors. I have to pick you up to carry you into the gate. I'm sorry, it's gonna hurt."

Victoria nodded and prepared for the pain. Ryan picked her up and tears ran down her face. She didn't scream only because she passed out.

Serenity walked over and opened a gate. The three of them left.

Dave Roberts had kept his eyes on Tempest the entire time. From the moment Serenity entered the room until she opened the gate and left, Tempest had drawn an ancient stone dagger, green in color, and held it between her and her sister. Why would she do that?

Tempe dropped her dagger back in its sheath. She pulled the two guards and Dave Roberts into a wind funnel, opened a gate and left. Bryce and Phoenix went with her.

Geoffrey stumbled back into the wall and tried to steady his breathing. What had happened?

A tall blonde male entered the room, "We need to leave. This place is gonna blow."

"You... you can't do that," Geoffrey whined.

"It's already done." The shifter grabbed Geoffrey and frog-marched him down the hall.

*****

Phoenix exited the gate in front of the Supreme Court Justices in the middle of a meeting. Stacks of paperwork on various cases and petitions were spread out in front of them. Phoenix looked around, no longer surprised his eldest sister opened a way into the internal layout of buildings she shouldn't have knowledge of.

Tempe dropped the wind funnel, and the three men fell to the floor. "We are done. Either you police humans who cause harm to shifters and humans working with shifters, or we will treat humans who break our laws the same as we treat shifters who break our laws."

Matthew Goldwin, one of the justices, stood up, "As I understand shifter law, you have three telepaths read their mind and, if they are guilty, they die."

"Exactly," Phoenix replied. "Shifters don't have prisons. The Three look into the mind of the person and determine the level of guilt. If there is a chance of rehabilitation and a shifter steps forward as guardian, the guilty are allowed the opportunity to rehabilitate, if not, they die."

"What are the odds a shifter would be willing to become the guardian of human?" Matthew asked.

"Very small," Phoenix acknowledged.

"But that means these so-called telepaths could lie and have you kill an innocent." Marie Pentax protested.

"They can't lie to the executioner." Tempe narrowed her eyes on the justices.

"You mean you don't think they would lie to you," Justice Pentax said. Tempest was the executioner.

"No, I mean they can't," Tempe pressed her lips together.

Pentax looked at the powerful shifter, and her eyes narrowed, "In addition to the powers we know about, you're a telepath as well?"

Tempe inclined her head in agreement.

"You lied on the forms," Pentax smiled in victory.

Bryce stepped forward, "And you want to bag and tag us. We will not allow that to happen. The question before us is what do we do about these men? Will you prosecute them, or do we kill them? They were torturing a human who works in one of our facilities."

Matthew Goldwin silenced Pentax with a look and answered, "You have instant justice. We have processes and procedures that take time. We also need proof, physical evidence to prosecute anyone. We don't have telepaths and, to be honest, many of us don't believe in them."

"Here's your proof. The AIB's own video of their interrogation." Phoenix dropped the disks on the desk in front of Goldwin.

Maria Pentax smiled gleefully, "It's not admissible in our courts. It wasn't gathered properly."

"The human courts need to catch up with reality. I have been ordered to assist in setting up acceptable laws and guidelines for authorized shifters to submit evidence." Bryce kept his eyes on Goldwin.

98

"And if we refuse?" Pentax asked.

"That's your choice. These three we leave with you, do what you will. Just know that we will be watching, and if you can't handle human on preternatural crimes then the next time we catch humans torturing anyone connected with the shifter community, I will kill. It's certainly easier for me to kill rather than detain." Tempe returned Maria's smile.

Bryce handed his new business card to Goldwin. This card identified him as the sovereign's legal advocate. "Discuss amongst yourselves and contact me if you want to work out a mutually beneficial arrangement."

Tempe opened a gate, and the shifters left. The gate exited on Bryce's property, Beryl Lane. In this case, it seemed like the best option and would cause no harm. They exited in the tower that served as both a lookout over the valley and a kid's playhouse.

"That was fun. I need to meet with Sage before returning to PAC HQ," Phoenix waved and headed for the entrance to Calabozo in Tempe's house.

Tempe looked over the valley, "It looks peaceful, doesn't it? I keep waiting for an invasion force, either other shifters or the humans. Funny, I'm no longer all that worried about the fae."

"Do you truly believe Rafael will make a play? He doesn't have the raw power needed to take on the Alpha Clan."

"I'm not sure he sees it that way. Rafael was never happy under Rayna's rule, but he understood she alone could take him out. He doesn't think Sage has built up the strength and knowledge to stand against him, one on one. Rafael seems to be waiting for some signal, and I think he's hoping I won't be around for the attack. He doesn't like me, but Rafael respects my fighting skills. Over the last few centuries, he's made comments about the other alphas getting weaker while I was the only one fighting. Rafael believes they've gotten rusty and are no longer a fighting force."

Bryce stepped up behind her and pulled her into his arms, "Not taking the prifs to the Farseen for the Freed Fae War means they haven't seen you guys in action for a long time. Perhaps the other alphas should showcase their talents more."

"That's one of the reasons Sage set up the teams for going out and handling issues."

Chapter 18

Victoria came awake with a start. She had been questioned and beaten and should be in a lot more pain than she was. Where the heck was she now? Victoria could open her eyes to see, but she was afraid to do that.

"It's okay, you're safe."

The comment came from a voice she didn't recognize. Victoria opened her eyes to look at the woman, obviously a preternatural. Even without her current bruises, all preternaturals made her feel decidedly average looking. Victoria pushed her bangs out of her eyes.

The woman handed her a clip for her hair and placed a hand on her arm. "I'm Lea, a sister of Tempest. Doctor Long and I treated your injuries, but you should move slowly for a few days."

"How? My ribs were broken, weren't they?" Victoria touched her side. It was tender, but she wasn't taped up, and nothing felt broken anymore. She pulled her bangs back with the clip and sighed in relief. She would never allow her bangs to be cut again. "You're a healer? I thought healers were a myth."

"We aren't common, but we do exist. Working with Doctor Long, I was able to heal you, but since you're human, your ribs will be tender and easy to break again for at least a couple of weeks."

"Cool. Don't suppose you could ask the crazies to leave me alone while I heal?"

Lea smiled in sympathy, "Wouldn't that be nice?"

Victoria nodded and tried to stand. She winced and became one with the bed. "Yeah, I think I'll just rest here for a while."

"I knew you were smart," Destin placed flowers on the table by the bed. "Don't worry about your place. Tempe had a cleaning crew set things right, and there are guards at your house now."

"Wow. I need guards? Why?"

"Have you talked to Tempe yet?"

Victoria opened her eyes wide. "Why would she need to talk to me?"

"Well," Destin cringed, but plowed on, "You sort of made the evening news."

"Me?"

"Actually, I made the evening news and someone, whom I shall find, leaked your photo, so now everyone knows you work for us." Tempe walked in and stood at the foot of the bed. "I'm afraid I did a poor job of protecting you."

"Honestly, I think you did a great job of rescuing me. I'm not sure I would have survived many more questions."

"That's kind of you to say, but now we have a problem. The hate groups know who you are and where you live. You must move."

"I just bought that house. I can't afford to move."

Tempe flinched at Victoria's response. The only reason the girl had trouble chasing her was her job, working with shifters. "We'll buy the house from you and help you relocate. You can't go back there."

"Relocate? You mean I lost my job, too?"

"No. Your job is secure. We'll work on getting everything else worked out. I called your parents, and they know you're okay. We're also guarding them. You won't be able to contact them until we work out a few details. Destin will bring you a more secure phone tomorrow."

"Secure phone? I'm being moved to a secure location, and I need a secure phone? What am I, a spy?" Victoria sighed, "I know it's not your fault, but geez, I like my little house. I just finished tiling my kitchen and painting the cabinets. It's perfect."

"That'll help with resale," Destin smiled, happy to be able to offer some good news.

102

Tempe and Victoria turned to stare at him and then looked at each other and shrugged. Men.

"Get some rest. We'll talk tomorrow." Tempe patted Victoria's foot and left.

Victoria sat for a minute and let all the bad news sink in. "So, did they trash my place?"

"Uh, yeah," Destin blew out air. "Ryan said it looked like they were looking for something specific."

"Oh no, surely they didn't." Victoria stood on shaky legs, "We have to go. I think I know what they were looking for."

"Okay," he caught her before she toppled over. "Let me call Tempe back and –"

"No! Not until I see if it's gone or not." Victoria walked over to grab her clothes, flashing her panties. Stupid hospital gowns. She turned and saw that Destin was now facing the closed window. Her boss had a sweet side. Too bad he had a girlfriend. She dressed quickly and only hissed a couple of times. Once dressed she asked, "You coming? Or are you going to rat me out?"

"You know Tempe, right? She won't be happy if anything happens to you."

"Then let us make sure nothing happens. I just want to be sure it's safe." She checked the hallway was clear before she angled toward the stairs.

"What are we checking on, anyway?" Destin asked as he opened the door to the stairwell.

"Nothing. Destin, go home. And you must be Victoria. You go back to bed.

Victoria looked up at nearly six and a half feet of gorgeous, most definitely crackers-in-bed worthy, male. She smiled. Any woman on the planet would gladly hop back into bed if he joined her.

"Hey, Fred. Whatcha doing here?" Destin gave him a pained smile.

"Making sure you humans don't go and do something foolish." Fred crossed his arms over his chest and planted his feet.

Victoria groaned. They wouldn't get past him without his permission. "Fred, is it? I have to check on something at my house. We'll be quick."

"No." No anger, no heat, just a simple no from the shifter.

"I have to make sure the crazies didn't find my research." She leaned on the wall to steady her shaking legs. Apparently, the drugs weren't out of her system yet.

"What research?"

"The part of my research I didn't tell anyone about. I can track individual gate signatures now."

"You can identify who opens a way? And you didn't tell anyone? Fred asked. His quiet tone didn't match the flash of fire in his eyes.

"I didn't want to show it to anyone until I was sure I had it right."

Fred glared at the human and spoke slowly and distinctly, "Are you telling me you worked on this at home? Where anyone could find it?"

"Yes," her voice squeaked. "But I also booby-trapped the safe. No one but me should be able to open it. I'm not a fool."

"That remains to be seen," Fred said through gritted teeth. Should was not a power word. "Let's go."

"You'll help?" Victoria looked up at him hopefully.

"I don't see that I have a choice, do you?" He tossed his keys to Destin and swooped Victoria up into his arms.

"Hey! I can walk." She tried to move, but he held her firmly in his grip.

"You can fall on those shaky legs, but I doubt you can walk more than a few feet." With Fred carrying her, they left the building, using stairways and less traveled routes. He placed Victoria gently in the back seat of his car before crawling in beside her. Pegging Destin with a glare, Fred muttered, "Drive while I call for reinforcements."

Chapter 19

Destin parked down the block from her house. "This is a bad idea, isn't it?"

"Yep, but I've left messages on every friggin' phone the local alphas have. At least one of them should get the message and show up soon. You stay in the car and wait for them. If anything happens, get away and call for help." Fred turned to Victoria, "You'll obey every order. Right?"

"Yes, sir!" She added a backward salute.

Fred rolled his eyes and opened the door. "Just don't get injured again. Your Aunt Naomi will kill me if you get hurt."

"I'll do my best," she said and hid her smile. Apparently, Fred had met her aunt and was impressed. Most people were.

Fred put his arm around her to keep her close. Humans didn't understand how fragile they were. They were easily injured, and they healed slowly. As they neared her house, Fred said, "Something's wrong. I don't sense any shifters inside your house." He tightened his grip on her, forcing Victoria to slow down.

She tried to move forward but Fred held her in place. She tapped her foot when he didn't move. "So?"

"So, there should be two shifter guards in your house right now. We're leaving." Fred turned and caught the business end of a non-regulation Taser in his stomach. He fell.

Destin saw Fred hit the ground and used the only tool he had available. He drove the car into two of the four assailants. One of the men flew into the windshield, cracking it. Hopefully, Fred would forgive him. Within seconds, one of the remaining guys pulled Destin out of the car and held him in a chokehold, whispering, "You could be useful. Come quietly, or we'll kill you and the shifter. Either way, we're taking the girl." Destin stilled and gritted his teeth. The zip ties used to bind his hands behind his back were pulled tight and cut into his skin. Victoria looked over in desperation as her hands were bound as well. They were thrown into the back of the van.

"Leave those two. If they were stupid enough to get run over, they deserve to be captured." The guy who whispered in Destin's ear issued that order. The other guy nodded and closed the side door before joining his friend up front.

No one noticed the butterfly that fluttered into the van and perched on a rope in the corner.

Destin looked around. Well crap. He didn't know they still made vans with no side or back windows. Even if their hands weren't tied, they wouldn't be jumping. The door didn't have a handle on the inside, and the driver's foot was heavy on the pedal. Fred wasn't with them, so he was dead or unconscious. Hopefully unconscious. Surely a Taser couldn't kill a shifter. Not with their genetics.

He was under strict orders to reveal his shield only in dire emergencies. Hopefully, Tempe would consider this an emergency. Destin worked out a simple plan. Before anyone could separate him from Victoria, Destin would set a shield and hope like heck Tempe could find him. Why had he never asked if anyone could sense a shield? That would be useful information to have right about now. With the zip tie on his hands, Destin couldn't remove the magical bracelet so Tempe could find him.

Destin twisted until his back leaned on the side panel and he pulled his feet toward his butt until his knees were nearly eye level. He wasn't sure what that position would do for him, but it was mildly comfortable. Victoria noticed and followed suit. That was good. At least Destin would have a contained area to shield.

The kidnappers would hear anything he said, so he couldn't tell Victoria the plan. Destin tried to look reassuring. Base on Victoria's response, eyes wide in terror, he failed at comforting looks. He glanced around the van for something to help and noticed a butterfly on the rope. Destin had heard about the butterfly

106

shifter. Anyone who spent any time around shifter kids heard the story. It was a cautionary tale about focusing during first shift, but he didn't believe it was true. How could someone get distracted during their first shift? And if there were a butterfly shifter, he or she would be some ninety-pound weakling. Oh yeah, in a pressure situation he turns to a butterfly for help. Time to focus on Plan A. Shield and hope help arrives before the air runs out in his shield. Depending on a delicate butterfly to save the day was definitely Plan B.

Eventually, the van slowed and turned onto a bumpy dirt road. Victoria and Destin bounced around the back. Destin growled and tried to protect Victoria from the jarring, but it was a losing proposition with his hands tied behind his back. Her face grew whiter with each bump, proving she still had some healing to do.

The van stopped, and Destin took a deep breath. He might be able to shield the entire vehicle. Then they might be able to get their wrists untied and, if the keys were left in the van, they could drive away. The driver got out of the van and took the keys with him, driving the first nail in the coffin of that plan. Crap!

The butterfly fluttered over and landed on Destin's knee, facing the van door. The little wings flapped softly.

"Maybe you should shake your knee to move it," Victoria whispered. "They seem like the type to pull the wings off a butterfly."

Destin shrugged and moved his knee. The butterfly hovered and turned to look Destin in the eye. Destin stopped moving his knee, and the butterfly returned to his stance on Destin's knee, facing the door.

Destin and Victoria exchanged surprised expressions. "Okay, that's just weird," she shrugged. Destin silently agreed.

The van door opened, revealing one the two kidnappers. No one else was around. The butterfly fluttered towards the driver, the only one with a gun. The driver was clueless until the butterfly shifted into the guy he had Tasered earlier. The muscled man tackled him to the ground, landing on top of him. Fred's knee connected to the driver's stomach at the same time his fist connected with jaw. The driver was out.

Fred turned to take out the other guy and stopped to enjoy the view. Destin and Victoria were grinning behind a shield, while the moron hit the shield and then shook his hand from the shock. Then he repeated the same process over and over again. Apparently, some people can't be taught.

Fred stalked over behind kidnapper number two and grabbed him in a chokehold. Once the guy was out, Fred tossed him on top of his cohort.

"Nice shield. If you drop it, I'll cut the zip ties." Fred pulled out a pocketknife.

Destin dropped his shield and grinned, "So you're the butterfly shifter I've heard so much about."

"I tell you what, you don't mention what I shift into, and I won't mention that you used your shield. Since I didn't know you could shield, I'll bet you were ordered to keep that a secret." One quick slice and Destin was free.

While Fred cut Victoria's ties, Destin looked at the cut mark on his wrists, "Deal."

"How about me?" Victoria looked up from inspecting the cuts on her wrists.

"You will keep both of our secrets, or we'll tell everyone you were running tests in your house instead of the secure lab," Fred snarled. "You could have been killed. These guys were not going to play nice."

"Geez, I know that." Just that quick she left the grateful train and disembarked in the dreary town of Annoyed. "It was one of those middle-of-the-night-ideas, and I didn't want to mention it until I was sure I was onto something."

Two birds shifted as they landed.

"Looks like we're late to the party. Guess I'm on cleanup," Ryan said. He grabbed a kidnapper without waiting for anyone to speak.

"I'll help." Fred offered. It was the work of a minute to tie up and load the two kidnappers into the van. Fred followed Ryan into the house to search for anything useful.

"Report." Tempe's tone was bland, but her eyes burned.

Victoria hung her head. "My fault. Destin said the house had been trashed, and I had to go check to see if they found my research. Yes, I was doing research at the house. I know I shouldn't have. You'll probably never trust me again."

"No, it's my fault. I shouldn't have agreed to help Victoria leave the hospital." Destin's shoulders slumped. It was the first time he had failed Tempe. He didn't like the feeling.

Fred walked back to the group. "Tempe, we need Destin and maybe Victoria. There's some equipment, as well as folders, and we can't make heads or tails out of 'em."

"Go, we'll discuss this later."

The humans ran for the house, glad to have a reprieve, even if it was a short one.

"So, I screwed up," Fred stared her in the eyes. He believed in being direct.

Tempe shrugged, "How so? Looks like you had everything under control when we got here. You and Destin should have been enough support with two shifters guarding her house. You know as well as I do that stuff happens. Did they see your shifter form?"

"Yes, and I know Destin can set a shield now."

"Well, I suspect you guys will keep each other's secrets. And it appears that Victoria is the queen of secrets." Tempe patted him on the shoulder and headed for the house.

Fred grinned and followed.

*****

Victoria looked across the table at Tempe, Ryan, and Sage, as well as a host of alphas, some she didn't know. Her side project was safe, but she had caused a lot of trouble. At least Fred and Destin, sitting on either side of her, weren't injured because of her actions. "What now? Am I gonna to be tossed in a cell? A cave? Six feet under?"

Laughter greeted her last question.

Fred leaned over and placed a gentle hand on her shoulder. "No one's going to harm you."

Rain, Fred's prif, leaned into his screen. "Fred?"

"She's safe. Because of her, we have a list of organizations with ties to the not so defunct AIB, as well as contact names within those organizations. Good info that we can use. And she makes a breakthrough about once a week. We need her working for us."

Victoria looked between Fred and the man who had spoken to him. What was she missing?

Sage smiled. "You're safe, Victoria, and we're going to keep you safe. You have options. If you still want to work with Destin, we can either assign you quarters in one of our facilities, or you can live with your Aunt Naomi, who is already living in a secure environment."

"I get to keep my job?" Victoria squealed.

"Yes, but no more unapproved projects. Anything you want to work on is fine, but you have to tell Destin everything you're working on," Sage explained.

"And you will do all work in a secure facility, even middle of the night eureka moments," Tempe added.

"That's great! I'll live wherever, and I promise all my research will be kept in the secure lab from now on. I've learned my lesson."

"You'll stay in Calabozo." Fred's tone left no room for discussion.

He was ignored.

"You sure?" Ryan chuckled.

"Yes, it will be better to have her where she has quick access to her lab."

"That the only reason?" Rain leaned back and grinned.

Fred glared at his prif, "It's enough of a reason."

"That works." Destin turned to Victoria, "I live there and can show you around."

"I'll show her around." Fred glared at Destin.

"As you wish," Destin smiled.

Victoria looked at Tempe and asked, "How did you find us?"

Fred held up his hand. "All of the sovereign's PAs wear a ring that allows the alphas to track us. Sovereign, if there's nothing else, I'll get Victoria settled in her quarters."

"Dismissed."

As Victoria left with Fred, she heard a lot of laughter but didn't know what it was about. Must have been some shifter joke. Before the door shut, she heard Sage say, "Enough. Torment Fred on your own time. We have other topics to discuss."

Chapter 20

Ryan opened the way, nervous about the trip, but pleased that she agreed to meet him away from the Northern Realm residence. He opened the gate from PAC HQ and exited at Saffron's herb garden.

Saffron looked up from her cuttings as her young nephew arrived. "Welcome." Ryan didn't speak, and she stood. "Tempest and I are not much alike, except that we don't think a lot of small talk. I suspect you don't either. Why are you here?"

"I seek your indulgence," he admitted and then winced. It sounded better in his head than it did out loud.

Saffron raised her eyebrow in a Tempesque fashion before returning to her garden. "At least you didn't ask for a favor."

He watched her cut herbs and breathed a sigh of relief. Of course, he was going to ask a favor. He just had to figure out how to word it properly. "I found something."

"Did you?" Saffron didn't look up.

"Yes, when I was staying in Val's quarters. We, Shawn and I, were admiring the... well, I found this." He held the journal in his hand but didn't offer it to her.

Saffron was pleased to know he was smart enough to not offer it to her. If he handed it to her, by fae law, it became her property until she gave it back, however long that was. "Did you find anything interesting therein?"

"That's sort of my problem. I can't read ancient fae. I only understand about one in ten words. Not effective."

"Did Tempest refuse to help you?" Saffron arched an eyebrow in disbelief, looking more like her sister than usual.

"No, I didn't show it to her. She is so closed mouthed about Val. I didn't want to upset her." Ryan paced around the garden, "And, of course, I know she will be upset when she finds out I had it and didn't go to her first." He dropped onto one of the stone benches, "You were there, in that time. Do you believe this diary will upset her regardless of what's in it?"

She laid down her cuttings, wiped her hands on her apron and joined Ryan on the bench, "Tempest and Val were closer than any other siblings I've ever met. I know that many believe she has blinders where his memory is concerned, but I don't. Show it to her. Ask her who should translate it for you. She may surprise you."

Saffron returned to her cuttings and said over her shoulder, "There's a chance she already knows what is in there. Val never could block her completely from his mind, and her mental shields never worked that well with him."

*****

Ryan took a deep breath and knocked on Tempe's new home office. The quads had moved to different rooms, and their nursery became Tempe's office. The old office was now the main entrance to Calabozo without opening a gate. It had become grand central station.

"Abandon all hope, ye who enter here... for here there be dragons." Despite the joking nature of her comment, Tempe's voice sounded irritated

Ryan chuckled and opened the door, "There be dragons out here as well."

"Spoil my fun," Tempe muttered. "Be forewarned, I've spent the last couple of hours talking to fools who have raised my blood pressure."

"I can come back later," Ryan backed toward the door.

"No, I'm just grousing. What do you need?"

"A favor. Might be better if I come back."

"Intriguing. You know I'm half fae, right?" Tempe leaned back and smiled.

Ryan snorted. "Of course, but you've never invoked the favor owed rule except with another fae."

112

"Perhaps I'll expand my horizons." She smirked and waved her hand in dismissal. "Nah, I'm just cranky. What's the favor?"

Ryan pulled out the journal and held it in one hand.

Tempe laughed. "You found Val's journal. Saffron will be pleased. I'm sure she placed you in Val's quarters for that reason."

"It's not doing me much good since I can't read it."

"Ancient fae is tricky," Tempe agreed.

Ryan sighed. This wasn't going the way he wanted.

Tempe grinned. "Val was short tempered. Mother suggested he keep a journal to help with that. Surprisingly enough, he tried it, and it helped. If you are looking for a translator, I recommend Jarvious."

"Jarvious?"

"He will provide the most literal translation, and being a bard, he will understand Val's writing better than most. Others might edit the content a little."

"If the journal was an open secret, why didn't anyone look for it?"

"Many fae did, Father included, but as far as I know, I'm the only person who knew about his hiding place and how to open the hidden drawer."

"You've read it." It wasn't a question.

"I read it after he died, mourning his loss. I was never sure why I returned it to its hiding place, except that I couldn't think of a safer place. I do think reading it would be of value to you. It might even help you understand the fae better," Tempe shrugged.

"Why don't you just tell me?"

"If I told you what was in the journal it would be my words. Val had a style of writing, and speaking, that reeled you into the story. He would have been a great bard, but Father crushed that dream, along with so many others."

*****

"Interesting place to meet," Jarvious commented as he joined Ryan on the rock overlooking the river outside of PAC HQ. It was the only outdoor area protected by the facility's shield and the preferred meeting place for any private conversations. The area was shielded from external irritants, like the humans watching from a distance, as well as from telepaths and other preternaturals within the facility. The only entrance to this protected area was through a guarded door off the main hall. It was the only place in PAC HQ where no one – not even a telepath – could listen in and was available on a first come first served basis. One rule governed its use. If anyone was waiting for the area, you kept your conversation to no more than 15 minutes.

"Isn't it?" Ryan kept his eyes on the river. "Cousin I'm going to ask a favor, and it's a big one. What would you like in fair exchange?"

"By the five realms, surely Lady Tempest trained you better than this. Do you know how many fae would love to have you owe them a debt?"

"Yes, hence I'm discussing terms first."

"Why me?"

"I need something translated. Something that's written in ancient fae. Since the person who wrote it was a bard, you were suggested as the translator."

"Ancient fae and a bard?" Jarvious cocked his head to one side. "You found Valiant's journal. The Northern Realm has looked for that journal for three thousand years. My brothers and I spent many a visit to Lord Ellwood's sneaking into that tree house to look for it. Most assume it details secrets of the northern realm or secrets about Lady Tempest and Lord Ellwood. You should take it to her."

"Lady Tempest is the one who suggested you as the translator. She read it after Valiant died and put it back where he hid it. I found it during my last visit to the Farseen." Ryan pulled the journal out of his back pocket.

"Are you nuts? Put that away!" His eyes darted around looking for anyone who might have seen the book, even though it should have been impossible. "I'll translate it since Grandmother recommended me for the task, but I'll do it at Beryl Lane. If anyone suspected I had it, they would tear apart my quarters, and possibly me, to get to the book. Keep it in her home, and I'll plan to visit a couple of times a week. It will take a while, but I'll get it done."

"And what do you want in return? I may be a shifter, but there's no agreement until I know what you want. No open-ended bargains."

Jarvious smiled, "I rather hoped you wouldn't remember that. To be honest, I know exactly what I want in exchange, full rights to write songs from any entry in the journal. Any bard would require that to translate the journal for you."

Ryan pursed his lips.

"Cousin, if Grandmother told you to have a bard translate it, she understood that would be the price. If, as you said, she has already read it, there shouldn't be a problem."

Ryan grinned, "Agreed."

"Our bargain is struck with no out clause." Jarvious smiled. "Val's songs will give me something every bard wants, a legacy of new songs. I'm surprised she didn't just translate it herself."

Ryan shrugged. "She said a bard would translate his words better than she could."

Chapter 21

Destin held the door open to the café for Victoria. "How are you settling in?"

"Pretty well." She grabbed utensils and a tray and headed for the breakfast sandwich line with Destin. "Fred's been a great help. I'm still amazed that this huge facility is on the other side of that guarded door in our lab, and I've only seen a small part of it."

Once they had their food and grabbed a table, she took a bite of her sandwich before continuing. "Is there anyone else who can transport me out of the facility if needed? I know you and Fred have agreed to escort duty, but what if you're both busy?"

"You will need an escort anywhere you go on the outside. You already agreed to this."

"Yes, but who do I contact if it's an emergency? I'm a planner. I have to know what the procedures are."

"Probably so she knows when she's ignoring them," Fred commented as he sat his tray down beside Victoria.

"Not fair. I wouldn't... okay, I obviously would, but I do need to know what to do."

Fred laid a cell phone between them on the table. "Here's your new phone. Contacts are already loaded. Speed dial one is for emergencies and will get you immediate attention. Don't use it to order pizza."

"Funny. You're a funny man." Victoria grinned. "I do need an escort to Uncle Theo's bar tonight after work. Tempe set up a dinner with my family. I haven't seen them since the kidnapping."

"Yep, it's on my calendar," Fred replied.

*****

Victoria opened the door at the heavy knock and discovered Fred had an entourage. She eyed all the muscle. "We need four bodyguards?"

"No, you need four bodyguards, in addition to the guards already in place at Harmony."

She closed the door and walked beside Fred as they headed for the transport room. The same van she used to get to and from work when she lived in the outside world. Two guards walked in front of them and two behind. They loaded into the van, and she relaxed into the seat. "Will someone explain how this works?"

The guard who was driving twitched his lips but didn't speak.

Fred shrugged, "Not until we're sure you stay."

Victoria watched as the van was suddenly bathed in light, something that had never happened before. The van pulled out of the garage and made its way through the parking lot and turned onto the main road, just like she was driving home. "Understandable, but a little disappointing. There's so much to learn."

"And you're the person doing most of the teaching right now." The other guard in the front seat turned to look at her. "The fae, witches, and vampires are demanding equal time with you, the human government is demanding that you be returned to them, the AIB and a host of other groups have a bounty on your head, alive if possible, but dead if it means no one else gets your brain."

"What? But I'm just me. I'm not worth all the bother." Victoria unconsciously moved closer to Fred, who put an arm around her.

The guard chuckled. "You've discovered a lot of the science behind the magic. Lots of folks are unhappy about that or want the info contained.

"Shawn, you're not helping," Fred rubbed the back of his neck and turned to Victoria. "Don't worry. I won't let you out of my sight."

"I don't want anyone hurt because of me." Victoria chewed her bottom lip.

Fred didn't know how to ease her mind, so he changed the subject. "The guard who can't keep his mouth shut is Shawn, a descendant of the Alpha Clan line. The driver is Kaleb, called the ice shifter by the reporters."

Victoria turned to get a better look at the driver. "I heard about you and saw the news footage from Tennessee and Texas. Impressive."

Kaleb grinned in the rear-view mirror.

Pointing to the back, Fred added, "You already know Ryan and Sam is another alpha. We'll protect you."

She eyed the guards warily before speaking to Ryan. "I never got a chance to thank you for rescuing me from the AIB, thanks. This all seems a bit much just for me to have dinner with my family. I'm not sure I'm worth all the bother."

"You are," Fred said as they pulled into the parking lot at the Harmony Bar. He hopped out and held the door open for her.

By the time she scooted over and exited the van, her guards surrounded them. She sighed, "I look like one of those ridiculous stars with staff hovering around all the time."

"Now you know how they feel," Fred murmured.

"Serenity opened the back door for us. Let's go." Ryan motioned for Sam to go first and he brought up the rear.

*****

"That was fun. Thanks, everyone, for giving up your evening so I could have dinner with my family." Victoria was happy, even with guards surrounding her for the return trip to the car. Sam was once again in the lead with Ryan bringing up the rear.

"Hey, Ryan..." His head turned toward the voice, and the world exploded.

Shawn, Kaleb, and Fred were Tasered and hit the ground, unmoving. Sam also dropped with three darts in his body. The attackers carried an unconscious Victoria through a way.

Ryan threw wind in the direction his name was called, set his shield as he ran, and followed Victoria into the gate. His shield protected him from the fire the fae used to block the gate opening. Once the flames dissipated, he could see he had walked into real trouble.

Non-aligned fae surrounded him. The one carrying Victoria spoke, "Drop your shield and surrender, or I'll kill her."

"You brought her to the Farseen just to kill her? You could have done that in the Seen." Ryan clenched his jaw and ran through his options. There weren't many.

"Indeed, she's worth more alive, but dead will net us a good fee for one hour of work. If you don't surrender, I'll kill her, just so we can focus on you. Your death will bring us both prestige and additional compensation."

Ryan wanted to wipe that smug smirk off the fae's face, but that would get Victoria killed. He dropped his shield and fell under a barrage of element manipulation and powers. No one noticed the butterfly that flew, grass high, away from Ryan. The butterfly swooped up and landed on Victoria's shoulder under her collar.

Ryan regained consciousness with a dry mouth and pounding headache. He didn't move or open his eyes. Perhaps he could gather information if the fae thought he was still unconscious. Once he determined there was no one in the room with him and he was on the floor, he cracked open his eyes. Dungeon. No windows, one door, broken wooden box, dirt floor, and one small vent about the size of his fist, probably for air.

He spat out dirt and sat up as best he could with his hands and feet in manacles. One tiny pull of wind and Ryan was able to confirm that the cuffs blocked magic. What realm was he in? Or was he with unaligned fae in one of the wastelands? Time to prepare for round two. Hopefully, his actions would be more impressive this time.

Chapter 22

Victoria groaned and sat up. The room was nice enough, large comfortable bed, some type of desk and windows. She checked her phone, but there was no signal. Guess that's why they let her keep it. She ran to the windows, opening them easily, and looked down. Good grief. Rapunzel didn't have hair long enough for this tower. No escape out the windows unless she grew wings. Victoria checked out the terrain, looking for a hint of where she was. Low mountains that didn't go above the tree line surrounded her, so there was a chance she was still in the southeastern United States somewhere in the Smokies. Except she was pretty sure such a huge castle looking building would be well documented in the States. An average looking river ran directly in front of the fortress, not helpful.

She looked up. Okay, she was in the Farseen. The dragons off in the distance and three moons cresting over the horizon gave it away. Another look at the river revealed some odd creatures, including some type of jellyfish that was at home in and out of the water. How peculiar?

She had studied everything she could on the Farseen, trying to map the area and determine where gates opened here. Victoria was sure Destin could already do that as he wasn't interested in the project. The scant information she was able to gather was not useful. She suspected that was precisely what the preternaturals wanted. Other than naming the five realms, no information was available.

And that brought her to another sad reality. Most humans who entered the Farseen were never heard from again. From what Victoria understood, a human in the Farseen was the property of the fae (ruling or lesser) who held her. At least if she were with the ruling fae, they would want her alive and working for them. She hoped. The lesser fae would consider her lunch. With a sob, Victoria sat down on the window seat. Tempe had warned her, but she hadn't believed it would happen. The fae had kidnapped her, and left her guards wounded or dead. Hopefully, her family had remained safe in the bar.

Victoria jumped when she heard footsteps. She wiped her tears away and faced the door.

"I told you I could do it, Balen."

"Shut up! No names." A whack accompanied the order.

"Sorry." The person not Balen didn't sound sorry, he seemed bitter.

The door opened, but Victoria had already schooled her features into a bored mask. Tempe would be proud.

"Ah, you're awake. Good. I brought you a repast." The voice of Balen belonged to a tall man with striped brown hair and grey eyes. Of course, he was handsome – all preternaturals were, but he was on the slim side. No bulky muscles for him.

Apparently, repast meant food. Balen lifted a cover off a platter to reveal a wide variety of produce and some type of fish. Her stomach gurgled, but she ignored it. "Why have you brought me here?"

"Come, little human, you aren't that foolish. You know why you're here. You work for us now. Behave, do your work, and you will remain here in comfortable quarters. Cause us any trouble and you'll be in the dungeon with scraps to eat. If you need motivation, we can bring some of your family here."

"No! The shifters will protect them."

"As they protected you? How nice."

Balen grabbed her arm. "You aren't the only one we captured. Do as I say, and none will suffer."

"Who? Who else do you have?" Victoria's voice trembled.

"Don't worry, you'll see who the first time you disobey me. I'll let you watch their torture."

"You evil, Ba… baboon." At the last second, she caught herself and didn't say his name. She wasn't sure why, but she believed it was important that she not admit to knowing.

The fae left the food tray and walked out.

Part of her training since moving into the shifter facility had been survival. Stay strong until an escape presented itself. That meant she needed to eat the food they gave her. Victoria wasn't a threat and doubted there was any reason to drug her now. She chewed on the fish and tried not to worry. Worrying about the other prisoners wouldn't do anyone any good. At least the food was tasty.

"Oh Fred, I hope you guys are okay," Victoria whispered.

*****

When the door was unlocked, Ryan remained sitting on the floor, leaning back on the wall. When the door opened, he turned a bored face to the fae. That they were using fae camouflage meant he would recognize them, or they thought he would. Perhaps they were from one of the courts. Of course, they could simply be vain, assuming Ryan could identify them.

The taller fae laid a platter of food on the box that apparently served as a table and opened the lid. The food smelled wonderful, and Ryan's stomach rumbled in spite of his wishes.

"Hungry?" The voice sounded pleased. Ryan rolled his eyes but remained silent.

"If you want food you have to earn it."

Ryan raised his hands to show the cuffs, but still, he said nothing.

"If you agree to our terms, the cuffs will be removed when you are earning your meal. If you don't agree, there's a chance we'll send Victoria here to join you, one piece at a time."

"You're saying I do everything you say when you say, or you'll kill your cash cow?" Ryan shook his head. "Not even you are that stupid. She's worth more than all of us if she's alive."

"If I understand the term 'cash cow,' then you are right, however, to use you, I must control you."

"If you harm Victoria in any way, I will kill you."

"Brave words from someone who can't use magic right now."

"A vow, from me to you."

122

The three fae who hadn't spoken began the beat down.

Fred flew back up the vent, leaving Ryan. He wanted to help, but if he shifted in the cell, they would both be captured. Never had Fred hated his shifter form more than now. Freaking butterfly! Regardless of form, he could only impact the weather in small ways, so his power was a bust. He could make a heat wave hotter or a cold snap colder in a small area, but he couldn't turn cold weather warm. He was fairly worthless as a shifter. It didn't take a genius to understand that his multiple black belts in karate, and all the time he spent in the gym, was his way of compensating.

He had regained consciousness just as Ryan ran for Victoria. Fred shifted and tagged along inside Ryan's shield. That may not have been the best choice. Perhaps if Fred had stayed in the Seen, he could have told Tempe what happened, and she would have already rescued them. Victoria and Ryan were in danger, and he was useless. Fred couldn't open a gate and had no method to contact anyone in the Seen. He needed someone he could trust in the Farseen, but who? And how would he find them? Fred didn't even know which realm he was in. He needed an identifiable landmark.

Fred exited the vent and flew up the outside of the fortress to check on Victoria. Hopefully, she had left the window open. Focused on his problems, Fred almost missed the ahool diving at him. Freaking Farseen bats! Unlike their Seen counterparts, the ahools flew day and night. He dove deep into another small vent where the bat couldn't reach him. Fred heard voices, and he fluttered closer to the sounds and listened.

"No sign of Lady Tempest yet?" One man gloated.

"How many times must I tell you, she's not a proper member of the court and doesn't deserve the title lady?" Anger rolled off the man.

The first man lowered his head in submission. "Sorry Father, but I must see her in court, and it would not do to slip there."

Fred peeked through the vent and recognized some of the players. Good thing he had studied up on the members of the Northern Realm court. Fred was surprised Balen's dad didn't see the flash of anger in his eyes. Balen would not remain submissive much longer.

"When do I claim Lady Star?" Spruce asked.

"If you had secured her interests when first you met, she would be yours now," Balen retorted. "You lost her to a shifter. Perhaps you don't deserve her."

"You can't blame me for losing Lady Star to a shifter when you lost Lady Saffron to Salix." Sarcasm coated Spruce's words.

Balen stormed around the room. "Yunnan is to blame! She was supposed to secure Salix's interest. Instead, she chases after his younger brother."

"Yes, she has been a disappointment. How she duped Lord Ellwood to approve Styrax to court her when I informed him I wanted her with Salix still amazes." Their father scratched his chin.

"Apparently, Yunnan is better at manipulation than all of us." Spruce grinned, pleased that Balen also had trouble acquiring his lady.

Balen laughed, "No she's not. She and Lady Star developed a friendship, and they do things to help each other. Oddest thing I've ever seen."

"I will deal with Yunnan's betrayal in my own time. Don't worry, my sons. You will each get the wife you deserve. Both of you go to court. We must keep up appearances."

"Will you open a gate for me, Father?" Spruce asked.

"It's not a gate, it's a way. You spend too much time in the Seen. No, if you can't do it yourself, you will walk. It's less than fifteen miles." Their father walked out of the room.

"Guess we run," Spruce sighed.

"You run, I'll teleport." Balen disappeared.

"You could have given me a lift," Spruce yelled to the empty room.

Fred flew back out the vent and up to Victoria's window. This time he paid attention to his surroundings and arrived without incident. Landing on the windowsill, he tucked himself into a corner where he could remain unseen.

Victoria sat on the bed, crying. If only he could go to her. But if he shifted, and told her she wasn't alone, a pixie would see him, and he would be captured. The best thing Fred could do for her and Ryan would be to get help. At least he had a plan. It wasn't a great plan, but it was a plan.

It didn't take long before Spruce left the fortress and ran down a path. Fred sighed in relief. Now he had a plan. Take the trail to the Northern Realm. As the kidnappers revealed information about themselves, Fred identified his location. The Northern Realm. Here he had a couple of contacts leaving hope intact for a little longer. Fred had also studied the layout, and it was the one realm where he might find his way around. Following Spruce, Fred flew away from the fortress and found a spot to shift. Flying into the wind as a butterfly he wouldn't even make five miles an hour, and Spruce was almost out of sight.

By the time Fred reached the river Spruce was long gone. Ryan and Joey had talked about how fast the fae ran, but until now, Fred hadn't believed. He took his butterfly form to cross the river, so he could stay dry and barely missed being the lunch of an iridescent jellyfish creature that moved in and out of the water with equal ease. The Farseen was more dangerous than he thought. Back in human form, Fred trailed the river, knowing it would take him to the backside of the residence where the family tree houses were. Staying on the trails would just alert everyone to his presence.

"What brings a lone shifter to the Northern Realm?"

Busted! Fred stopped and gritted his teeth. So close to the castle, he let his guard down. He was tired, hungry, and still unsure how he would find Lady Saffron. And now he was caught. He turned, expecting to see a Northern Realm warrior. Instead, he saw a nymph, no, a mermaid. Well, he didn't know what she was. So much for Star's book on the lesser fae, nothing like the female before him was in it.

"You're not one of the shifters who has visited of late. Who are you and why are you here?"

"I'm looking for Lady Saffron. I have news from the Seen." It wasn't a lie exactly. He did have news to share, and he was from the Seen.

"I think you must learn to lie with the truth better than that. State your business and your name. I'll see if Lady Saffron will see you." Fred didn't respond, so she replied with a poem.

"Lady Saffron is my patron, you see.
No harm to you do I intend.
I shall depart and leave you be,

If your plan is to pretend."

Fred repeated the poem in his head, and asked, "Are you Kailani?" She backed away, and he could have slapped himself. Since she was of mixed heritage, she would be fair game for most of the Farseen without Lady Saffron's patronage. "I mean you no harm. I'm Fred, the sovereign's personal assistant. One of them anyway. I'm not here on the sovereign's authority, but I have news that might interest Lady Saffron. I would be grateful for any assistance."

Kailani stopped moving away, "Are you offering me a boon?"

"A what?"

"A boon, a favor in exchange for my help?" Fred sighed. What choice did he have? "This boon must be something I can do for you. Not something I would ask the sovereign or Lady Tempest to do. I am a normal shifter and not a strong one at that. I doubt you will find my boon valuable."

Kailani smiled, "Agreed. The deal is struck with no out clause. With Lady Saffron as my patron, I don't need anything. I just like the idea of a shifter owing me a boon. Stay here while I check with Lady Saffron. My friends will sit with you."

Fred watched three water dragons slither out of the river and position themselves around him. Now, what did Star's book say about water dragons?

Chapter 23

"What does that term mean?" Balen demanded.

"How many times do I have to explain this?" Victoria's voice rose in irritation. "I know the human – mostly English or Latin – words for scientific terms. I can't translate them to fae, and apparently, you can't either. I don't know how to explain the tracking of gates without using scientific terms."

She rubbed her forehead and tried to think of some way out of this mess. Balen and the other fae were getting irritated, and that was probably a bad thing, but Victoria had a feeling it would be much worse if she gave them the knowledge they wanted.

"I've had enough." Balen stood and walked toward the door. "Guard her until I get back."

Victoria turned toward the two remaining fae. "Do you have names, or should I call you Fae One and Fae Two?"

"Huh?" The one who had called Balen by his name and the lead whiner asked.

"Wordplay. You know, from the Dr. Seuss book The Cat in the Hat, Thing One and Thing Two. Oh, never mind. If you have to explain a joke, it's not funny. What are your names?"

"You don't need our names. If you must address us, master will do." The reply came from the mean looking fae who appeared older than the others, although appearances didn't mean much with beings who could glamour.

Before she could find a suitable cutting remark that wouldn't get her beaten, Balen said through the door, "Conceal your face."

Victoria watched as the faces of the fae suddenly looked blurry. She blinked her eyes, but it didn't help. Balen, also blurry faced, entered the room pushing a clear faced Ryan to the ground. His hands were in cuffs behind his back, and his feet were in cuffs as well. Ryan landed face-first on the floor with a loud thwack. He rolled over, and a fresh cut on his lip was bleeding. Without the blood, it would not have been noticeable. Ryan was a mess of bruises and cuts.

Victoria gasped and ran toward Ryan, but Balen blocked her. "As you can see, your failure to comply has already cost Ryan. Do you want to watch us beat him this time?

"Don't listen to…" Ryan groaned. Balen kicked him in the side.

"Stop it! It's not Ryan's fault I can't explain the science so that you can understand." Victoria pushed against Balen, but he didn't move. "Perhaps if you were to bring a smarter fae into the room, they would understand."

Ryan, still on the floor, laughed. "Doubt it." Fae One kicked him again and he moaned.

"Please be quiet," Victoria whispered.

"You do the same," Ryan retorted.

"No, she will talk." Balen grabbed her by the hair and pushed her toward the board. "You will explain all the science you have identified – starting with tracking ways – or Ryan will suffer. Each time you explain something so that we don't understand, Ryan will pay. Do I make myself clear?"

"Yes, but for me to do that I have to provide you with some basic scientific principles. That will allow me to use certain words that I know you will understand."

"Fine, just get on with it."

She looked over at Ryan. "Sorry, but I can't watch them beat you and not do anything."

*****

Two hours later Ryan continued to watch as Victoria taught science to the fae. At first, it was confusing because some of the information sounded wrong. Eventually, he remembered enough from his studies to realize that she was feeding them bad information. Not much, just enough to keep them from successfully tracking gates. It was impressive, and he hoped she could keep it straight. Had Victoria been informed that some fae could recall any experience with perfect clarity?

Ryan had to get the cuffs off his wrists and ankles. Although the ankle cuffs had a chain long enough to allow him to take small steps, he was useless with his hands cuffed behind his back.

"Enough!" Fae One stood. "We have somewhere to be."

"Who's taking Ryan back to his cell?" Fae Two asked.

"Leave him for now. Let him see how nice he could have it if he cooperated." Balen was the last to leave.

As soon as the door shut, Victoria ran to Ryan's side. "What can I do?"

"Give me a second." Ryan grimaced and stretched his body.

"Uh, can't you use magic? Open a gate or something?" Victoria had assumed he was waiting for them to be alone before taking her to safety, but he wasn't doing magic or anything.

"Love to, but these cuffs prevent the wearer from using magic of any kind. I think there might be just enough chain in the wrist cuffs." Groaning, Ryan contorted his body and slid his wrists down his legs and over his feet. He stood with his hands in front of his body. "Better. I don't suppose you have a bathroom in your penthouse suite."

She blushed and pointed to an interior wall, "That door."

Ryan emerged a few minutes later. He was relaxed. "I feel a lot better now." Still cuffed, he shuffled over to an open window and whistled low, "No wonder you didn't try to go out the window."

"Exactly."

"At least I know we're in the Northern Realm wastelands."

"How?"

Taking pleasure in the simple act of pointing, he said, "See that horseshoe curve in the river?"

Her eyes followed where his finger pointed and nodded.

"There's only one river horseshoe curve, surrounded by woods, in the Farseen. It's between the Northern Realm residence and the Northern Realm wastelands. I'm guessing we're less than fifteen miles northeast of the residence, in the wastelands."

"The wastelands? I thought humans shouldn't be in the wastelands, too dangerous."

Ryan huffed, "They're too dangerous for shifters, too."

"So, we're stuck. No escape."

"I didn't say that. I'm working on it." Ryan wasn't sure what he was working on, but she didn't need to know that. If he had his powers, this would be easy. If he had his powers, they would never have been able to hold him. Ryan had begun to realize how much he had come to depend on them. Until the cuffs were removed, he might as well be human. Even if they escaped, danger would be everywhere, possibly more outside of the fortress than inside.

"I guess I should explain myself."

Ryan had been so busy wishing for his powers back that he had forgotten Victoria would be scared and confused. "No. Even if you don't see them, pixies are watching us with orders to report everything we say."

"Okay," she chewed her bottom lip. "I'm sorry I got you into this. Who else was taken?"

Ryan barked a laugh, and his ribs responded in pain. A couple were cracked or broken, but at least they didn't puncture his lungs. "We're it. I ran into the gate after you. The others were unconscious."

She sighed in relief, "You sure?"

"Pretty sure. Being Tasered hurts, but a single – even supercharged – shock shouldn't be deadly to a shifter."

"That's a relief. I was so worried about Fred... and the rest," she added hastily.

A grin flashed across his face, before his thoughts returned to the task of escaping. His stomach growled. "I don't suppose they left you some food or water."

"You haven't eaten?" She hurried over to a cabinet, pulled open the door, and revealed a feast of raw produce and dried meats. "What do you like?"

"You are a goddess! Anything." Ryan eased himself into the chair at the desk. He bit into a piece of fruit and groaned with pleasure. He downed the first mug of water and then proceeded to eat while Victoria poured more water into the mug. As his stomach filled, Ryan noticed he was getting sleepy. "Crap!"

130

"What's wrong?"

"They drugged the food or water."

"I've been eating, and I'm fine. The fae did, too."

"That's the trick. It must be a drug that only works on shifters, not humans or fae." Ryan stood, which was a mistake. He stumbled and fell to the floor unconscious.

Chapter 24

"Crap indeed." Victoria moved Ryan's legs onto the bed properly before checking his breathing and pulse, both were fine. At least he landed partially on the bed. She would not have been able to lift his dead weight by herself. It was hard enough to get his legs on the platform.

Even with Ryan in his unconscious state, confidence filled Victoria. She was no longer alone. Companionship made a big difference. She looked out the window and watched the sunset. The colors were beautiful, but probably no more impressive than dusk in the Seen. When had she last viewed a sunset back home? Victoria searched the tower room again and confirmed there was nothing to help remove his cuffs. She did find something of interest, but it was useless until Ryan regained consciousness. By the end of the search, it was full on dark, and the stars were breathtaking, probably a result of the lack of artificial light in the Farseen. Victoria stargazed for a while and laughed at herself for looking for known constellations in the Seen. The fae still hadn't returned, so wherever they went, they weren't in a hurry to resume their lessons.

She sighed, set the candle beside the bed and lay down beside Ryan. She had never shared a bed with a man before, but it was the only one, and she should probably rest while rest was possible. She must have nodded off immediately. She awoke to a rising sun.

"Good morning sleepy head," Ryan said from the open window.

She hopped out of bed. "I can't believe I slept so hard. We need to get going."

"Going?"

"Look what I found."

"Hmm…" Ryan peered down the stairs that were behind a secret door. "You know this could be a trap, right? Right now, you're fairly safe. If this is a test, they might toss you down to the dungeon where I was. You don't want to be there, trust me. If this is an old staircase that they don't know about we might make it into the wastelands, and there's not much I can do to protect you." He held up his hands to display the cuffs still on his wrists.

"I don't see we have a choice. I trust you at half strength more than most people at full strength. If you weren't trying to protect me, you would have already started down the stairs, right?"

Ryan didn't respond, and Victoria smiled, "I'm going. I expect you to follow me." She grabbed the candle and began her descent. Pulling the door closed behind him, Ryan followed.

Victoria muttered under her breath, counting steps. She estimated the tower was five stories high. Using a rounded average of fifteen steps per floor, they should reach the bottom in seventy-five steps. Step eighty-five marked the bottom of the stairs. A small circular room with a single tunnel was the extent of the room.

Ryan sighed as he jumped the last step, once again the thump of contact was loud. He was amazed that their captors hadn't heard him. After the first few steps, Ryan had quit trying to walk and started jumping from step to step. These stairs were steep, and there wasn't enough chain between the cuffs on his ankles for him to step down normally, so he had jumped or hopped down.

"Too bad there are no windows. We don't have any idea where this tunnel goes, although at this point it doesn't matter." Ryan moved down the tunnel. "Stay behind me. If anything attacks, stay back."

"You don't have any more magic than I do at the moment. You'll be fodder." She didn't want to be fodder, but it didn't seem fair to hide behind him.

"You're the brains. I'm the brawn. Brawn gets to be fodder first."

"I don't remember that from Tempe's survival guide," she retorted.

"You must have missed it. It's in there." Ryan smiled.

Victoria rolled her eyes and followed.

*****

"Lady Saffron. Ridge. Unknown fae." Fred bowed and gritted his teeth. He had been prepared to pay whatever price Lady Saffron placed on his head for her help, but he didn't want to owe Ridge a favor. He didn't even know the third fae's identify.

"Fred, this is Salix. Kailani told me of your news from the Seen, while both Ridge and Salix were with me. They refused to stay behind but were not invited." She smiled, probably at his obvious relief that he would not owe them anything, before asking, "What news do you have from the Seen?"

"Fae – wearing faceless masks – appeared in the Seen and kidnapped a human scientist. Ryan was captured when he entered the gate to rescue her. They are being held in a fortress east of the river. Balen, Spruce, and their father seem to be the brains behind the kidnapping. The others had the markings of fae mercenaries." He pointed behind him toward where the fortress was. "I am unable to contact the Seen or open a gate." There! He got the information out without making a request.

Salix grinned, "Nicely said, but I don't think I've ever heard anyone identify those three as the brains before."

"Last time I passed the fortress, six seasons ago, it was empty. If they are using it to hide activities from the realm, it's my problem to address." Ridge turned to Salix, "You and Lady Saffron take Fred to safety, and inform Lord Ellwood and Lady Tempest of the problem while I go to the fortress."

"No!" Fred's voice was sharper than intended. "That is, I need to go with you. Victoria's scared and Ryan's wounded. I don't have a lot of magic to call, but I can't go to safety while they're in trouble."

"Then shift and let's go."

"I'm more useful in human form."

Ridge raised an eyebrow, but didn't respond, except to say, "Follow me." He opened a gate and entered.

Praying he was doing the right thing, Fred followed. The gate exited at the base of the mountains behind the fortress. Much better than running back.

"Shifter, how did you escape? This fortress, while old, is known for keeping its prisoners."

"Er, I wasn't a prisoner. They didn't know I was there."

"What's your shifter form? A small bird."

"I take a small flying form, yes."

"Can you fly to where your scientist is being held? Check and make sure she's still there and let her know I'm coming to rescue her. I know a couple of tunnels that Pinus and his boys probably don't know about."

"Pinus?"

"Balen and Spruce's father."

"Got it. I'll sneak up to the fortress and shift."

"It would be better if you shifted here."

Fred ground his teeth. "I don't think so."

"You're the butterfly shifter, aren't you?" Ridge didn't change his expression at all.

"How do you know about me?" Fred paled. He hated for anyone to know his shame, but especially powerful preternaturals.

"Anyone who knows many shifters knows about the butterfly shifter. Frankly, I don't see what all the fuss is about. I would like to change my form and being able to fly would be nice."

"Not as a butterfly," Fred muttered.

"If, as I suspect, you used the vents to fly between a room where they kept your scientist and the dungeon where Ryan is surely kept, only a flying creature the size of a butterfly would fit. I stand by my statement."

Fred almost grinned. Ridge might have fallen out of favor with Tempe, but he had been kind to keep his laughter, and even his smile, to himself. Most didn't once they learned what his form was. "How do you know so much about this fortress?"

"I built it. This was, at one time, my home and anyone staying here now is trespassing. I should have guarded the place, but I left it for travelers as a place of safety in the wastelands. My oversight. I will address it. Now go, check on your friends."

Fred shifted and flew up to Victoria's window. Balen screamed, and Fred slowed his approach.

"Where are they? The food would have put Ryan to sleep. They didn't pass the guards, and the manacles aren't here, so he's still wearing them and has no magic."

Not waiting to hear anymore, Fred flew back to Ridge and shifted. "They're gone! Escaped apparently. Balen said the manacles Ryan is wearing doesn't allow him to use magic."

"Which window?"

"The only open window on this side of the fortress."

Ridge smirked. "They found one of the hidden staircases. Come, let's get to the escape tunnel. It comes out deeper in the wastelands. I'll deal with Pinus later." Ridge opened another gate, and they left.

Chapter 25

Ryan hobbled as quickly as he could, hampered by the cuffs. So far, they had been lucky, and nothing had attacked. He didn't want to know the odds of their luck holding. They had pushed out of the tunnel further back up the foothills of the Northern Wasteland Mountains. He needed to get Victoria across the Kaveri River and into the relative safety of the Lord Ellwood's residence. Ryan sighed. He was in such dire straits that Lord Ellwood looked like a suitable safety net. He had to get these cuffs off, but Ryan needed another preternatural with the strength to break them to do that. Such a lovely mess he had gotten himself into. Problem was, Ryan wasn't sure what he could have done differently.

"It's not your fault." Victoria slapped at a huge bug with mosquito traits and continued walking through the brush. "If you weren't here, I would still be back at the fortress."

"I doubt it. You're the one who found the stairs."

"Yeah, but I wouldn't have had the courage to use them on my own," she admitted. She let go of the branch she was holding too soon, and it smacked Ryan in the face. She cringed, "Sorry. How can we remove the cuffs?"

He rubbed his jaw where the branch hit him. Ryan watched the blood drip from his fingers to the ground. "With the key, unless you have the magic necessary to break them."

"But there should be something –" Victoria's voice trailed off.

Noticing her worried look, Ryan added, "Don't worry about it. We'll be to the Northern Realm soon."

"If that's supposed to make me feel better you guys shouldn't have told me stories about Lord Ellwood and the Northern Realm."

Victoria had muttered her response, but Ryan's shifter ears picked it up just fine. He pressed his lips together to keep his laughter at bay and continued to hobble toward the river. As they neared the sound of running water, Ryan began to see a positive outcome for this adventure. He would owe someone in the Farseen a huge favor, but it would be better than having something happen to Victoria. Once they returned to Calabozo, he would demand that she remain in the facility. It was harsh but less harsh than her dying during another kidnapping.

An enormous red dragon, one the same size as Tempe, landed in front of the duo.

"What an odd couple to be wandering the Northern Realm Wastelands. It has been a long time since a human has wandered the wastelands without a patron." The dragon grinned at Ryan, "A patron from the Farseen, I should have said. Ryan, third in the Alpha Clan and protégée of Lady Tempest, you should know better than to wander such, especially encumbered as you are."

Ryan gritted his teeth but didn't speak. If the dragon hadn't already attacked, she wanted something.

"Hey! Even encumbered, as you so rudely pointed out, he saved me." Victoria glared at the dragon.

"He might have saved you from someone else, but he looks a bit banged about, and he hasn't saved you from me, yet." The dragon smiled showing lots of sharp teeth. "Ryan, I offer fair trade. I will remove the manacles from your hands and feet, and you will find something of mine that has been taken to the Seen."

"What was taken?"

"It matters not. It is mine and must be returned to me. I will give you full details once you agree. I also vow that I, and those under my will, shall leave your human unharmed this day."

"If we are to trade, I have need of your name and designation."

"Indeed, Lady Tempest has trained you well. I am Ralliner, Supreme Matriarch of the Reds."

138

Based on her size, he wasn't surprised, but it was good to have verification. "Ralliner, to accept your quest with no other information given, I require that this human, Victoria Nelson, have the protection of you, and those under your will, any time she is in the Farseen, regardless of her reason for being here, for the rest of her life."

"Well played, young alpha. The deal is struck with no out clause. Once the manacles are removed, you have one rotation of the Farseen planet to arrive, alone, at my lair for instructions." The manacles dropped from his wrists and ankles as the matriarch flew away. Seven smaller reds followed her. Ryan had noticed only five. He still had a lot to learn.

"Do you even know where her lair is?"

"No," Ryan rubbed his wrists, "But I know who to ask. Let's get you home." He opened a gate, took her hand, and walked onto the pad at Calabozo.

Ryan had to scream for his passcode to be heard over the alarms from his unscheduled appearance. The obnoxious sound lowered in volume but didn't cut off completely. The guards' weapons remained focused on Ryan and Victoria. Loane entered the room flanked by Sam and Eli. Ryan huffed out air but opened his mind, not that he could keep his powerful great-aunt out of his head even if he tried.

After a few seconds, Loane smiled. "Ryan is cleared, and the sovereign is waiting for a report."

The alarms cut off, and the silence was greeted with relief by everyone in the room.

As they walked down the hall, Sam asked, "Where's Fred?"

"No clue. He was unconscious when I entered the gate." Ryan looked at Sam and groaned. Fred was resistant to electrical charges and must have followed Victoria. Ryan had left someone behind. "I gotta go back. Tell Sage…"

"Tell me yourself." Sage stood. As Raven replaced her in the command chair, Sage headed for her office.

Ryan sighed and followed her.

Chapter 26

"They didn't know you were here. Impressive." Ridge said as he rose from the bushes he and Fred had hidden behind.

"I told you that. Why didn't we join them? You could have removed the cuffs from Ryan, and he wouldn't have owed a favor to a dragon."

"Many would rather owe a favor to a dragon than to me." Ridge grinned. "I'll open a way to Beryl Lane and return you to your duties."

Thankfully, Ridge led the way. Fred still wasn't sure he should trust this fae. When Victoria was in danger he didn't care, but now she was safe, and he could worry about his own skin. The gate opened on a walking trail used between Beryl Lane and Vitvarg Farms. Ridge walked to the edge of the shield and tapped it, sending sparks into the air. Few could see the shields that had been placed over the territory of preternaturals. It appeared that Ridge was one of the few.

Tempe arrived moments later, appearing beside Fred. "You alright?"

"Yes."

She turned to Ridge, "What was your part in this?"

"Only that my fortress was used without my knowledge. I assisted Fred in tracking his comrades and then returned him here, unharmed, after they left the Farseen. That is payment enough for not tending to my holdings properly." Ridge bowed, "I take my leave, Lady Tempest. Peace be present with you."

"With you as well," Tempe inclined her head. After Ridge left, she turned to Fred. "Ryan and Victoria are already in Calabozo. We should join them." She held out her hand. When Fred took it, she teleported them to the room in her house that contained an entrance to the facility and commented, "Perhaps we can enter without setting off all the alarms, as Ryan did."

Fred nodded and provided his palm print and passcode. Tempe did the same, and they breezed through with no alarms, although Loane was there to verify Fred was himself.

When they entered the sovereign's office, Victoria was just completing her report. "Balen was the only name I heard. I called the others Fae One and Fae Two. Fae One seemed to be in charge. The ones who never spoke seemed to be muscle."

"Pinus was Fae One. Balen and Spruce did whatever he said." Fred grabbed a seat.

Ryan, with a blush running up his cheeks, looked over at Fred, and admitted, "I wouldn't have left you if I had known you were there."

Fred looked around. His shifter form was known to everyone in the room. "How could I have let you know I tagged along? I knew if I shifted to human the pixies would notify their masters that I was there."

"Not in the dungeons," Ryan explained. "Pixies won't enter them for some reason."

"Wish I had known that." Fred stretched his neck. "Question, Tempe. Ridge and I caught up to them just as Ralliner struck her bargain with Ryan. Ridge didn't intervene – according to him – because most would rather owe a dragon a favor than him. I think there's more to it."

"If Ridge had interfered during the negotiation, the dragons would have attacked. Ralliner wants something from the Seen, and I suspect that's what she bargained for."

Ryan finished chewing a bite of sandwich one of the PAs gave him, and said, "Yep, I need to return to her lair as soon as we finish here."

"How soon?" Tempe leaned back in her chair.

"I have a full rotation of the Farseen planet from the time the cuffs came off."

"Good, we have time to discuss after everyone reports in."

A short time later, after everyone else left the conference room, Sage turned to Ryan. "What do you have to do for Ralliner?"

"Find something that was taken from her." Ryan leaned back and closed his eyes. He opened them slightly and glanced at Tempe through his eyelashes, "Is that what she wanted you to do?"

Tempe laughed. "No. But I believe our tasks are related. A member of the Northern Realm stole something from Ralliner. She didn't tell me what, but she demanded that I deliver the thief to her."

"Demanded?" Sage leaned forward. "Why is this the first I've heard of it?"

"I was there as a daughter of the Northern Realm. Since I've been staying at Father's when Star visits, I've taken over my old rooms, and I'm participating in court as a member of that court, I am bound by fae law to support the realm as required. Ralliner requested me and expected me to get the job done without creating an incident." Tempe shrugged. "It worked. I captured the thief, he confessed before Lord Ellwood, and I delivered him to Ralliner to meet dragon justice."

Sage narrowed her eyes on Tempe, "Which means?"

"The punishment for stealing from a dragon is death. Any ruling fae knows this. Heck, any lesser fae knows. I'm not sure how the fool managed it, but he stole something."

"What?" Ryan asked.

"No one asked. It didn't matter. Old bone or magnificent jewels, the price for stealing from a dragon is the same."

Ryan leaned back in the chair, never taking his eyes off his aunt. "Do I know the fae?"

Tempe shrugged, "Cupressus was a hanger-on in court, but I doubt he befriended any shifters. He was a bit of a snob."

*****

Victoria had been subdued throughout the entire briefing, and she walked back to her quarters, defeated. Fred didn't like it. Victoria was impulsive and opinionated, never defeated. His rooms were just down the hall, so they walked together.

"You okay?" Fred leaned on the wall by her door as she provided her palm print. "I'm sorry I couldn't let you know I was there, but you didn't need me. I wasn't any help at all."

She lunged at him and threw her arms around his neck and sobbed into his shoulder. "I'm the one who's sorry. It's my fault, all of it. I shouldn't have asked to go to the bar. I should have realized you were there."

"It's alright." He finally had her in his arms, and she was scared. Not exactly the emotion he had wished for. At least no one else was in the hallway. Fred held her gently, rubbed her back, and let her cry.

Chapter 27

Ryan approached Ralliner's lair with steady strides. Since he didn't know where he was going, Tempe had opened a gate for him to a location a mile away from the nest. She had told him to walk down the path into the mountain pass and not into the woods. According to Tempe, the long walk would indicate he wasn't concerned walking into a matriarch's stronghold in human form. Well, looks could be deceiving. Ryan concentrated on keeping his breathing as steady as his steps. As he approached the largest cave entrance he'd ever seen, two dragon guards uncoiled.

One lowered his head to look Ryan in the eye. "Welcome young alpha. Enter in peace. Congregate in peace. Leave in peace… or make the blood price so high your enemies will desire peace. Ralliner awaits you." Both dragons stepped back, and Ryan walked into the dragon's lair.

As he progressed deeper into the cave, a young dragon stood before each fork in front of the tunnel he was not to take. It certainly removed any doubt as to the direction he was to take to find Ralliner. Thirty minutes later the tunnel opened into a large cavern, complete with a river running along the far side. The water came out another tunnel to his left and flowed toward another tunnel on the right. Based on the sound, the tube on the right turned into a waterfall. Since there were no waterfalls in the Northern Realm wastelands, he suspected the waterfall was inside the cave.

"I have come to fulfill our bargain," Ryan bowed.

"And I have prepared for your arrival. Two sketches, drawn by the thief, have been placed on a rock to your left." Ralliner moved to a sitting position.

Ryan picked up the drawings, each on some type of leather. One was a sketch of a relatively average looking guy. The other was a sword. He looked over the photos in detail before turning to Ralliner and raising an eyebrow.

Ralliner grinned. "Lady Tempest must have taught you that expression. The human is the one who currently has the sword. The sword is one of the Five Swords of Virtue. I must have the sword back. It is dangerous if wielded by the wrong person."

"Dangerous, how? And what does the phrase 'the wrong person' mean?" Ryan looked at the drawing of the sword again but wasn't sure why he bothered. He had heard of the Five Swords of Virtue but had assumed they were a myth and didn't pay attention to the details. Ryan would have to rectify his shortsightedness about that and other things. Many tales he had assumed were just stories had turned out to be true of late.

"Your questions are wise. The Sword of Veracity is a weapon no one should wield."

"I assume there's more to it than a sword that ferrets out the truth."

"Indeed, young alpha. Veracity remakes the universe so that the words spoken by its wielder become truth."

"It… you're telling me that the person holding that sword can change everything?"

"In essence, but there are rules. First, the wielder must know and say the correct incantation to bind the sword to his will. Second, the wielder must state his will out loud, in a specific format, to invoke the magic of the sword. Third, the sword will work for each wielder one time only. It is commonly believed the Sword of Veracity forces all to tell the truth to the wielder."

"Well, that's something," Ryan shook his head. "How many know the rules?"

"I suspect many fae know there are three rules, and they may even know what I have told you of the rules themselves, but they may not believe the truth. The three fae to whom the sword was presented to know the incantation to bind the sword, and the words to speak to invoke the magic of the sword to wield it properly." Ralliner brought her head down to eye level with Ryan. "And no, young alpha, I will not tell you who those fae are."

"Fair enough, and I've figured out who the wrong person is for myself. Everyone. No one should wield that sword. Who thought creating such a sword was a good idea?"

Ralliner blew fire over Ryan's head. "My father. He lost a bet with the five realm lords' millennia ago. In payment, he crafted a sword for each realm based on a specific virtue, but since he was tricked into losing, he didn't craft them as each lord expected. I managed to recover all five. One of my foolish clutch mates traded the sword to a ruling fae for a boon. Both have been dealt with."

Ryan didn't ask about the fae or the dragon. Even though it was probably a foolish thing to do, he couldn't help but ask, "Where are the other four swords?"

"I will show them to you so that when you hear the song of the fifth sword, you will know it to be the true sword." Ralliner waved her left wing lightly, and a large boulder disappeared. Four swords were displayed in front of the wall. They appeared to hang in the air, unconnected to wires or the wall. The center of the display was empty, clearly where the missing sword belonged.

Music slowly circled Ryan. He could feel the song of each sword, different, but with an underlying tone that was the same. He would definitely know it if he found the right sword.

"The missing sword is Veracity. To the left of where it should be hanging is the Sword of Tenacity, as long as the sword is in the hand of the rightful wielder, all – including the wielder – will place complete confidence in his words. On the far left hangs the Sword of Invincibility. It prevents all harm to the wielder; however, each time the sword saves the wielder from harm, someone close to him dies. On the right, the Sword of Diligence gives the wielder complete focus, but once the wielder releases the sword, he will be in a daze until the next sunrise. Further right, the Sword of Alliance unites any creature in the presence of the rightful wielder, but the effect goes away as soon as the sword is sheathed." Ralliner flicked his wing again, and the rock reappeared.

Ryan shook his head. Each sword had a massive downside. The obvious lesson in all this was never trick a dragon. "May I take the two drawings?"

"They are yours, young alpha, to aid you in your quest. Return both with the sword. A word of warning. If others discover what you are looking for, and why, there will be a host of preternatural interference. Many would like to claim any of the five swords, regardless of what they do or don't do."

Ryan gathered up the images, bowed, and left the presence of the matriarch. He reversed his steps, relieved to see the whelps. At least he wouldn't make a wrong turn on the way out.

A short time later, in the sovereign's conference room, Ryan faced Sage and Tempe, "Dragons don't share info, do they?"

Tempe shrugged, "They consider knowledge to be power, why?"

"One of Ralliner's clutch mates stole an item and gave it to a fae. The fae sold it, or traded it, to a human in the Seen."

Tempe nodded. "Then her clutch mate, as well as the fae, are dead. Your task, in payment for her help, is to find the stolen item and return it to her. Are you required to return the human to her as well?"

"No, just the item. Ralliner didn't seem to think the human was important."

"As far as the dragons are concerned, the human didn't know dragons were involved. It was the clutch mate and ruling fae who broke dragon law."

"What was stolen?" Sage ground out the words.

"A sword." Ryan leaned back and closed his eyes.

"One of the five swords Ralliner guards?" Tempe demanded. Ryan nodded, and she said, "Which one?"

He tossed the picture on the table. Wondering if the drawing was accurate, he waited to see if Tempe would identify it.

"The Sword of Veracity," Tempe murmured, her gaze remained on the drawing for a few seconds before she shook her head, "That sword does not do what many believe."

"So, I've been told."

"If anyone finds out about your quest, you will have a huge target on your back, although anyone with any skill will wait for you to find the sword before revealing themselves."

"I was told that, too."

"Well, I haven't been told anything. Explain," Sage demanded. Ryan finished his rundown of the Five Swords of

Virtue, and Sage looked over at Tempe in shock, "Why didn't the realm lords destroy the swords?"

"Unmaking a magic sword created by a dragon is not within the power of any fae witch. Only a powerful dragon could destroy the swords, and no dragon will willingly destroy such a treasure. The best that can be done is to have the swords hidden and protected from use."

Sage leaned back in her chair and pursed her lips. "Could one of us take our dragon form and destroy it?"

Tempe shook her head. "Two reasons why that's a bad idea. One, I doubt that we could. In dragon form, we have access to some dragon magic, but we lack the full magic of a dragon. I tested that after I first shifted to a dragon. Second, Ryan is charged with returning the sword to Ralliner. If he doesn't the dragons will enter the Seen and attack all shifters, just as they would attack a realm if one if one of its subjects broke an agreement."

"I thought dragons couldn't open a gate to the Seen?" Ryan sat up and placed his elbows on the conference table.

"Most can't, matriarchs can," Tempe said.

"And why didn't Ralliner attack the Northern Realm after the sword was stolen?" he asked.

"Why attack when you can have the eldest daughter of the Northern Realm take care of the issue for you?" Sage muttered.

"An accurate assessment," Tempe agreed. "I didn't tell you about Ralliner because it was a Northern Realm issue, and she made it sound as if returning the fae to her would resolve the entire mess. She wanted the thief, and she didn't want to start a war to get him. I have repeatedly refused to discuss shifter business with Lord Ellwood, and he must have faith that I refuse to discuss Northern Realm business with you."

"I didn't realize what a tightrope you walk there."

"It's why I hate going to the Farseen, too much political maneuvering. Ryan, as a full-blooded shifter you have no restrictions. It is expected that you will share all information with your sovereign."

Ryan chuckled, "So that's why you drag Joey to all those meetings as the Sovereign's Squire. They expect him to report back, and it gets you out of the middle. And I'll bet they don't pull you into court discussions as much because he's there."

Tempe grinned, "It does tend to work in my favor."

"Why didn't Ralliner ask you to track down the sword? Seems like she could have made that part of the bargain with you." Sage eyed her powerful sister.

"Starless night! You know how to wield it!" Ryan's eyes rounded. "You know the incantation to bind the sword to your will, and you know the proper phrasing to reform the universe."

Tempe shrugged. "Lord Ellwood, Ridge, and I are capable of wielding Veracity for its true intent. You must make sure none of us touch it. What Ralliner apparently didn't tell you is that the sword calls to any fae. It's intoxicating. The desire to use the sword is overwhelming. Ralliner knows better than to allow us access to the sword. I have never shared the knowledge of the sword with anyone, and I doubt Lord Ellwood or Ridge have either. It's simply too dangerous. The three of us nearly killed each other trying to control the sword. Val and Rayna were the ones who prevented us from using the sword."

"So, the Sword of Veracity was given to the Northern Realm."

"Yes, The Sword of Alliance was presented to the Central Realm. The Sword of Diligence went to the Eastern Realm, the Sword of Invincibility to the Western Realm, and the Sword of Tenacity to the Southern Realm." "Tempe smiled wistfully. "Did she show you the other four?"

"Yeah."

"Isn't their song beautiful?" Tempe's head moved as if she were humming to herself.

"Yeah."

Tempe shook her head, as if to clear away the cobwebs, and stood up. "Never let me near the sword. From this moment on, do not tell me how your quest is going, even if I ask. If you need help, shifters are your best bet. All fae are drawn to the swords even if they don't know how to wield them. Wizards of the Seen have the same reaction to the swords as the fae do. I have no clue how vampires or other preternaturals of the Seen will react. Let's not find out." With those words, she left the conference room.

"I wonder what else Ralliner failed to tell me?"

Sage shrugged, "No clue. Find the sword and take it directly to Ralliner. No side trips. Work no other issues until this is resolved. Let me know if you need my help, but otherwise, we won't discuss it again. I'll let the others know you're working a special project, and they are to provide you whatever you need without question."

Ryan left and walked down the hall toward his quarters. His first big solo mission and it was a doozy. It would have been nice to ease into such a big task. Then again, perhaps everything he had already experienced was leading up to this moment.

"Ryan!" Destin grabbed his arm. "I've been calling your name since you turned down this wing. You must have been a thousand miles away."

"In another dimension, actually."

"Return to the Seen, please. I wanted to go over the new security measures for Victoria."

"Get Sam and Fred to look them over. I'll be out of pocket for a while."

Destin's phone pinged, and he checked the message. "Aha, just got the word. Good luck to you."

"Thanks." Ryan stopped walking. "Hey Destin, can you do some type of facial recognition search on the Internet, using a drawing?"

"You mean like on TV? Sort of, but it's not as quick as the crime shows make it seem."

"Great. I'll be in your office in thirty minutes. No one else can be there."

"Aha, a covert assignment. You can count on me, sir." Destin gave a mock salute and walked away. Ryan barked a laugh.

Thirty minutes later, Ryan entered the small briefing room that had become Destin's office. He spent so much time in conference calls on sensitive, technical issues that Sage had demanded he take over the space as his office. Not surprisingly, Victoria was in the room, and their discussion was so far over Ryan's head that he might as well be sitting in a cave. "Sorry to interrupt."

"No, we're just discussing an idea I had," Victoria smiled. "See you guys later."

Destin quickly cleared his desk as she walked out the door. "Got the drawing?"

Ryan pulled the leather out of his vest pocket and opened it up.

"Is this a joke?" Destin raised an eyebrow in a Tempesque fashion. A habit most of the family had developed.

"No. This is deadly serious, why?"

"You want me to do a search for Parker Lee? Why don't we walk down to the Norm Lab and talk to him?"

"What?" The Norm Lab was what the shifters called the lab where the normal humans worked.

Destin pointed to the sketch. "That's a drawing of Parker Lee. He's a methodical researcher. Not brilliant, like Victoria, but his results are solid."

"Are we that bad at vetting people?" Ryan growled in frustration.

"What's he done?"

"I need to talk to him. Call Parker Lee to the small conference room in the lab. I'll meet you there." Ryan turned and walked out the door.

"Seriously?" Destin said to the closed door.

Chapter 28

Ryan walked into the conference room and Destin scowled. Finally, some answers. Ryan hadn't told him anything, just issued an order and left. His cousin needed to remember that humans didn't have to follow his orders without explanation, although most did.

Parker Lee sighed, "I guess this means I've lost my job. I liked it here, but I understand."

"Huh?" Destin looked over in surprise.

"You aren't even going to deny it?" Ryan sat down across from Parker.

"No need. You've obviously found out, or I wouldn't be here. We don't call this room the firing room for nothing. Everyone who enters gets fired. Did you think we hadn't noticed?"

"First tell me where it is and why you acquired it, then we'll discuss your future with us."

"What are you talking about?" Parker looked confused now.

"You know what. Where is it?"

"Where is what? I thought I was here because you found out my idiot brother is a member of the AIB or whatever organization has replaced it. We haven't spoken in years, but I can see how you would consider me a risk."

"Brother?" Destin leaned forward. "Do you have a photo of him?"

Parker barked a laugh. "No. We were never close, but unless he's gained a lot of weight, I'm sad to say I probably still look like Clay. Once I reached adulthood, strangers frequently mistook us for twins."

"Oh, thank god," Destin breathed a sigh of relief.

"What's going on?"

"Both of you stay here. I'll be right back." Ryan walked quickly out of the room.

Destin turned to Parker. "I need to know everything you know about your brother."

"I told you his name. That's pretty much it. We don't keep in touch. I have no info on his current whereabouts or who his friends are. He's three years older than me. Even as a child, he was a predator. You know the kind I mean. We had a dog when we were young. Something happened. Our parents never allowed another pet in the house. I was a lot older before I figured out why. His only friend followed him around, and they bullied everyone they could."

"Is there no way for you to get in touch with him?"

"If anyone knows how it would be Uncle Jess. He's a predator too." Parker leaned back as Ryan entered the room, "So what did Clay do?"

Destin shrugged.

Ryan opened a file. "We're still tracking him, but it looks like Clay is living in rural West Virginia."

"Okay. I'll ask again. What did Clay do?"

"He has something that doesn't belong to him. I need to return it to its rightful owner."

Parker scoffed, "Good luck. He's tricky and mean. Don't trust anything he says." He cut his eyes toward Ryan and asked, "How fired am I?"

Ryan paged through the file. "We asked for full disclosure when we approached you about this job. You left out a militant brother and uncle. Both are members of the IGI, and it looks like your brother still works for the AIB. They aren't as defunct as the news reports have indicated. What do you think we should do with you?"

Parker sighed, "Don't you have at least one family member that you don't claim in public?"

Destin barked a laugh.

"A couple, as a matter of fact." Ryan grinned.

"Look, this is a great job. I have access to exceptional technology and work with the best people. The work is challenging and worthwhile. I'm sorry I didn't mention Clay or Jess, but I haven't spoken to either since the funeral for my parents, five years ago, and that conversation was a fight."

Ryan tapped the file, "Yeah, a loud one. The funeral director was appalled. Said it was the worst family fight he had seen in thirty years in the business."

"We're overachievers."

Destin leaned forward, "You got that information awfully fast."

"Yeah, well, we already had it. The person doing the background check didn't interview or research his brother and uncle, believing they were out of Parker's life. I'll be addressing that oversight." Ryan turned back to Parker, "For now, you're on lockdown. No project work and you're staying in a holding area. If everything works out, you'll get to keep your job."

"No joke?" Parker looked up hopefully.

"No joke, but your activities are severely restricted for now."

"If there's a chance I can keep my job, I'm good with that." Keeping his focus on Ryan, Parker added, "I'll have to tell Elaine, my girlfriend. She'll go nuts and call the cops if I don't show up tonight."

"You can call, but I'll have to listen in."

"Understood." One phone call later Parker turned to Ryan, "Where am I staying?"

"Right here. A cot will be rolled into this room, and we'll bring you books to read. No computer, no TV, no phone. Sorry."

Parker nodded, "One request."

Ryan raised an eyebrow.

"If Clay figures out I'm helping you, Elaine and her daughter are in danger."

"Don't worry, I already assigned guards to them."

"Thanks."

Adam, one of the guards that the humans saw frequently, walked in with a cot, followed by a young woman. "Parker, this is my daughter, Willow."

"Hello, give me your reading and food preferences." Willow looked over at Ryan, "Could he have a DVD player?"

Ryan shook his head. "No remotes of any kind, but we can put one of the screensavers up on the screen in this room. Let Willow know your preference." The screensavers – as everyone called them – were external camera views, new stations, or other public camera views throughout the world.

"We could run DVDs from another room into the screen. I'll volunteer to keep the movies coming." Destin commented. "How about a marathon? Star Wars. Lord of the Rings. James Bond. Anime." Destined snapped his fingers together and grinned. "I know, rom-coms. You name it, and I'll bet someone has it on DVD."

"How about Harry Potter? Elaine's daughter loves the books and the movies. I've never watched them. Seems like a good time for me to learn a little about her favorite movies."

"That's sweet," Willow smiled.

"Might want to make a list. I'm not sure how long this will take," Ryan said as he walked out of the room.

Chapter 29

Ryan ghosted through the pasture. He had flown around in his bird form for hours, but there had been no movement in or around the farm. According to procedure, Ryan should have called for backup and should have set a shield. But, come on, he was chasing humans for cripes sake. No reason to waste the energy or the manpower. Ryan had already lost enough time. It took nearly two days to track down Clay Lee. Clay might be a bully, but he was a smart one. Paid for everything in cash, lived off the grid. If good old Uncle Jess hadn't been bragging in a bar, owned by a witch who wasn't out, about something from the fae that would propel his nephew to greatness, Ryan would still be searching. Lucky for him, the witch called the High Wizard Coven, and the high wizard told the rest of the Tetrad. Sage had called with the news.

He approached the tidy lawn around the farmhouse. Ryan had expected to find a rundown farm. No such thing. The farmhouse had solar panels, so did the barn. An impressive, and expensive, water collection system was also in place. It looked like a lot of the homes owned by preternaturals who could no longer trust the government to provide such services. The animals were well tended, as was the vegetable garden. Heck, pretty flowers hung from pots on the front porch. The land was owned outright, and taxes were paid by a corporate account.

Ryan took human form as he hit the last step to the porch of the back door. He took a deep breath and cursed. Ryan turned just in time to catch the bat with the side of his head.

156

Ryan shook his head and immediately regretted it. Pain exploded behind his eyes. The rest of his body was immobile. Tied up again.

"What do we do with him? He's too strong to be trapped here for long." A voice Ryan didn't recognize carried through the door.

"Don't worry about him. As long as those cuffs are on his wrists and ankles, he has all the power of a normal human."

That voice Ryan did recognize, and it confirmed what his nose had sensed earlier. It also explained why the farmhouse was so green. The fae liked green technology.

Ryan groaned and tried to roll over on his back, but his hands were cuffed above his head with the chain running around a bed pole, and his feet were cuffed in such a way that he was forced to remain on his stomach. At least he was on a bed, a vast improvement over the dungeon from his last capture. Unfortunately, that was the good news. The bad news was he couldn't move at all. If the alphas found out about this, he would never live it down.

Might as well get it over with. Ryan pitched his voice to be heard outside the door, "Hey Spruce, I know you're here. How about you take these cuffs off, and we go for it, one-on-one?"

"He knows who you are?" The unknown male squeaked.

"Shut up!" Spruce hissed before he opened the door. "Awake at last. You will regret interfering."

"Is that the best you've got?" Ryan turned his head to face the door. Spruce stood a bit in front of his human companion. At least Ryan had visual confirmation that Clay and Parker looked alike.

"Brave talk considering your magic is bound. Do you even know why you're here? You stand in the presence of greatness." Spruce smiled.

Ryan twisted to eye Spruce as best he could, "Don't you mean veracity?"

"Aha, so you do know. I'm surprised you came here knowing what can happen."

"And I'm not surprised you don't know what the sword truly does." Ryan bunched his muscles and released the tension in hopes of relaxing his shoulders. It didn't work. "When I get out of here, you're a dead man. How's that for truth?" Ryan turned to Clay. "You know, Spruce here is a preternatural, right?"

Clay grinned, "Of course I know. He's fae, but we have the same goal, remove all aberrants from my world. Earth is for humans only."

"You're a fool." Spruce kicked Ryan in the knee and walked out with Clay on his heels.

Ryan sucked back a grunt. He would not be walking on that knee anytime soon. Ryan tried to meditate and push the pain away to no avail. His knee was still throbbing in time to the pounding in his head.

Glass, either a window or door, shattered downstairs. Based on the amount of glass that continued to break, Ryan bet whoever it was started the brawl in the kitchen.

"Fool," Spruce yelled. "You thought to defeat me?" Spruce lowered his voice, and Ryan strained to hear the rest. "The only question is, once I kill you, do I notify Star or let her worry? I'll have to think about that and decide which will serve me best. But there's no need for you to worry about your children. I'll raise your sons as my own. I don't blame them for their father's arrogance."

Ryan heard Joey's voice, but it was too soft to make out the words. Joey must have said something Spruce didn't like. The next sound was a gunshot.

Even encumbered, Ryan tried to use magic and move. The cuffs shocked him, and his knee rejected all movement by adding explosions of shooting pain to the ever-present throbbing. Ryan passed out from either the cuffs or the knee, perhaps both. When he woke, again, Ryan heard ragged breathing. He turned his head and saw Joey, still bleeding from a gunshot wound to the leg. "Hey man, how you doing?"

"Been better. We came to help, but I think I made it worse." Joey sucked in a deep breath as if answering the question took all his reserves.

"Don't tell me Star used her ring to find me? She's not with you, right?"

"What? No! Well, she used her ring to find you, but we sent her home as soon as we found the farmhouse. Kaleb came with me. I don't know what happened to him." Joey tried to tighten the makeshift bandage he had created from his t-shirt. The flow of blood slowed but didn't stop.

"How long before more people show up?" At this rate, everyone would know he was captured by that dweeb Spruce, for the second time no less.

"Don't know. Sage was reluctant to send anyone. Something about an artifact that no one should hold."

"Yeah. So far I'm doing great on my first solo mission."

"At least you weren't shot," Joey retorted.

"Did you look at my knee?"

"Yeah, it doesn't look so good."

Kaleb walked into the room. "I've iced down just about everyone. That fae…"

"Spruce." Joey supplied.

"Aha, that explains it. Spruce took off running, and I decided to help you rather than chase him down."

"Good call. Get Joey to safety." Ryan pulled on the wrist cuffs, still unable to move.

"But..."

"No buts. Joey's shot and I can't use magic as long as these cuffs are on, so I'm useless. Don't suppose Spruce left the keys?" A peck at the window caught Ryan's attention. He tried to turn toward the sound but only managed to strain his shoulder. "What's at the window?"

"A golden eagle." Kaleb opened the window and punched out the screen. The eagle flew in and shifted. "Hey Phoenix, excellent timing. Can you do anything about Ryan's jewelry?"

Ryan groaned. Phoenix would tell everyone. He would never live this down.

"Not sure. Let's see if the cuffs run from my awesome null powers." Phoenix touched the cuffs. Nothing happened for a few seconds. Finally, they vibrated and fell away. Ryan sighed in relief. When he started to roll over Phoenix stopped him. "Don't move. That knee needs to be braced."

"Whatever." Ryan tried to move, but Phoenix held him down. He would have pushed Phoenix away, but his knee upped the shooting pain. It appeared the knee was in charge at the moment.

"Stay still. Hang on a minute," Phoenix disappeared down the hallway but returned quickly with a board and twine. "Kaleb, can you set his knee?"

Kaleb snorted, "Wrong twin. Blake's the medic, and he's in Texas now."

"Fine." Phoenix set the board at the back of the offending knee and tied it in place with the twine. He looked over his handiwork and grimaced. "Sorry man, but it's gonna hurt when we move you. Can you open an earth side gate to one of our medical facilities?"

"Yes, but if I pass out, it will close on us."

"Oh goodie," Phoenix responded with all due sarcasm. Where the traveler ended up, or what happened inside a collapsed gate, was anyone's guess. No one had ever been seen again after such an event, and no remains were ever found. "Open the gate to Calabozo, Joey and Kaleb will go through before I help you stand."

"Good plan," Ryan muttered, but he opened a gate.

Before they could complain, Phoenix pointed them toward the swirling mass. "Go, we're right behind you."

Joey hobbled through the gate on his good leg, leaning heavily on Kaleb. Phoenix turned back to Ryan. "Close it. They would never have left if they thought we weren't going with them."

Ryan still hadn't moved, but he breathed a sigh of relief, "Thanks, man. So, what, you gonna do, carry me?" Ryan didn't sound hopeful. He was taller and outweighed Phoenix by at least thirty pounds, and they were a long way from any town.

"No alpha, you're both going to die."

Ryan turned and snarled at the humans wearing AIB patches. Phoenix faded to shadow as Ryan set his shield, then let loose his magic. Now that the cuffs were gone, he was ready for some payback. Using wind, he tossed the AIB, one at a time, through the still open window. They landed in the pond.

"Did that feel good?" Phoenix reappeared next to Ryan.

"As a matter of fact, it did." Ryan slowly slid his injured leg over the side of the bed. It didn't hurt too badly. Phoenix's wrapping helped. Ryan stood, and pain coursed through his leg.

160

Phoenix caught him before he fell back on the bed. "Think of me as your left leg until we get to my car. I stashed Lea at a hotel about three miles up the road. She's not pleased that I made her wait there."

Ryan's groan was weak as he tried to put weight on his injured leg.

Phoenix growled at his nephew. "Lean on me. I won't break. Don't put weight on that thing until after Lea heals it." As they slowly descended down the stairs, Phoenix asked, "What do you want me to do with the AIB?"

"Leave them," grunt, "It's our fault for opening a gate they could track. I'll talk to Star about that." A few minutes later, they finally made it to the car. Ryan muttered curse words trying to twist his leg into the sports car. Sweat dripped into his eyes. "You know, there's nothing wrong with an SUV."

"Yes, yes there is." Phoenix started the engine and flew down the road.

Ryan wiped the sweat off his forehead, hoping he didn't look as weak as he felt. Injured as he was, it might be hard to get in and out of, but the sports car moved fast. Lea had waited for them at a rundown hotel. She healed Ryan's knee, ribs, and head, and he took a little nap. After a shower he joined his aunt and uncle at the table.

"Take care for a couple of hours yet," Lea said between bites.

"I know the drill," Ryan replied. Healing left the healed shifter vulnerable to further injury for a few hours. He sat down and joined the feast of pizza and soda. Once they finished eating, he turned to his aunt and uncle, "Thanks."

Lea clicked her tongue. "You're welcome. Next time follow procedures and call for backup. Phoenix, give me your keys. I'm ready to return home."

"Take care of my baby." Phoenix tossed her the keys, and she left.

Ryan narrowed his eyes at Phoenix. "How are you getting back to Tennessee, New York, PAC HQ or wherever you're going?"

"I'm not. I'm going with you."

Ryan gritted his teeth at the one shifter who didn't have to obey orders from anyone. "No, you're going back to your job as the public face of the shifters."

"Right, 'cause going solo worked so well for you the last time. Besides, you're tracking some dangerous magical artifact, right?" Ryan nodded, and Phoenix added, "And I'm immune to magic, right?"

"Yeah, but…"

"But what?" Phoenix leaned on the door and asked into the silence.

"Give me a second. I'm trying to think of a suitable response," Ryan muttered.

Phoenix grinned. "How about, gee uncle, you're right. You're exactly who I need on this mission."

"I'm pretty sure that's not what I was thinking." Ryan frowned before he sighed and admitted, "But you could be useful. Let's go get a rental car and continue the search."

Phoenix pulled another set of keys out of his pocket. "Done. I thought my car might be a little too obvious."

Barely noticing his knee at all, Ryan grinned, and followed his uncle out the door. Lea did good work. He hoped to reach her level of healing one day. Of course, for that to happen, he would have to study medicine. Ryan planned to put that off as long as possible.

Chapter 30

"Direction?"

"Back to the farmhouse." Ryan glared at Phoenix. His most irritating uncle wouldn't back down. Ryan had been reduced to passenger status.

Phoenix kept his expression bland and pulled out of the hotel, heading back the way they had come, proving he could occasionally be gracious about a war-of-wills win. "Tell me about this mission." After Ryan finished the update, Phoenix sighed, "So, we're looking for a sword that can remake reality, hopefully, to destroy it?"

"No, I'll return it to its rightful owner."

"Hmm, don't you think it should be destroyed?"

"Yes, I do, but the dragon supreme matriarch it belongs to wants it back."

"For future reference, lead with 'the magical artifact belongs to a dragon.' It will eliminate most questions for your audience."

"It does, doesn't it," Ryan grinned. They exited the car back at the farmhouse. After a thorough search of the house, they were once again in the room Ryan was held in. "Grab the cuffs. I'm not sure if they will regain their power, and I don't want Spruce to use them on me again."

"Seems wise," Phoenix murmured.

Ryan glared at his uncle, but no smile touched his uncle's lips as he picked up the cuffs. Ryan's eyes narrowed, but all he said was, "Let's check the barn. I don't want to start this search over again."

*****

Back in Calabozo, Ryan let loose a disgusted sigh. "Nothing. I'm back where I started. No leads."

"That sounds like I'll be here longer." Parker offered up his own sigh. He had been in the little conference room for two days before they moved him to an actual prison cell. At least here Parker had a bathroom without needing to call for an armed escort. So far, he had watched Harry Potter, Indiana Jones, Twilight Zone, Star Wars, and every Star Trek movie ever made. He was now watching the original Star Trek TV series.

"Well, actually, we have a possible plan. It's dangerous, so you need to think about it before you agree."

"I'll do it. Anything to get out of this cell," Parker agreed immediately.

"Listen to the plan first," Ryan ordered. "Do you think your brother and uncle would buy your disillusionment with preternaturals?"

"Doubtful. Clay's a bully, but a smart one."

"I was afraid of that."

Parker leaned back in his chair. "He might buy that I'm afraid."

"Explain."

"I could contact my uncle. Tell him I was fired for not revealing the family relationship to known IGI/AIB members and then explain that I'm afraid the shifters are going to kill me because I know too much."

"You think they'll care?" Destin's tone indicated that he didn't.

Phoenix frowned, "They won't, but if they think Parker has intelligence they could use against preternaturals, they will check it out."

"And they just might beat the info out of you." Ryan shook his head. "No, too dangerous."

"I know it's dangerous, but what other choice do we have? There must be some way to keep a tracker on me."

"Not one they won't find," Phoenix argued.

164

Ryan leaned forward, "Maybe we do. I've got a plan that just might work."

Chapter 31

Parker pulled into the parking lot, cut the engine, and sat for a moment. A week ago, he would have laughed if someone had told him he would be on a covert mission. He wasn't the hero type. Parker got out of the car and headed into the dive – no one would give this place bar status – absently scratching his shoulder blade. He looked around, impressed by Ryan's information. He had been shown photos, and told the names, of most of the people in the room, including the bartender. Parker's uncle sat at a corner table, back to the long wall, so he walked over and sat down. He ignored the person hiding behind a newspaper at the next table. How cliché.

Uncle Jess barked a laugh, "My little nephew finally grew up and saw the world for what it is." Aside from his beard moving into Duck Dynasty status, Uncle Jess hadn't changed much.

"I'm glad I amuse you." Parker dropped into a chair with his back to the corner wall, leaving both of them with a view of the room, and the door.

Jess nodded, "At least you've acquired some street smarts."

"Had to," Parker retorted. "They're after me."

"Why? What have you learned?" Clay leaned over from the next table. He didn't drop the newspaper.

Parker scoffed. "Nothing. I did a lot of support work for Victoria Nelson, but I wasn't allowed in her private lab."

"I told you he wouldn't be part of the inner circle."

The man sitting next to Clay smiled. "Oh, I think he'll be able to tell us a few things."

166

Parker didn't so much as twitch. Dave Roberts, senior, was a big deal in the AIB and the briefing Parker received included what happened to Victoria under Roberts' orders. After her kidnapping, new security procedures were put in place for humans working at the facility and Parker suspected their homes were watched. He didn't mind. He liked the added security. "I'll tell you anything I can."

"Yes, you will."

Parker shuddered, no longer sure he would be able to pull off the deception.

*****

Ryan and Phoenix flew through the sky, following the truck down the back roads of West Virginia. On the plus side, both took a golden eagle form. On the negative side, golden eagles didn't nest in West Virginia, and summer was the wrong time of year for them to be passing through. Hopefully, no one would notice, but Ryan wouldn't count on it. Since the big preternatural reveal, humans developed an irritating policy of assuming any animal, not in its normal habitat, was a shifter. The fact that they were frequently right made it no less annoying for the shifters.

Ryan emitted one short high-pitched piping note and dove for the cover of some trees. Phoenix followed, and they watched the truck stop at a checkpoint a mile down the road. With their superior eagle eyesight, they observed the check-in process and watched the guards rough up Parker.

The truck passed the first checkpoint, and they retook flight. This time, Ryan set a shield of invisibility around them. They flew past the first and second checkpoints with no problem. The third checkpoint was the entrance to the building. The building boasted some type of laser shield. The birds banked left and landed in another stand of trees. This time they headed for sturdy branches where they could shift to human.

*****

"You guys really did drink the Kool-Aid, didn't you?" Parker looked at the last of his family in disgust. He wasn't surprised he was roughed up, but he was surprised his brother and uncle didn't help.

Clay glared at Parker, "And you don't know what you're dealing with. For example, we tried to grab your girlfriend and her daughter to bring them here, for their own safety. They have shifter guards on them. Your girlfriend is feeding them."

"Of course, she is. She knows I work for them and they probably gave her some story about keeping her safe while I'm missing." Parker matched Clay glare for glare. "You do realize since I didn't return home, she called my office. I'll bet the shifters are searching for me now."

"They sure are. You're just lucky we have a safe place to hide you."

*****

"Suggestions?" Ryan asked. Seemed silly, but the rank structure in the Alpha Clan was strict. If he didn't ask, most alphas wouldn't offer a suggestion, they simply waited for orders.

"Forgot who you were with, uh?" Phoenix smiled. As the only alpha not tied to rank, he didn't need to be asked to offer his advice. When Ryan didn't speak, he added, "Fine. We need to get through the checkpoints. Find someone off duty, you glamour to look like 'em, and bring me in as a trophy found in a bar or something."

Ryan nodded, "I agree, but for once if I tell you to leave, get Parker out of there and get gone."

"No deal, but I promise to make sure Parker is safe before I disobey."

Ryan shrugged. It was better than he expected from his most disobliging uncle.

A couple of hours later, Ryan drove down the road conveniently wearing the face of one Evan Miller. It went nicely with Evan's wallet, security badge, and car. Thinking of the car made Ryan cringe. It was a 1966, mint condition shadow blue Mini Cooper. Evan took care of his car.

Using glamour to look like an average Joe, Ryan struck up a conversation with Evan. It didn't take long to discover that Evan only worked for the AIB because they had the only jobs available in the area. Evan had already lost the family farm. Unlike his father and his father before him, Evan wasn't a farmer. Shortly after, his wife left and took the kids. He needed money, so Evan took the only job available. He was getting ready to sell the Mini Cooper – his father's true baby – and move on. Evan didn't have the stomach for the AIB job, and the car was his only way out. He had

168

decided to take it for one last spin before delivering it to the buyer. Ryan vowed to himself that he would get the car back to Evan in mint condition.

"Nice car." The guard said as he approached the vehicle.

"It was Dad's. What's in the back seat is more interesting. Met him in a bar." Ryan had pitched his voice a little deeper and hoped it would be enough. He didn't have the fae ability to absorb languages or mimic accents and voices.

The guard peered in the back and laughed at Phoenix, trussed up like a Christmas turkey. "Lucky dog. You'll get a promotion for this. How did you capture him?"

"He's immune to magic, not tire irons." Ryan made use of the fact that the news stations had run a video of that immunity a few months ago.

"Smart thinking. You're clear." The guard sent a hand signal to the other guard, and the gate opened.

Ryan drove through and did a repeat at the second gate. At the third gate, he was greeted by an AIB herd, led by Dave Roberts.

"It's a night of surprises," Dave grinned. "Take Phoenix to a holding cell."

Watching Phoenix being dragged down the hallway still pretending to be unconscious, Ryan almost missed the guard's order, "Handprint." Ryan walked over and placed his hand on the scanner. Typically, glamour wouldn't pick up prints, but he had studied Evan's hands and hopefully matched the prints with his glamour. The device flashed green.

Dave patted him on the back. You've done well this evening. We just received a tip about Phoenix being in the area.

Ryan grinned. Phoenix had called in that tip.

Handprint notwithstanding, Ryan was questioned for hours on how the capture occurred. Finally, he was allowed a few minutes to himself. Ryan listened to the conversation on the other side of the glass. He would find Phoenix and Parker in the same area. He walked into the restroom and into a stall. He set his shield of invisibility and breathed a sigh of relief that his use of magic didn't kick off any alarms. He moved down the hallway and followed the signs to the holding area. The facility was set up like an office building with signs to everything. The first thing on his to do list when he returned to Calabozo would be to remove what few signs there were or at least turn them into codes.

"When do you meet up with him again?" Dave Roberts asked.

Ryan stopped and listened.

"I need to leave now to make the meeting," Clay said.

"I want that sword. Understand? Get it."

"Easier said than done. Since he arrived here, he guards it at all times. I can't get close. There's some type of shield." Clay glared back. He didn't like Dave's superior tone.

"Why hasn't the fae used it himself?"

Don't know. Spruce said he didn't want to draw attention, so I think other fae will somehow know if he does."

"Find out if they will know if we use the sword," Dave said.

"Find out yourself," Clay muttered. "Oh right, you can't. I'm your contact with the fae. Remember that."

"Yes, you are," Dave agreed as he walked off, "For now."

Clay snarled at Dave's back before turning and walking toward the exit.

Even though it was the plan, Ryan debated what to do, save his friends or chase the sword. With a prayer that his strategy would work, Ryan followed Clay, hopefully, to the sword.

*****

Evan Miller woke in the bushes behind the parking lot. His head pounded, and his eyes were full of sand. At least that's what it felt like. He rolled to a standing position and discovered his head was not on board with that plan. Evan dropped to one knee and clutched his head. After a few minutes, he stood again and surveyed the parking lot.

Joe, or whatever his real name was, had knocked him out, taken his wallet and his car. The Mini Cooper his father had prized, had been the only thing Evan had left that he could have used to escape the job with the AIB.

Evan stood in the middle of the parking lot with his hands on his hips. He reached for his phone, only to discover it was gone. The back door of the bar opened, and he didn't even look around. He had nothing left to steal.

"Hey, man. You ok?" The man tossing trash into the bin looked over at Evan.

"Car stolen. So, no, not ok."

"Sucks, man." The guy went back into the bar without offering to help.

Shoulders slumped, Evan dusted off his pants and took the first step in his three-mile walk to his apartment. At mile one the family farm, the one the creditors took, stood on his right. Yet another failure. As he walked, Evan was reminded of all the questionable actions he had taken for the AIB. He wouldn't go back there. Evan's hand was on the door knob before he remembered his apartment key was with his car key. Joe, the thief, had his keys.

Evan looked at the door to his garden apartment for a few before walking two doors down and knocking. Hopefully, his elderly neighbor would remember all the times Evan had helped out by carrying groceries and running errands. He knocked three times before he heard shuffling on the other side of the door.

"It's two am. Go away. Come back at a reasonable hour."

"Sorry, Mr. Abernathy." Evan placed his hand on the door jam. "My wallet, keys, and car were stolen. I had to walk home and need someone to call maintenance to let me in."

"Miller, that you?"

"Yes, sir."

Mr. Abernathy moved the curtain back and looked at Evan before unlocking the door and stepping back. "Come on in, Son. I'll get you some water while you call maintenance. The number is by the phone. Heaven knows I have to call them often enough."

Evan sighed in relief and followed his neighbor into the apartment.

Chapter 32

Phoenix watched the butterfly flitter into his cell. "Keys?"

Fred batted his wings but didn't shift to speak. He wasn't sure if shifting inside the cell would set off alarms."

Phoenix nodded his understanding. "I'll fade to shadow and you, in that spiffy AIB uniform you're supposed to have on, will walk Destin out like he's on his way to more talks. You've explored the facility, right?"

Fred waved his wings up and down, irritated at the question.

"Okay. Sorry. Let's get this show on the road." Phoenix faded to shadow and watched Fred shift, retrieve the keys, and release him. Phoenix frowned at the bruises on Parker. "Your brother?"

"No, Dave Roberts had some muscle-bound idiot pound on me to see if I forgot anything. I'm okay with torching this place." He limped out of the cell.

"Sorry, the sovereign wants it intact for intel," Fred explained, "But don't worry. No one else will be trapped here for interrogation." He grabbed Parker's arm and marched down the hallway. No one stopped them until they turned toward the parking area.

"Where you goin' with that prisoner?" The burly guard was no match for Fred in height, but his muscle mass more than made up for his lack of inches. Both men stood ready to fight, like well-trained bouncers. If it came to a fight, it would be a good one.

Fred shrugged. "To transportation. Roberts doesn't want him near the shifter in case a rescue is attempted."

"Roberts does plan ahead." The guard stepped out of the way.

Fred nodded and moved on. They made it to the parking garage where Phoenix tapped him on the shoulder, pushing them toward a Mini Cooper. Phoenix unlocked the car and dropped into the shotgun seat, still invisible.

"Nice car." Fred helped Parker into the floor of the back seat, covered him with a blanket, and climbed into the driver's seat.

"Yeah, I hope you don't have to scratch it to get us out alive. The owner, Evan Miller, isn't a bad guy, just a guy in a bad situation."

"Okay, let's do this." Fred drove toward the exit and was immediately stopped. Apparently, they checked leaving as well as arriving. He rolled down the window and said, "Whatcha need?"

"Why are you in Evan's car?" The guard wasn't smiling.

"He was worried about this baby. Asked me to drive it back home. He'll follow shortly with my car."

The guard started to argue but then shrugged and motioned them through. The other checkpoints weren't a problem. A couple of miles later Phoenix took form.

Parker pointed to a man on the side of the road and asked, "Is that the sovereign's bodyguard?"

"Sure is." Fred slowed to a stop and rolled down the windows. "Kyan, I didn't find any other prisoners."

Kyan peered into the back seat, "Who did this to you?"

Parker shrugged, "A guard, with Roberts' blessing."

Kyan stood back, opened the door, and created an earth side gate. "Fred, take Parker to medical. Then he'll meet with Loane and the sovereign."

Parker's eyes widened. He never expected to meet the sovereign. He tripped exiting the car and bumped into Fred. So much for calm, cool, and collected. He entered his first gate, surprised to exit on a platform inside PAC HQ. At least it looked like pictures he had seen of the facility. While Fred talked with the people who surrounded them, Parker looked around in amazement. Huge facility, and lots of activity. He couldn't believe he was here.

And then they were off. Fred led Parker down a corridor toward another checkpoint.

Chapter 33

Ryan followed Clay. The bird form just got more and more useful, although if he had a smaller form, bug maybe, he could have hidden in the car. Ryan would have to work on that. He didn't know how far they were going, and he was tired from the previous flight. Not to mention hungry. He hadn't eaten anything since the burger at the bar when he was talking to Evan. That was hours ago. Between the glamour, shifting, and keeping invisible, Ryan needed to eat soon, or they would hear his stomach, even if they couldn't see him.

Eventually, Clay arrived at another farmhouse. This one was more run down.

Ryan flew to one of the trees that framed the front entrance and set his shield, remaining invisible. He could feel the presence of fae. Hopefully, they couldn't feel his presence through his shield.

Spruce walked out the door and glared at Clay. "You're late."

Clay frowned but admitted, "Yeah, Dave called me in. He's still fishing for info on the sword."

The smirk on Spruce's face widened, "Our deal was made with no out clause. I know that doesn't mean much to you, but to fae, it's binding. I can't double cross you and make another deal with Dave. Don't worry."

Clay smiled and followed Spruce into the house.

Ryan shook his head. If Clay died, Spruce could then deal with Dave. Somehow, Ryan doubted Clay would have included his continued status of living as part of his bargain. No time to worry about Clay right now, anyway. He needed access to the house. He eyed the open window, but it was a bit too obvious. After his fourth trip around the house, searching for another way in, he surrendered, and flew slowly inside, tripping a sensor.

A net caught Ryan, and he hit the ground, losing his invisibility in the process. The trap wasn't unexpected but angered Ryan anyway. He dropped his bird form to increase the odds of escaping the net. Most fae would be able to identify the bird as a shifter.

"The way you follow me I'm beginning to think you like me." Spruce's smile widened when Ryan rolled his eyes. "Still looking for the sword? Everyone in the five realms knows about your quest. You can't keep a thing like that quiet. I'm surprised Ralliner gave you the task. You must owe her a great debt."

Still, Ryan said nothing.

After waiting a few seconds for Ryan to reply, Spruce laughed. "No matter. I think I'll let you see the sword you're tasked with retrieving."

Ryan looked up then. If the sword were here, he might be able to wrap this mission up. It would be a relief. The sword's song called to him and he sat up.

Spruce entered the room with the sword in his fighting arm and frowned. "I didn't know the sword called to non-fae."

"I suspect there's a lot about that sword you don't know," Ryan said.

"Perhaps, but I can be taught." He raised the sword toward Ryan and said, "Tell me why you're searching for the sword."

Thinking the truth might help him, Ryan answered, "Ralliner didn't want to send a fae on the search, and since I was in her debt, she sent me on this quest."

Spruce nodded, "I thought as much. She helped you to escape the fortress with Victoria. I was impressed you managed that."

Ryan nodded as if Spruce had figured it out.

"How can I get Star to meet me away from the shifters?"

Ryan raised an eyebrow but didn't speak.

Spruce gripped the sword tightly and asked again.

Ryan responded through gritted teeth, making a show of fighting the power of the sword, "Leave a message on her private email saying I'm dead if she doesn't show up. Star would never leave a friend in danger, even if she knows it's a trap."

Once Ryan provided the email address, Spruce grinned, "Excellent!" Before he closed the door, Spruce added, "You are dead if she doesn't show up."

Still in the mesh, which contained his magic rather well, Ryan glared at the door. First cuffs and now a net. This was getting ridiculous.

*****

Kyan's team overran the AIB facility quickly. A few escaped, Dave Roberts senior being one of them, and some loyal AIB member had let loose a virus that destroyed some of the computer files, but overall it was a successful mission. Destin's team was hard at work rescuing whatever data they could.

Kyan looked over at Phoenix who was engrossed with his cell phone. "What are you doing?"

Phoenix looked up from his phone, "Waiting for an email. Aha, it just came in. Uncle, I need a gate to Calabozo."

Kyan stood in from of him and growled, "I know about Ryan's mission, and I know you're helping him. If you get stuck, call me."

"Aw, Uncle, you do care. Gate, please. I'm on a deadline." Kyan opened a gate, and Phoenix waved over his shoulder and left. After passing through the checkpoints at Calabozo, he headed straight for Star's quarters and knocked.

The door opened quickly, revealing an agitated Joey. "No. This is not happening. Star is not going to be anywhere near Spruce."

Phoenix pushed his way into the room and closed the door. "Don't yell the secret plans in the hallway. Seriously, some things the sovereign's squire should just know. Besides, Star isn't going."

Joey cocked his head to one side, "Uh, what?"

There was a knock on the door. Phoenix opened it and said, "Joey, meet Teirra, Char's daughter. She shifts into a jaguar."

Joey stared at the dark-haired beauty. She looked nothing like Star. "Can you glamour?"

"No, I can open a gate within the Seen and have some control over the weather. As my uncle said, I shift into a jaguar."

And with that lovely Brazilian lilt, she sounded nothing like Star either. Joey turned back to Phoenix. "How's that going to work? She doesn't look like Star. She doesn't sound like Star. She can't open a gate to the Farseen. I see a lot of holes here."

"I'm the distraction. If Spruce is as fixated on Star as everyone says, he'll focus on the jaguar, allowing Ryan time to take the sword," Teirra said.

"And where is Ryan?' No one answered, and Joey rubbed his forehead. "Like I said, a lot of holes.

Chapter 34

Spruce paced around the open field, getting the feel of the sword, keeping Ryan in his field of vision. The net should be strong enough to contain the shifter, but the cuffs, wherever they were, would have been a better option. There was no doubt that the cuffs worked on the shifter, and the net wasn't nearly as powerful. It was a known fact that the net couldn't hold any of the shifter half-breeds born to Lord Ellwood, but it worked fine on the average shifter. No proof of its effect on a full-blooded shifter of the sovereign's line was available.

Spruce smiled in anticipation of Star's arrival. Lady Tempest wouldn't come. The sword would keep her away. She, Lord Ellwood, and Ridge were afraid of the sword for some reason. Yes, he felt safe in his demand for Star to meet him. With the sword in his hand and Star by his side, Lord Ellwood would welcome him and perhaps even approve of his methods. After all, he had tricked Lady Tempest and the Alpha Clan. Even the Forest Lord had failed at that. Spruce was finally moving up in the world and soon everyone, even his father and brother, would have to give him the respect he deserved.

The way opened, and Star walked through in jaguar form, with a shifter male by her side. Spruce yelled, "Should I kill Ryan now? You didn't follow my instructions."

"Easy," Phoenix said. "Don't you recognize me? I'm no threat. I'm just here to take Ryan back as we expected him to be injured."

Spruce stared at Phoenix. There was something strange about him. He never fought, but served as the sovereign's spokesperson, dealing mostly with humans. And he never seemed to get hurt if magic was tossed. The humans said he was immune to magic, but that didn't make sense. No one was immune. Of course, if other alphas were around, they would be the ones on the receiving end of a magical bomb. Perhaps Star asked her uncle to come and help Ryan. It's something she would do. She worried about others. That's the first of her bad habits he would break.

"Once Star and I leave, you may do whatever you wish with Ryan." Spruce turned to Ryan, still inside the net, and raised the sword to point at him, "Does Phoenix have any powers I need to know about?"

Ryan strained at the net, but answered, "Phoenix turns to shadow but commands no aggressive power."

Spruce grinned. "Come Star. We have much to discuss." She hesitated, and he added, "The agreement was you in exchange for Ryan."

She meowed low, hung her head, and padded toward Spruce. Once within striking distance, she lunged.

Spruce fell back as her claws scrapped his left arm. The sword, still in his right hand, cut into the jaguar's side.

Phoenix grabbed the net, nullified its magic, and took off running to the jaguar's side. Ryan leaped to his feet with the net still covering him and used telekinesis to pull the sword to him even while he opened a gate to Calabozo.

Spruce, sprawled on the ground, watched as Phoenix took the bleeding jaguar through the gate Ryan opened. He jumped to his feet to follow, but the gate closed in his face. Spruce screamed. He turned to Ryan, "Is Star alright? I have to know."

Ryan cocked his head to one side. "Do you care? She's a means to an end for you."

"She's much more than that."

"Interesting. I won't know her status until I return home, and I have to return the sword to its guardian first." Ryan pointed to the new gate he opened, "And you're coming with me."

*****

Ryan, net over one shoulder and the Sword of Veracity in his arm, marched Spruce toward Ralliner's lair. Three unaligned

180

fae mercenaries attacked. Ryan found he was more irritated than surprised. He froze Spruce in place and tossed the net on one of the fae. While the fae untangled from the no-longer-magical net, Ryan used wind to push one fae off the bank into the fast-moving river. Ryan turned to face the third with the Sword of Veracity gleaming in the sun.

"Drop the sword. You can keep Spruce," the fae grinned.

"I'll keep both." Ryan again used wind and tossed the fae who managed to get out of the net into the river. He joined his comrade, moving down the rapids and over the Psyche falls. Too bad they were only fifteen-feet tall. Both would survive, probably wouldn't even be hurt.

The remaining fae dropped into a fighting stance and pulled a beautifully detailed short sword. This sword also sang. The fae smiled at Ryan's confused look. "You are not the only person in possession of a dragon made weapon. Give me the Sword of Veracity, and I'll allow you to leave unharmed."

"Right, 'cause Ralliner won't be mad that I gave it up," Ryan scoffed.

"Then I shall kill you and take the sword. I have never been defeated with this sword drawn."

"That's because you've never faced me." Ryan had no clue where those words came from. He was not nearly as experienced with swords as the average fae and it was a bad idea to brag before a fight. He raised the Sword of Veracity in his hand, and it sang. The sound grew louder until the song of the short sword could not be heard. Ryan charged.

The fae faltered. Without the song of the short sword to guide his steps, he wasn't as sure of his fighting skills. The fae's defensive moves were no match for Ryan's attack. Ryan lunged, and the Sword of Veracity connected with the short sword. The fae lost his grip on his weapon. He ran into the woods as the sword fell at Ryan's feet.

Ryan looked at the sword in his hand. He wasn't sure what happened. He had never wielded a sword so well and never so aggressively. Ryan bent down and picked up the short sword and stuck it through his belt.

Ryan, once again, marched Spruce toward Ralliner's lair. Spruce was now wet from where Ryan melted the ice off his body.

The two dragon guards smiled wide showing their large white teeth. The dragon on the left asked, "May I help you with your burden? The long sword, the short sword, the fool, perhaps all three?"

Spruce slid closer to Ryan who pushed him away. "I need no assistance. As you see, I have returned with the object Ralliner requires."

The other dragon blew smoke, "You may give the items to me. I shall return them to Mother."

Ryan shook his head, "My quest. I shall return the sword to her."

More blue smoke accompanied the dragon's laugh. "Indeed, young alpha. Enter in peace. Congregate in peace. Leave in peace... or make the blood price so high, your enemies will desire peace. You are earlier than expected, but Ralliner awaits you."

As Ryan and Spruce walked into the lair, the whelps once again guarded the forks in the tunnels, allowing them to make good time. They entered Ralliner's chamber and Spruce sucked in air, "I never expected to be here."

Ryan raked Spruce with an incredulous stare, "You tried to wield a sword that belonged to Ralliner, and you didn't think you would end up in her presence? You are a fool."

"Why am I here? I didn't steal the sword from her. The one who did is already dead. I've broken no dragon law." He turned to run and found himself facing the business end of the Sword of Veracity.

Ryan grinned evilly, "After I return the sword to Ralliner, I'll return you to Lord Ellwood."

Spruce groaned, and Ryan's smile widened.

Ralliner chose that moment to shoot up out of the river, spraying water on her visitors. Since dragons could exit the water without splashing, Ryan assumed she did so for a purpose. He suspected she did it because she could.

She took no notice of Spruce as she took the sword from Ryan. "You have impressed me, young alpha." She revealed the wall with the swords and the Sword of Veracity flew to its assigned spot. "I also require the two leather drawings."

Ryan pulled the drawings out of his pocket. He was glad Tempe had warned him they would have to be returned. He was happy to be rid of them. Knowing that the leather was the tanned pelt of the fae who stole the sword was downright creepy. Even creepier, the fae had been forced to draw them on his skin while he was still alive.

He held out the short sword, "Is this another dragon sword? I took it off a fae who attacked me for the Sword of Veracity. Veracity swallowed up its song. I think that's how I defeated the fae."

"The Patron's Sword. It likes you, young alpha." She reared back on her legs. "This sword was presented to Valiant the Bold by Tulvir, supreme matriarch of the greens. Since Valiant's death, the sword has moved from fae to fae, looking for a new master. While others could wield it, they could not call forth the true power of the sword. The Patron's Sword has chosen you, alpha. Veracity didn't defeat it. The Patron's Sword surrendered to you. It will remain faithful to you until your death or until you disappoint it. Wear it well, Ryan, bearer of the Patron's Sword."

Ryan stood there in shock. Somehow, he acquired a sword explicitly made for Val. Hopefully, that story made Val's journal.

Ralliner dropped a ring in Ryan's hand. "Give this to your human. As long as she wears it, we shall provide for her safety in the Farseen. Once the ring is on her finger, no one can remove it, save me. I expect we shall see more of you in the future. Until next time, young alpha." Ralliner dove back into the water. This time there was no splash.

How long would the dragons would refer to him as a young alpha? Ryan turned and pointed Spruce back out of the lair.

"No reason to return me to the Northern Realm. After we leave this lair, we'll each go our own way," Spruce offered.

"It will be my great pleasure to return you to the Northern Realm, telling Lord Ellwood exactly what you tried to do."

Spruce gulped.

Chapter 35

As expected, Spruce tried to make a run for it after they left the dragons. Prepared, Ryan grabbed him, opening a gate to the Northern Realm's receiving rooms. A breach of protocol, sure, but he was done with Spruce. Ryan exited the gate with his prisoner, and the Northern Realm guards remained wary but relaxed. A bit disappointing. After all, he was a shape shifter and an alpha. Ryan had expected weapons aimed at him, maybe even an attack. He looked over at the Master-At-Arms, Ash, and saw Ridge standing next to him. They were both smiling until they saw the sword he pointed at Spruce. Ridge did a double take and Ash's mouth dropped open.

Ridge was the first to reclaim his bemused expression and to speak. "Ralliner told us something of your adventure, but it appears she left a few details for us to discover ourselves. Leave Spruce with Ash. Lord Ellwood awaits your testimony, Ryan. Lady Tempest, Lady Star, and her consort are here.

"Is she alright?" Spruce asked. "Is Lady Star alright?"

No one answered, and Ridge shut the door in his face.

"Ryan!" Star hugged her cousin.

"Man, you look a little worse for wear," Joey grinned, patted him on the back, and whispered, "I'm told I can't challenge Spruce, but I don't get it. He tried to take milady. It seems like I should be able to seek justice."

"You aren't looking for justice. You seek revenge. We haven't had a blood feud in the Northern Realm in nearly one thousand years. I have no desire to see that record broken," Ridge said.

Joey snarled, but Ryan agreed with Ridge. Fae blood feuds could last centuries and frequently ended only when one of the feuding families died out. Ryan moved forward and bowed to Lord Ellwood. Only then did he present his grievance against Spruce. He included the actions of Pinus and Balen as well.

"You have had an excellent quest," Lord Ellwood leaned backed in his chair. "Pinus and Balen presented themselves to my rule shortly before you arrived. Spruce used the sword to control them."

Ryan sputtered, "The sword doesn't control people!"

"True," Ellwood agreed. "It remakes truth to match the wielder's words; however, most people believe it forces everyone to tell the truth to the wielder, and so they told Spruce what he needed to enact his plan."

"You know Spruce didn't act alone."

Tempe stepped forward to stand on her Father's right side, facing Ryan. "Did you see any fae except Spruce wield the sword?"

Ryan balled his hands into fists and ground out his answer, "No."

"Lord Ellwood, you have heard testimony from four people of the Seen. We will return home and await your verdict."

"Safe journey, daughter mine." Ellwood inclined his head. Before they left, Ellwood added, "I see that you now wield the Patron's Sword. Wield it wisely, Ryan, grandson of the late Lady Rayna."

Ryan tilted his head but didn't speak. He didn't know how to respond. He needed to get in the Seen and find out about the short sword that everyone else seemed to know more about than he did. Maybe Jarvious completed the translation of Val's journal. Surely, receiving a dragon made sword would merit a mention or two in a journal.

Tempe led the shifters out of the receiving hall using the main entrance to the Northern Realm to go outside. Ryan looked around in amazement. This part of the residence was old. Since it was older than any structure back home, he wasn't sure why he had expected it to look new, except that most structures in the

Farseen maintained a shiny new appearance. Ryan had wanted to see this, but the shifters used a gate to arrive and all excursions from the residence left from the other side of the mountain. Until now, there had been no reason to enter or depart from this entrance. They stood in a courtyard halfway up the mountain. Each step down to the ground floated in place. There were no handrails or any structure to steady footing going up or down. Unless you flew, there was no way to access the guard tower that rose up in the middle of the circular steps. This entrance was on the other side of the mountain from the family tree houses, so they weren't visible. Massive trees dotted the landscape, but most of the undergrowth was cleared. No one could approach the steps unnoticed, and no one could use those steps without being seen.

"At least we don't have to go down those," Joey muttered nodding toward the steps.

Star patted his shoulder, "I love these steps. They're fun."

"Yeah, but you can fly," Joey retorted.

Ryan looked over and nodded his agreement with Joey, thankful he had a bird form and could fly.

Tempe nodded to the guards before she opened a gate back to Beryl Lane. Ryan held his tongue, saving his questions until they were back in Calabozo, sitting in the sovereign's office.

They walked into the office, and Phoenix looked up from his laptop. "Sage will be here shortly. She's meeting with the Tetrad and the human reps."

"And what a fun meeting it was," Sage said as she breezed into the room and took her seat at the head of the table. "We're going to layoff every human who works for us but isn't related by blood or marriage to a shifter. We simply can't continue to protect them in their daily lives. Yes, we lose good researchers, but it's too dangerous. Those who have been exposed, like Parker, will remain under our protection and can keep their jobs." She drummed her fingers on the desk, "Everyone is demanding time with Victoria. The humans were ready to drop bombs to get her but backed off. I reminded them what happened with the last bomb that was dropped on my location." She grinned, "I didn't think I was the type who enjoyed scare tactics, but apparently I am. I liked the look of fear in their eyes." She focused on Ryan, "Report."

Ryan watched his young aunt, amazed at the change in her. She had become the sovereign, confident and sure, or at least able to maintain that appearance. Ryan finished his report, and asked Tempe, "Any idea what Lord Ellwood will do?"

Tempe shrugged, "Pinus and Balen will be applauded for reporting Spruce's actions to the Forest Lord, putting the good of the realm above their family as it were. Spruce will be reprimanded publicly for his use of the sword. Privately most fae will ridicule his failure to attain Star while wielding the Sword of Veracity. He was not the one who stole the sword from the red dragon supreme matriarch. His only crime was failure. No one expects a ruling fae to ignore the call of any sword of virtue. Your testimony, and that of Phoenix, Victoria, and Fred will be portrayed as that of the people of the Seen, with their lack of knowledge of how the swords work." She smiled at Ryan's loud sigh but continued, "Lady Star's testimony only proves that Spruce was using the sword to attain her, his love, and the fae understand that males do foolish things for love."

"And your testimony?"

"I could only speak in generalities and hearsay. I had no contact with the sword, the kidnapping attempts against Victoria, or Ralliner's use of you."

"How about a true telepath? Their word is good."

"You know why they aren't used in these types of actions. If a true telepath were called in every time two parties disagreed, no one's thoughts would be their own."

Ryan snarled, "They get off, no repercussions?"

"Not completely. While many fae will believe the lie they tell, Lord Ellwood will not. Neither will Ridge. They owe restitution to Ridge for using his fortress for their own means without approval. I doubt Ridge will be kind in his demands. Lord Sky may have a reaction since Star is a lady of her court, but they failed, and Star is safe, so she won't go to war."

"Fred's report of Pinus commanding his sons didn't have any impact?"

"They explained that Fred misunderstood, and they had no choice but to help while Spruce wielded the sword."

Disgusted, Ryan turned to Sage, "Anything else, or can I go get cleaned up?"

"Just one more thing. How many swords did you acquire?" She pointed to the new short sword.

"I suspect that sword is why the Northern Realm sent this. It arrived just before you did." Phoenix leaned down and picked up a scabbard and belt, tossing it to Ryan.

Ryan shrugged. "Apparently, the Patron's Sword picked me when I fought the fae who was wielding it. Right now, that's all I know."

Everyone turned to look at Tempe.

She grinned, "Val received that sword from a dragon at the same time he acquired the name 'Valiant the Bold.' As long as the wielder is the most in tune with the sword, it will fight for the wielder even if it's in someone else's hands. Congratulations, Ryan, I suspect the fae will write another song about you."

"Huh? What do you mean, another?"

"You're the hero in the 'Cold Iron Attack,' a song about removing the iron from the Farseen and saving the bodies of the children for proper burial. You are also depicted as the only intelligent male in a court of fools in a well-received, but never to be mentioned in any court, ballad about young men in court making fools of themselves over a lady." Ryan stared at her, open-mouthed. Tempe added, "I'm sure Liron can sing both of them for you."

Phoenix laughed out loud.

Sage looked down at her tablet to hide her smile. "If there's nothing else, you're dismissed."

*****

Showered and fed, Ryan tracked Phoenix down in the command center. "Where's the Mini Cooper?"

"I was just going to return it. Fred washed and waxed it. Said it was the least he could do after driving it." Phoenix held out a wad of cash in his hand. "Evan deserves a bonus for the inconvenience. How we gonna do this? The car has been reported stolen."

"I'll take care of it." Ryan took the cash, wallet, phone, and keys and headed out.

A short time later, he arrived at the barn the car was hidden in. Under cover of darkness, Ryan drove it to a nearby cemetery. After placing the items in the car, except for the car key, Ryan shifted to his eagle form and flew away. The next day, he found Evan busing tables at a Mom and Pop diner.

Ryan, glamour firmly in place, walked up to the counter and ordered a soda. Drinking it quickly, he left money for the waitress and walked by Evan. Ryan asked, "Mister. You Evan Miller?"

Evan shrugged. "Yeah, kid. Why?"

"A man gave me $10 to give you this letter. Must be important." Ryan left quickly.

Evan opened the envelope, and the Mini Cooper key fell into his hand.

"Who was that teenager?" Cindy asked. "He ordered a soda and left $10 on the counter."

"Don't know, but he gave me the key to my stolen car." Evan opened the letter and read the short note.

Evan,

Sorry for the inconvenience. Your car is fine and will be found on Elm Park Road, parked in front of the marker for your parents' gravesite. Check out the glove compartment.

Evan read the note a second time and pocketed it. It was probably a joke. As if his world hadn't crashed around him enough, someone decided it would be fun to have him run around chasing smoke. When his shift was over, Evan walked down the street to the sheriff's office. "Afternoon, Maggie. Is Charlie around?"

Charlie walked out of his office. "Sorry. No sign on the Cooper or anything else. No one has tried to use your bank card or anything."

"About that. I got this today at work." Evan handed Charlie the note.

Charlie shook his head. "You think it's a joke."

"Yep."

"Let's check it out anyway." Charlie grabbed a fingerprint dusting kit, and they left.

A few minutes later the two men stood in the cemetery, looking at the Mini Cooper.

Evan walked around the car. It was in pristine condition. "I don't think you're gonna find prints."

"Not sure I want to mess up the detail job by trying." Charlie scratched his head. "Check out the glove compartment."

Evan opened up the passenger side and pushed the button on the glove compartment. Nothing happened. He never locked the thing. Perplexed, he used the key to unlock it and open it up. A stack of bills lay on top of his wallet.

Charlie whistled. "Are those hundreds?"

"Yep." Evan scratched his head and looked through his wallet. "Everything is here."

"You sure?"

"I only had my driver's license, my veteran's ID card, debit card, and Visa card, plus thirty-four dollars and some change. Not a lot to verify."

Charlie picked up the stack of hundreds and flipped through them. "The bills have the blue security ribbon on them. I don't think they're fake, but we can verify back to the office. We have one of those advanced scanners now."

Back at the sheriff's office, Charlie returned the bills to Evan. "They're good. You are holding fifty $100 bills."

"This doesn't make sense. They stole my car, returned everything, and paid me $5,000 for my trouble?"

"Looks like." Charlie scratched his head. "Maybe you should drop the complaint. I can say it was kids on a joy ride and you agreed to not press charges. If I continue to look for the perpetrators, I have to put the car and money in evidence."

Evan looked at the money and back at Charlie. "Can I do that?"

"Sure. Although you were inconvenienced, it looks like you've made out all right in the end."

"Boy, that's the truth." Evan looked at the money again. He could leave and start new. He had been working at the diner for three days, and while he appreciated the work, he wanted out of town. Evan had always wanted to live at the beach. Any beach. Now he had the starter money to get there and find a job. "Cancel my theft report. Looks like I wasn't robbed after all."

Charlie smiled and patted Evan on the back. Once Evan left, Charlie walked into his office and shut the door. He pulled out his personal cell phone and selected a number from his favorites list. He went straight to voicemail. Not a surprise. The person he called was in high demand. "This is Charlie Benson of the Wallkill River Clan. Evan Miller got his stuff back and has dropped the charges. Perhaps next time you could ask me for help before committing a crime in my jurisdiction. Just a thought." Charlie disconnected the call and went back to work.

Chapter 36

A week later Ryan was, once again, the shifter in charge at PAC HQ. It was nowhere near as exciting and prestigious as one might think. His calendar was so full he might have time to eat lunch running between meetings today, mail was overflowing, and he had to admit, if only to himself, that he was disappointed. Almost no one knew about his quest for the Sword of Veracity. Most of the Alpha Clan didn't even know. He didn't want accolades, much, but it would be nice to be appreciated for his efforts. Most of the family assumed Ryan had gone on some type of mini-vacation and received a dragon made sword as a gift from someone in the Farseen. Aside from a few raised eyebrows, no one commented. And that brought his to another question. How many of Tempe's mini-vacations over the years had been shifter business?

The computer pinged, indicating another meeting had been added to his calendar. It started in seven minutes. He checked the location, and attendees, and smiled. Ryan moved with purpose down the hallway, waving people off, so no one stopped him. Ryan arrived at the entrance to the shielded outdoor area in PAC HQ, the guard nodded and opened the door for him. Jarvious was already there. Ryan joined him on the rock overlooking the river.

"Our bargain is complete. Your copy of the translation is in Tempe's home office, and mine is in a secure location." Jarvious cleared his throat, "It's very telling. I didn't realize how difficult life with Lord Ellwood was. While a few of the entries, mostly of battles, will make excellent songs, it will be a while before I sing them. I want to do this right, and that means with deliberation."

"Our bargain is complete. Nothing owed on either side." Ryan closed the bargain with the words that prevented either side from trying to get more out of the agreement. He smiled. He was looking forward to reading the journal. Perhaps it had more about the sword.

His watch beeped.

But it wouldn't be today. "Gotta run. Another meeting." Ryan headed down the hall for a meeting he was not looking forward to. He walked in to find the argument had started without him.

"The realms simply want equal time with Victoria Nelson. She has made incredible advances." Theron, master-of-the-hunt for the fae queens, leaned back in his chair and smiled. Truth be told, he didn't care, and he didn't think the queens did either. He was here to keep tabs on everyone and report back.

"She's human. She belongs with her own kind. She belongs with us," Aubrey Ewing stated.

"She's standing right here and can decide for herself where she goes," Victoria growled. "My brain is not for sale to the highest bidder. I trust the shifters more than I trust you, Ms. Ewing. And as far as the realms are concerned, those that kidnapped me are still free in the Farseen." Victoria glared at Theron. "I don't trust you either."

Murdoch leaned back and took a sip of the already cold, standard issue, institutional coffee, and grimaced. Why couldn't someone create a spell to keep a hot beverage at the right temperature? Setting his cup on the table, he said, "The wizards are satisfied with the data we have received from the shifters. We have no need for" air quotes "equal time with Ms. Nelson."

"Of course not, wizards and shifters have long been friends. You probably share their research facility," Aubrey retorted.

Ryan shut the door, not quite slamming it, "No they don't. The wizards don't have access to our facilities, and we don't have access to theirs. We meet here, at PAC HQ."

"Where's Tempest?" Aubrey demanded.

Ryan laughed, "I'm the senior shifter rep at PAC HQ today. If you want Tempest, you need to schedule a meeting for the first half of the second full week of this month. That's when she's scheduled to be here. I would prefer it if you would. For today, you're stuck with me."

Liran grinned, showing his fangs, "The vampires are also satisfied with the reports from the shifters on Victoria's progress."

Aubrey stood and faced Ryan, "I must speak to Victoria alone to make sure she isn't being controlled."

"She may speak to anyone she likes. Ask her, not me."

Before Aubrey could ask, Victoria shook her head. "I will not speak with you alone. I don't trust you. You think it's okay to poison another dimension with nuclear waste and to spy on another's mind. There is nothing more to say." She walked out of the room with her bodyguards in tow.

"We aren't finished. Order Victoria back here," Aubrey demanded.

Ryan crossed his arms in front of his chest. "First you say we're controlling her and now you want us to. Sorry. She has boatloads of free will."

Aubrey Ewing stormed out of the room. Murdoch smiled, tipped an imaginary hat, and left as well, followed by Liran.

Ryan looked at Theron and raised an eyebrow, "What do the fae want?"

"The queens want nothing in addition to the reports you already provide. What the realms want is as varied as the realms themselves. No queen will take Victoria Nelson."

"But the queens won't dictate to the other fae." Ryan didn't ask it as a question. It was a statement. The queens didn't involve themselves in the daily running of the realms. Tempe seemed to think it was a good thing, but he wasn't so sure. Surely, the queens weren't as petty as some of their subjects.

Theron looked at the sword on Ryan's belt and grinned, "Congratulations. I heard the Patron's Sword found a worthy wielder." Theron left before Ryan could respond.

Ryan felt the blush rise up his cheeks, wishing his fair skin didn't show a blush so quickly. He still wasn't sure why, but Tempe had been insistent that the sword be belted to him any time he was on the sovereign's business.

Chapter 37

"Hey Bryce, Tempe around?" Ryan left Tempe's office and walked into the kitchen, immediately checking for food. PAC HQ shift complete, he planned to return to his quarters in Calabozo and finally read some of Val's journal, if he could find Tempe and locate the darn thing. He had expected to discover it in the safe where the alphas left stuff for each other. It wasn't there.

Bryce looked up from the coffee maker, "She's in Calabozo. I thought it was an alpha meeting."

Ryan looked at his watch, "Crap! I'm late!" He ran for the entrance to Calabozo.

Ryan keyed in his passcode and used the fireman slide. It had been put in as a joke, but it was the fastest way down if speed was needed. And he definitely needed speed today. Ryan rushed through the next checkpoint and ran for the sovereign's office. Upon arrival, Ryan took a moment to breathe deep. He quietly opened the door, praying he could sneak in late to the Alpha Cyn meeting. No one looked up as he closed the door and slid into the nearest seat while the Sovereign spoke.

"...it's unanimous. Ryan will represent the shifters at the Summer Solstice Assembly, to be held in the Southern Realm." Sage looked over and smiled.

"Huh? What?" Ryan's forehead crinkled. "Tempe attends all the solstice crap with the fae since we became friendly."

"The wielder of the Patron's Sword was specifically requested, so I asked to be relieved of the duty." Tempe turned bland eyes on him.

"You asked to be relieved? You're going to leave me in court by myself! What if Asp and I get into it."

"I suggest you don't. Asp invited Sara, and she'll be there."

"Can I kill Asp if he gets too close to my cousin?" Ryan muttered.

"If you think you're ready to take on Father Aldous, sure, try and kill his son, but Asp is rather impressive in a fight." Tempe leaned in close and added, "You will be responsible for Sara on this visit, so perhaps you might want to think of ways to gain her cooperation."

Ryan placed his head in his hands and sighed, "Is this my punishment for being late?"

"No, you would have gotten that assignment anyway." Sage didn't look up from her tablet. "Your punishment for being late is escorting Victoria to a series of meetings this coming week."

"We agreed she wouldn't leave Calabozo." Ryan leaned back in the chair. This day was going from bad to worse.

"No. You demanded Victoria remain here, but I don't bow to your demands. She needs to meet with various groups to keep the peace. All meetings will be at PAC HQ. Pick your team of six for support." Sage left the meeting.

Joey followed the sovereign, giving Ryan's shoulder a semi-apologetic bump of support as he passed. Serenity and Bliss each patted his shoulder on their way out.

The door shut, and Ryan glared at Tempe. "Come on. I have to go right back to PAC HQ and then turn around and leave for the solstice. And I guess I should ask, what is the Summer Solstice Assembly really about, and what am I supposed to do there?"

"Both the summer and winter solstice assemblies are parties for unmated, adult fae to meet, get to know each other, and build alliances. These gatherings are more free-form than anything you've attended so far. Since I married Bryce, I have been attending as a chaperone for the Northern Realm. Now that shifters are invited, you will be responsible for all shifters in attendance."

"Please tell me this isn't a keg party. How many shifters will I have to watch out for in this free-form gathering of unmated adults nightmare?"

"You'll receive a list of the invitees from the Seen this afternoon. It's the first year they've invited shifters. This needs to go well." Tempe stood and patted his shoulder on the way out.

Ryan groaned.

Chapter 38

"Can I veto some of the invitees from the Seen?" Ryan marched into Tempe's office without knocking since the door was open.

Tempe raised an eyebrow, "You have received a list of who was invited, but they have all received their invitations already. You are neither president nor king of the shifters to veto anything. Who do you think should not attend?"

"Have you seen the list?"

"No, once you were identified as our rep, all communication funneled to you. Is it that bad?"

"You tell me. Sara and Bridget. Shawn. Phoenix. And let's not forget the one human on the list, Victoria. I also want assurances that I am not responsible for the invited wizards. Murdoch was invited, so he's on the hook for them, right?"

"Wizards are a surprise and yes, if Murdoch is the highest rated wizard on the list, he has to supervise his own. Victoria changes things. She will need a full complement of guards with her, maybe the same six you use at PAC HQ. And, of course, you should let Ralliner know the human under her protection will be in the Farseen."

Ryan plopped down into a chair and eyed his powerful aunt. "It occurs to me if I ask you to be one of the guards it will look like I don't trust myself, or worse, the sovereign doesn't trust me."

No smile touched her lips, but her eyes twinkled, "Indeed."

"I was afraid of that."

198

He didn't say anything else, and Tempe shifted gears, asking, "Would you like the translated journal?"

"Not now. I go back to PAC HQ tomorrow for three days and then to the Southern Realm for what sounds like two nights of frat parties where I will be too busy watching my cousins to enjoy myself. I think I'll leave it with you until I return." He pulled the belt and sword from his hip and laid it on the table. "I need to know more about this sword, and I don't have time to research."

Tempe stretched and got comfortable. "When we were just past our teens, Val frequently ran through the woods in his wolf form. He heard a cry. He moved toward the sound and peered between the underbrush. A thin, whelp-sized green dragon was under attack from three adult river dragons. Without asking for any details, Val shifted and attacked the adults. He had understandable issues with adults preying on the young. Val and I had the same base powers, but, of course, his presented differently. He enchanted the river dragons, something unheard of and never repeated to my knowledge, and took the green whelp to a cave we used as our sanctuary when we wanted to escape court life or our family. Once the whelp recovered, he returned to his flock, and Val returned to the residence. He didn't mention his adventure. Father would not have approved of helping the weak."

"A few weeks later, when the three moons were in various stages of waxing, a guard entered the evening repast to announce Tulvir, the green supreme matriarch, waited at the steps to the main Northern Realm entrance to speak with Valiant the Bold. All eating stopped. As you know, the supreme matriarchs normally send for a ruling fae, they don't show up at a residence asking to speak to someone. There was only one Valiant in the room, and all eyes turned to him. Father demanded to know what was going on." Tempe sang,

> The feasting hall grew still and silent
> The green supreme matriarch waited.
> She demanded to meet a fae of the realm
> Valiant the Bold, she had indicated.
>
> Valiant shrugged his shoulders and left the hall,
> To meet the dragon matriarch.

Those in the feasting hall followed, too,
Even the Northern Realm's patriarch.

Silently waiting, the crowd looked on,
Valiant spoke for all to behold,
"Valiant is my name, 'tis true,
But none have called me bold."

The dragon smiled with sword in hand,
"Valiant the Bold, I call you thus.
Three river dragons you fought alone
And defeated them with no fuss.

River dragons for my son you fought
They singled him out, you knew not why.
You rushed to his aid against great odds.
My son is dual born, I cannot deny.

You stood as his patron, no fear for yourself
This sword I present you, forged by my fire.
Keep yourself worthy and pure of motive
And it will defend you when times are dire.

The Patron's Sword I have crafted
For one with others to protect.
It will fight for you, my friend
Unless you offend it with willful neglect.

Regardless of who wields this sword
It holds its faith to you.
Be a patron for the underdog,
And it will ever be true."

Valiant the Bold accepted the sword
And bowed to the dragon with flourish.
He wielded the sword with bravery and honor
And never lost a skirmish.

Ryan's eyes cut to Tempe, "So that's why dual-born fae sought out the favor of Rayna and Ellwood's children. Val's sword."

"It helped, and we embraced the calling as siblings. Our gift to those who weren't as lucky as we were."

"Lucky?" Ryan's eyebrow rose in a fair imitation of Tempe's favorite expression.

She grinned, "Compared to the dual-born lesser fae, yes, we were lucky. Father was hard on us, but no one else was. Our powers were stronger as a result of our dual-born status. That is rarely true for the lesser fae."

Ryan nodded, "I get that. So, I'm to protect those born of dual heritage?"

"Not exactly. You've protected others your whole life, and that is the true purpose of the sword. That is why the sword chose you."

"And why must I wear it on the sovereign's business?"

"For now, you need to wear it all the time. At this point, most preternaturals have heard the story. If you are seen without it, many will think it has deserted you as quickly as it has everyone who's held it since Val's death."

"He had it until he died?"

"Yes, and no one ever bested him with a sword, not while he wielded the Patron's Sword."

"But Ellwood killed him with a sword, right?"

"Yes, and only Father can sing of that battle. The Patron's Sword was not with Val when I found him. Until you walked into Ellwood's chambers wearing the sword, I had not seen it since Val left to face Father."

"You didn't look for it?"

"I didn't care. For a while, I blamed the sword for making Val cocky in battle, but that wasn't true. By the time I accepted Val's death I had made sure I wasn't welcome in any court." Tempe stretched in her chair, "Anything else you want to ask?"

Ryan huffed, "You know there is. In Val's tree house there were carvings of him and a long, thin, green dragon. Was that the dragon he saved? Why did the river dragons attack the young green?"

"Val and Kulvir shared many quests. They remained friends until the day Val died. I have not seen Kulvir since the day we spoke of Val's death. Kulvir is, or was, part green dragon and part river dragon. That's why the others attacked. The fae do not like different unless different is strong enough to kick serious butt."

Ryan nodded and left her office. Just once he would like to hear that someone in the Farseen lived happily ever after. Guess the fairy tales were wrong about that.

Chapter 39

Victoria opened her door and growled at the shifters. "No. There's no way I need six guards, plus Ryan."

"Do you remember what happened after dinner with your family?" Ryan's lips twitched. "You had four guards then. Now you have six, plus me, as you stated."

"I have Ralliner's ring. Isn't that protection enough?"

"We're in the Seen. The reds will not protect you here." Ryan headed down the hallway.

"Well crap," she muttered, twirling the ring on her right index finger. In place of a stone sat a silver dragonhead with rubies for eyes. Twin bands made up the feet and hands on the sides of the double banded ring with scales engraved on the bands. All in all, a Goth looking ring. She wasn't sure how it worked but the ring self-adjusted to her finger as soon as she put it on, and that sucker was going nowhere. Not even she could take it off. Good thing Tempe had warned her to pick the finger for the ring carefully. She eyed the guards. The alpha Serenity was the only female, so Victoria suspected she now had a bathroom buddy. She smiled at Fred, pleased he was one of her guards. Kaleb, the ice shifter, and Shawn, of the previous sovereign's line, were back. Quill and Jes, both male alphas, and Gerbold, also of the old sovereign's line, rounded out the guards.

Victoria shrugged, at least she could do some research, "Gerbold, I understand you control electronics. Let's talk about that." She grabbed his arm and moved down the hall behind Ryan, tossing questions at Gerbold.

Fred growled and rushed to catch up. The rest followed.

On the gate platform, at the appointed time, Ryan opened a gate and led them into PAC HQ. Once verified, they moved quickly to one of the glass conference rooms. Victoria still didn't know how it worked. The two glass conference rooms were set up so that everyone could see inside, but no one outside could hear what was said in the room, and somehow lips shadowed so no one outside the room could read lips. She didn't know if the magic was fae, wizard, shifter, or vampire, but she wanted details. As with tracking gates in the Farseen, Destin wasn't interested, meaning he already knew how it worked. He was as curious as she. There was so much to learn. She needed the shifters to trust her enough to give her all of their data. She took her seat between Ryan and Fred and waited.

Aubrey Ewing walked in as if she owned the place. Her aides followed, with Tad and Rhett Nelson in tow. Victoria stared at her brothers, and both offered up weak smiles. She glanced over at Ryan, his face was a mask, but he nodded to both of them, and they replied in kind. He wasn't surprised they were here. She fumed. Now he was keeping secrets about her family. That must stop.

"Aubrey, we see so much of each other now, I think we should use first names, don't you?" she asked sweetly.

Aubrey Ewing faltered before she placed a smile on her face and agreed, "Indeed, Victoria, there's no need for formality here."

Tad shook his head slightly, but Victoria ignored him. She stood and laid her hands flat on the conference table. "Excellent. Well, Aubrey, why the hell are my brothers here?"

Tad rubbed his forehead as if he had a headache. Rhett donned his expressionless lawyer face, something all lawyers seem to acquire before they take the bar.

Aubrey smiled, "You believe the shifters can offer you so much more than we mere mortals can. I thought you should be reminded of your human family."

Ryan cleared his throat to speak. Victoria glared, and he remained quiet, although his lips twitched. Turning back to Aubrey Victoria smiled, "As a veiled threat to harm my family, you've done well. Rhett and Ted are dear to me. Unfortunately, you've made a grave error."

"Have I?" Aubrey didn't look concerned.

"Yes, I feel threatened by you, and by extension, the United Nations, and other mere mortals. If humans plan to use my family to force me to do their bidding, then the best thing for me to do is talk to the fae." She held up her right forefinger with Ralliner's ring on it. "You see, in the Farseen I have the full protection of Ralliner, supreme matriarch of the red dragons. In the Farseen, I'm safe from threats from humans as well as fae. Our meeting is at an end. I will recommend that any new discoveries made in the shifter labs not be shared with humans. It is, of course, up to the sovereign. She will do as it pleases her. And Aubrey, if any of my family are harmed or meet any type of accident, I will go to Ralliner in the Farseen and offer her whatever she wants in exchange for her entering the Seen and hunting you – specifically you – down." Victoria retook her seat and drank a sip of water.

"As threats go, I believe Victoria's was superior," Ryan stood. "Ambassador Ewing, your meeting with Victoria Nelson is at an end. Fred will send the transcript to the human leadership on the agreed to distro. Thank you for your time."

"What?"

Tad grinned, "I warned you, Ms. Ewing. Our baby sister has never been one to give into peer pressure or threats."

"You'll never work again, Doctor Nelson. Neither of you will."

"Good day, ambassador." Fred was already at the door holding it open for her.

She stormed out of the room, with her aides following behind her. Tad and Rhett remained.

Victoria's heart dropped. What had she done? Tad was a biotech researcher with the U.S. government, and Rhett was a state lawyer. "You both knew you would lose your jobs if I didn't agree to whatever she wanted, didn't you? Why didn't you tell me?" She jumped up and took a swing at Ryan. She landed a solid hit, but he showed no outward sign that she had hit his massive chest. "And why didn't you? You knew this would happen."

Fred put his arms around her to prevent Victoria from hitting anyone else. Lucky for him, in that position she couldn't see his smile.

Ryan did a better job of hiding his amusement. "We weren't sure what she would do, but we suspected. I met with your family ahead of time, and they said they didn't want you pressured. We, your family, and some of the Alpha Clan, decided to let this play out and perhaps we would get a feel for their plans. You moved into the offensive a bit faster than we anticipated."

Victoria stomped on Fred's foot. His grip loosened, and she turned to face him. "Did you know?"

"No, absolutely not. I was in the dark. I've only seen your brothers once. The night we took you to meet your family for dinner."

"How about the rest of my guards?"

Ryan let his smile show this time, "I'm the only one in this room, besides your brothers, with prior notice."

"Well, okay then. I guess the rest of you are in the clear."

Shawn grinned, "On the plus side, once the other representatives hear what happened, and you know they will, it should cut down on the posturing."

Ryan looked down at the incoming text. "That didn't take long. The Northern Realm has asked that their meeting be rescheduled to now since the humans are done. I said yes since we have this room for the day."

"Let the games begin," Gerbold leaned back and smiled. He loved a battle of intellect with a worthy opponent.

Within five minutes Lady Saffron, Ridge, and Salix walked in alone. Victoria looked up in surprise. No aides, just senior members of the Northern Realm court. How interesting.

Lady Saffron sat and faced the shifters with a smile. "The Northern Realm is satisfied with the reports the sovereign sends out on scientific progress. Our request is for training in your sciences, and we expect Victoria to teach at least forty percent of the time."

Victoria raised an eyebrow, something everyone who spent time with Tempe eventually copied. "I tried to teach science to some Northern Realm fae, and they couldn't understand. It was a waste of time."

206

Salix's lips twitched, "We have a list of possible students and leave it to you to pick five for training. I think you will find the fae on this list to be of acceptable intelligence." He handed the list to Ryan. "We will, of course, expect you to offer no subterfuge to your students."

Victoria blushed.

"Subterfuge is customary during a kidnapping, but when training allies, accuracy is expected." Ridge grinned. "We agree to send the students to the Seen for training, but I would remind you that Ralliner lives in the Northern Realm. None would offer you harm while you wear her ring. It would be suicide to do so. We have an excellent facility for advanced training in what you call the hard sciences."

"What level of training do you expect?" Victoria asked.

"You will find the fae on the list to have completed studies equal to a master's degree in at least two of the hard sciences of the Seen," Salix answered.

Ryan looked over the list, surprised to find that many had attended major universities in the Seen and completed master's programs. A few even held doctoral degrees. Even though she wouldn't know the fae on the list, Ryan handed it to Victoria and waited. She nodded, he said, "Training is acceptable. We'll work out the details on location and timing once the five are chosen." He leaned forward, "I need to inspect your training facility, but I'm not saying we'll use it."

"Of course," Ridge nodded.

Victoria looked at Salix in surprise, "You're on this list."

"Yes. I'm here in case you wanted to question a prospective student to test our general level of comprehension. I think you will find I'm a bit more versed in the Seen sciences than those you tried to train before."

"You would have to be," she huffed. She drew something on her tablet and pushed it over to Salix and asked, "Four identical masses are connected by four identical springs and constrained to move on a frictionless circle of radius "b." How many normal-modes of oscillations are there? What are the frequencies of small oscillations?"

Ryan looked over, "Huh?"

"And it's on," Fred grinned. To the rest of the room, he said, "Prepare to feel like a scholastic failure."

Salix looked at the drawing and answered the question. He answered the next nine questions as well, covering subjects from engineering to math to physics, doing all calculations in his head.

Victoria smiled, "You're in the program. Are the others on this list at your level?"

"I haven't studied with all of them, but I would say yes. We've all completed the same level of scientific training available to us."

Victoria smiled. With any luck, they would teach her some of the science of magic.

Chapter 40

Which to take? The red look-at-me dress? Perhaps the sea green I-am-an-island dress? Both were comfortable and appropriate, according to Serenity, and they made her feel good. When facing a castle of beautiful people, feeling good about yourself became top priority. Victoria put on the sea green and stuffed the other into the weekend bag. She didn't have a clue what she was doing. Victoria was going to a party in the Farseen with fae, shifters, and wizards. She rarely attended parties in the Seen with humans.

At least the rest of the meetings with the fae realms had been simple. They all wanted training. Worked for her. The wizards, vampires, and shifters had come to some agreement on a shared lab, so Victoria didn't have to worry about them anymore. The humans were the only problem. Victoria's threat, aimed at Ewing, had caused a ruckus, but what did they expect? As far as she was concerned, if you threaten family, playtime was over.

Victoria checked her makeup, opened the door, and joined her posse in the hallway.

Sara and Bridget joined them at the same time. Sara's eyes were shining, "Is everyone ready? This will be great fun."

"Oh yeah, fun," Shawn grumbled. To Ryan, he added, "You aren't giving Asp permission to be with Sara, are you?"

"Silly, this trip isn't like that. I've talked to the fae at PAC HQ, and we're all encouraged, nay expected, to enjoy ourselves." Sara's eyes danced.

"Expected to… Oh no. That's wrong, right Ryan?"

"Sorry man, Sara's right." Ryan patted him on the back. "However, I expect everyone to maintain decorum. No fights, no anything that could start a war. Don't make me pull out this friggin' sword."

Phoenix chuckled, and even Shawn grinned. That sword had become quite the calling card. A number of fae had already tried to goad Ryan into wielding it.

"And don't do anything I wouldn't do," Tempe said as she joined them. "Have fun but do remember that you represent all shifters. Lady Saffron is attending, and if you have any questions about propriety ask her. She will speak the truth to pay back a debt to me. And remember, if you do anything to cause Ryan to wield the Patron's Sword, I'll be waiting for you when you return, and I won't be happy."

"Somebody shoot me," Shawn whispered.

"If it comes to that, one of the fae probably will," Phoenix grinned, "with an arrow dipped in something dreadful."

Tempe patted Shawn on the shoulder, "While it is acceptable to spend the evening with someone if you wish, please keep in mind what we've discussed. The fae are good with picking a partner for political gain. Choose wisely. Choosing no one is acceptable."

"Yeah, choose no one. I like that option. Order Bridget and Sara to do that."

"I could," Tempe agreed, "But then I would order you to do the same."

Shawn's face fell. Lady Snowbell would be there.

"Come on people, it's a party," Phoenix grinned. "I'm rather okay with being seduced for political gain."

Ryan rolled his eyes. Phoenix would drive him to distraction during the solstice assembly. He just knew it.

"As the oldest shifter there, try not to be a bad influence." Tempe's smile belayed her comment. She nodded to Ryan, and he opened the gate event and led them in.

Victoria walked through and stood beside Ryan as she had been instructed. Due to Ralliner's protection, she was expected to be on Ryan's right. The reason was immediately apparent. A small red dragon sat directly in front of her facing the fae. He couldn't have been more than fifteen feet long. The dragon was a teenager.

The dragon turned and bowed, "I am Montore, descendant of Ralliner, supreme matriarch of the reds. I am old enough to take down a wall and young enough to fly through most of the castle. The ring will call to me if you feel threatened."

Okay then, guess subtle wasn't part of the plan. Victoria hadn't expected so obvious a threat to the fae, but they didn't appear to be surprised. Neither was Ryan. She glared at him for all the good it would do. She had to make him understand that he had to communicate with her.

Before anyone else could speak, another gate opened, and the wizards arrived. Murdoch nodded to Ryan, and Ryan replied in kind.

The master-at-arms for the Southern Realm signaled the guards to stand down. Nymphs moved forward to take luggage while pixies fluttered around.

Lady Dawn, looking stunning in a cross between a sundress and a spider web, moved forward, her arms spread wide. "Welcome, revelers, to the Southern Realm and the Summer Solstice. Tonight, we take our repast on the beach. Follow me."

Ryan and Murdoch stepped off the platform together and followed Lady Dawn. Victoria walked beside her dragon guard, the other guards spread out strategically. The cave didn't look like a cave at all. The light from the rocks was stronger than candlelight but provided lovely shadows. The plant life was incredible. Even though it wasn't her field of expertise, Victoria wanted to study the ecosystem here. As they neared the cave entrance, it began to look more like a cave. A boulder cut like a door moved to the side as they approached, and then they were outside.

The three moons were beautiful, and while none of them were full, they cast a beautiful glow on the white beach, and dark water. Tents were set up with food and drink. Tables and blankets were available for eating and relaxing. Victoria noticed some of the smaller tents were closed, and she blushed. The fae didn't waste time.

Lady Dawn leaned over and whispered, "Some of the revelers have requested but not yet received permission to court from their realm lords. This is their only time to be together without the rules of court that govern our daily actions."

Victoria nodded. Tempe had explained that, but still it seemed odd to her that adult females could not see a male without the permission of their realm lord. Made a girl wonder just who the guys were seeing.

"I shall be atop that ridge, listening for the ring." Montore bowed and flew to a position overlooking the beach and the residence.

Victoria's guards closed in. Lady Dawn smiled, "All guards are invited to enjoy themselves as much, or as little, as their duties allow." She drew Victoria with her. "Come, many have asked for an introduction to you. Once that is out of the way, you are free to enjoy yourself." Her sparkling smile turned on Ryan, "It's nice to be without guards for once."

It was Ryan's turn to blush. Phoenix's laughter didn't help.

The introductions continued forever. Victoria wasn't sure if everyone wanted to meet her or if they were following the crowd. Being a science nerd, Victoria had never been so admired. Perhaps brains were more highly prized in the Farseen than in the Seen. Doubtful, it was probably a requirement to meet the teacher. As the introductions slowed down, she noticed the shifters and wizards were still in a tight huddle.

After introducing herself to Victoria, Lady Snowbell of the Northern Realm slid an arm into Shawn's and asked, "Are all of you guarding Lady Victoria? Surely, some of you are free to enjoy the evening."

"Some of us are," Phoenix grinned. "Shawn, perhaps you should go with Lady Snowbell, so we don't look like we're running in a pack."

Shawn nodded without taking his eyes off Lady Snowbell and followed the wise advice his Uncle Phoenix provided. As soon as he was out of sight, Rune approached Bridget. That seemed to break the ice, as various fae approached the shifters and wizards. The conversations were tentative at first but grew more relaxed as food and drink were consumed.

Ryan stood back and watched, not sure how approving, or disapproving, he should look. Everyone currently focused on food and drink, but at what point should he draw a line, or two. He watched Phoenix show a female fae how to dance to the hip-hop that suddenly blared from concealed speakers. With Murdoch's assistance, Phoenix had connected his iPhone into a hidden sound system. Surely magic was involved. What were the odds electronic connectors matched between the Seen and the Farseen when connectors didn't match within the Seen? Heck, what were the odds the Farseen had connectors for electronics? He hadn't seen anything to indicate they did.

"Well met. "Asp stopped beside him. "You're frowning at Phoenix. That's not who I expected you to watch this trip."

Ryan rolled his eyes but didn't speak. After all, he wasn't here to start a fight with Asp, although the urge was nearly irresistible.

Asp cleared his throat and continued, "Although normally frowned upon during solstice, I'm declaring myself. I desire to spend solstice with Lady Sara. We have found ourselves to be compatible in many ways."

Ryan glanced over at Sara, who was eyeing them with distrust.

Asp followed Ryan's eyes and grinned. "She's angry I'm telling you. She feels it is none of your business, but given our background, I prefer the truth to speculation. And to be clear, I will not back down if you disapprove."

"Fair enough. If you hurt my cousin, we'll speak again."

"Of that, I have no doubt," Asp walked away, his arm slipping easily around Sara as if he had held her many times before.

Ryan sighed. If this ended badly, Cousin Shawn might kill him, unless Uncle Ben got to him first. A growl to his right shook him out of his contemplation. He moved quickly past a tall fae to stand between Victoria and Fred. "Anything I need to know?"

"Yep, tell Blondie here to step away," Fred growled.

Victoria rolled her eyes. "You're being ridiculous."

"Well met, Acer," Ryan said with a sigh. "Fred, Acer is from the Northern Realm and a student for Victoria's upcoming classes. He's also a brother of Lady Tempest."

"Huh? Her only fae bother died centuries ago." Fred didn't take his eyes off Acer.

Acer grinned. "The fae do not distinguish between siblings who share both parents and siblings who share only one. Lord Ellwood is my father." He pointed to an open table, where three fae looked on in anticipation. "There are a few of us here who wish to discuss science, instead of revelry, if our future professor is so inclined. You may, of course, sit with us."

"Oh, well, that's okay then." Fred relaxed. Talking to eggheads instead of watching idiots hit on Victoria would be a good thing.

Victoria shot him a look that said he would pay later and walked toward the table with Fred on her heels. Her other guards maintained their distance.

"You might consider a guard who isn't so attached to her," Acer observed.

"Yeah, tried that," Ryan muttered. Fred had promised he wouldn't cause a scene, but it was evident to everyone his interest in Victoria was personal.

Ryan continued to walk the beach, keeping an eye on everyone. He watched Lady Dawn out the side of his eye. She also kept an eye on everyone. Made sense. Since she was the eldest daughter of the Cavern Lord of the Southern Realm she probably had duties to attend as the solstice was being held in their realm. Ryan had watched her send away numerous suitors and was pleased Asp wasn't one of them. Asp had been true to his word. He and Sara hadn't left each other's side. Ryan looked around, hoping Shawn wouldn't notice. He found Shawn and chuckled to himself. Shawn wouldn't, not any time soon. Lady Snowbell still held his interest.

"Would you care for some drink?"

Ryan swallowed his curse. He hadn't even heard her approach. That could be dangerous. He couldn't afford to drop his guard, especially here, with so many depending on him. He smiled and took the cup, "Lady Dawn, you have rushed about all evening tending to others. Have you eaten?"

"No, we could take food and sit on the hill. There we can watch over the others."

Ryan winced, "That obvious?"

"'Tis expected," Lady Dawn smiled showing a perfect dimple that drew his eye. "It's the first time full-blooded shifters and wizards have been invited to solstice. Murdoch also watches."

Ryan shrugged. He suspected Tempe asked Murdoch to keep an eye on him to make sure he didn't get distracted. He would have been insulted, but one glance at Lady Dawn, and he understood. Ryan watched Lady Windy, a member of the Central Realm air guard, approach Murdoch and grinned, "Yeah, let's check out the food."

Sitting on a blanket, on the hill overlooking the beach, Ryan relaxed. Lady Dawn was intelligent, as well as fun, and lovely to watch. She tensed, and he followed where her eyes led.

"Pagan does not have Father's permission to court Lady Fawn. I have to stop them." She moved to stand, and Ryan gently gripped her arm.

"Perhaps I don't know all the rules, can you stop them? During solstice?"

She ground her teeth, "No, I can't. But she must be careful. Father will send Pagan away from court if he finds out and doesn't approve. Although no one should tell, someone will, if only to seek Father's pleasure."

"Yeah, I wondered about that."

She grinned, "If we were to make use of one of the tents, it would create a rather large incident." She moved a little closer, until their lips almost touched, and added, "No one could blame us for a kiss. It would sound foolish to mention a mere kiss during solstice, especially to their realm lord."

Ryan grinned and closed the distance between their lips. Just when the kiss was getting good, Montore screeched and dove toward Victoria. Ryan jumped up, pulled Lady Dawn to his side, and said, "Teleport us to Victoria."

They arrived to find a fistfight, no weapons, no powers, just fists. Montore's wings circled Victoria. She was safe. She wasn't even the source of the fight, just a nearby onlooker. Ryan nodded to the dragon and pulled the Patron's Sword.

The sword's song weaved its way through the crowd. Slowly, all but the two combatants stopped moving, waiting to see what he would do with his new weapon. With a disgusted sigh, Ryan used wind to break the two apart and sheathed his sword.

Pagan was the first to move. Ryan grabbed him before he could take another swing at the male.

"Let go!"

"I don't think that's a good idea." Ryan tightened his grip.

Asp moved in and grabbed the other fae roughly, receiving a kick to the thigh for his trouble. "Odell, kick me again, and I'll feed you to Montore."

"I would enjoy a snack," Montore said agreeably.

Asp glared at Odell and Pagan. "Have you lost your minds? Fighting at solstice?"

"Look at Lady Faun's arm," Pagan shouted, "He bruised her." Pagan struggled, but Ryan's grip remained firm.

A blush rose up Lady Faun's face while the spectators looked at her arm where a bruise was forming.

Asp growled, "Did you harm Lady Faun?"

"She belongs with me." Odell whimpered, and Asp tightened his grip.

"You idiot. She belongs with the one she chooses." Asp looked toward the residence as the warriors approached. "It might be helpful if Montore left the scene. If you cannot add to the explanation, spread out. Let's not end up posturing the first night of solstice."

Ryan nodded to Montore, and he flew back to the hill with Victoria and Fred in tow.

"Jarvious, you promised to sing another song of past battles fought by Lady Tempest. Let's go to the bonfire." Murdoch led most of the others away.

Haven, advisor to the Southern Realm, approached the group. He looked at Lady Dawn, then Lady Faun, and finally at Ryan and Asp who were still holding Pagan and Odell. He spoke to Pagan, "What happened? Choose your words carefully."

Pagan snarled at his eldest brother, "Odell grabbed Lady Dawn, and I hit him."

"Advisor, there's more to the tale." Asp stepped forward, dragging Odell with him. "Lady Faun and Pagan were walking on the beach. Lady Sara and I passed them a few minutes before it happened. I didn't see him, so Odell must have been lying in wait to jump them. While I didn't see the entire exchange, Pagan was protecting Lady Faun, as he always has."

Advisor Haven narrowed his eyes on Odell. "Did you harm Lady Faun?"

"I was trying to save her from that fool." He pointed at Pagan.

216

"I didn't ask to be saved, you putrid, licentious, disreputable, boorish, miscreant. You are never to approach me again for any reason," she yelled and then kicked him in the knee hard enough that everyone heard the break.

Ryan pressed his lips together to keep from smiling. Sara walked over and placed a gentle arm around Faun, "Come, we'll put ice on your arm to keep it from swelling."

"The sap of the red weeping bush would be better." Faun took refuge in her knowledge of healing plants as another blush moved up her face. She had caused a scene during solstice. Father would not be pleased.

"Okay, we'll get some of that," Sara agreed, walking Faun away from the men.

"Advisor," Lady Windy approached. "Pagan did throw the first punch but only after Lady Faun screamed when Odell grabbed her arm. The fault cannot be Pagan's."

"Truly, I would have done the same had a lady with me been grabbed in such a manner," Asp commented.

Ryan released Pagan, sure that he needed to keep his mouth shut. He wasn't certain how fae politics worked in this case, but he felt for Pagan. The kid was just protecting Lady Faun.

Asp released Odell at the same time. Before Asp could speak, Odell tackled Pagan and punched him. This time Asp and Ryan looked on as the warriors broke the two apart.

"Bring them both," Haven demanded. "We'll discuss this in my chambers."

"That's probably not good," Ryan commented as they left.

"No, Haven will be hard on Pagan just to prove he's not biased in favor of his youngest brother." Asp watched them walk away, "Sometimes family ties are not helpful."

"I hear you."

Ryan and Asp joined the group around Lady Faun. She turned on them and glared. "What happened? Where's Pagan?"

"We released them, and Odell took another swing at Pagan. Haven took them both away," Ryan said.

"What? I must go. It's not Pagan's fault." She stood to go to the residence.

Lady Windy blocked her path. "If you go to defend Pagan, there are those who will say you protected him because he was too weak to defend himself. Allow him his dignity."

"I won't just wait."

"Yes, you will. You must. Pagan will be back soon enough." Lady Windy patted her shoulder and walked over to join Murdoch.

Eventually, the crowd lessened, leaving Faun with Sara, Dawn, Asp, and Ryan. Faun sighed, "You guys go take a walk or something. I'm fine here."

"No, the minute we leave you, you'll do something truly reckless." Lady Dawn sat and got comfortable.

Sara looked over at the men and shrugged, "Why don't you guys grab us something to snack on."

While Ryan loaded a couple of plates with snacks, Asp gathered up drinks and found two trays, giving Ryan enough room to fill another plate. As they walked back, Asp muttered, "If Odell's still alive after solstice, I may beat him myself. He ruined a promising evening."

Thinking about that kiss Ryan didn't speak, but his head nodded in agreement.

Chapter 41

Riding on Montore's back, just after sunrise, Victoria was giddy with excitement. She had never experienced giddy before. She liked it. Flying through the Southern Realm on the back of a dragon was glorious. She looked back at Fred. He looked a little green. Surprised, she asked, "What's wrong? You take a flying form. Surely you don't get motion sickness."

"I don't when I'm doing the flying. This isn't flying. This is riding." Fred burped, looking greener than before.

Montore dove and landed on a mountaintop, commenting dryly as Victoria and Fred disembarked, "If you must be sick, please do so on the ground."

Ryan, in dragon form, landed. Once Lady Dawn was on the ground, he shifted and handed Fred a root. "It works like ginger in the Seen. Chew on it. You'll feel better."

Fred accepted the root, and while chewing, stood on the edge of a cliff. Now that he wasn't riding through the air he could look at the scenery. They were on a mountain peak overlooking a valley north of the Southern Realm where a river forked in two directions. The one closest to them was the widest. While he tried to decide if he was looking at sea or river merfolk playing with the hippocampus, he saw an odd-looking dragon approach. "Hey, Ryan, you know him?"

Ryan looked down at the long, thin, jewel-toned green dragon flying up the side of the mountain. "I might."

The dragon landed as far away from Montore as possible. Montore didn't attack, and the green tucked his wings and spoke,

"Wielder of the Patron's Sword. You are the first, since Valiant the Bold, to whom the sword has sworn allegiance. It chose you, and therefore, I choose you. I am Kulvir. The sword will call to me each time you enter the Farseen. If you desire my presence, think my name and I will come. I have had many centuries since Valliant the Bold's death to hone my skills. I am pleased to be of service."

"Well met, Kulvir. I'm Ryan, perhaps we could meet once my solstice obligations are completed."

"That will serve us both well. Remember, think my name and I will come." Kulvir dove off the side of the mountain and flew away.

Lady Dawn watched Kulvir fly away. "The songs I've heard said he died when Valiant the Bold did."

"He did not die. He was, as he said, honing his skills." Montore's claws scraped the rock as he moved to stand by Ryan. "He is now powerful, and few dragons will aggress against him. While he looks weak and frail, he is neither. His magic is more powerful than most."

"But he watched you warily," Fred commented, looking a little less green.

"It is said he does not enjoy killing. Had I attacked the half-breed, he would have killed me with ease. Ryan, wielder of the Patron's Sword, you have acquired a powerful ally."

Ryan watched Kulvir disappear. Reading Val's journal just moved to the top of his to do list after the solstice. Hopefully, it had the details he needed. He clapped his hands together once, "Okay folks, the sunrise ride is over. Let's head back for breakfast on the beach."

They landed on the hill overlooking the revelers. Many had taken sunrise walks on the beach. Victoria smiled, wondering how many were walking to reduce speculation on where they spent the night, or with whom. She turned to Montore, "I enjoyed the ride. It was wonderful."

"Yes, the ride pleased me this day," Fred added. He felt silly using the phrasing of the fae, but Tempe had told him it would be expected.

"I found it interesting as well. I had never had a two-legged on my back before. And Ryan, know that I will speak of your conversation with Kulvir." Montore lay down on the hill, to resume his vigil of the revelry.

Ryan nodded. He wasn't surprised.

"Come, we must hurry." Lady Dawn ran down the hillside. The others followed.

Ryan didn't know what was so urgent until he saw Faun yelling at Odell, who was walking with a cane. Faun moved fast and cracked Odell's good knee.

"Is there a reason for this display?" Lady Dawn slowed to a walk and moved to stand beside her sister.

"Yes, there is," Lady Faun snarled. "This…"

"Lady Faun, Odell is surely worthy of the words you are about to say, but I would prefer you refrain from saying them at this time," Lady Saffron walked up to stand between the sisters.

The crowd quieted. Lady Saffron had displayed more power of late, and many were waiting to see if she would rival Lady Tempest for mastery of her gifts and displays of temper.

Lady Saffron glanced at Phoenix, "Brother mine, take Lady Faun for a short walk to cool her understandable temper."

Phoenix didn't bat an eye at Saffron's order but rushed to comply. He had never been called brother by Saffron before, but in this setting, it did make sense.

Phoenix took Lady Faun out of sight. Only then did Saffron turned on Odell. "I cannot say there are no males so foolish in the Northern Realm, but I can say most would plan their actions better. If a lady rejects you by breaking a kneecap the night before, do not expect her to embrace you the next morning. I tire of this foolishness. Nephew, I will be satisfied if you remove this male from my sight. Asphodel will surely assist." She turned and walked over to a table laden with fruit, devoting her full attention to the culinary options before her.

Asp grinned and walked with Ryan to where Odell was hugging the knee that didn't have a cast. "I, for one, wish to see your aunt satisfied. Ryan?"

"I try to keep on the good side of all of my many aunts. Makes life easier." Once Ryan explained the method to Asp, they seized Odell, lifted him in a fireman's carry, and headed for the residence. Once they were out of earshot, Ryan groused, "Why are we always cleaning up after this fool?"

"Perhaps your aunt believes we will not kill him for ruining our solstice, but if I see him again this day, I shall demand reparation," Asp said. Odell whimpered, and Asp squeezed the leg tighter as they approached the guards. "This only hurts half as much as it could."

Features schooled into a mask, one of the guards asked, "Did he approach Lady Faun again?"

"He did," Asp smirked. "Is Advisor Haven available? If not, can we dump him in the dungeon?"

"Bring him and follow me," Haven snarled from the open door, followed by a mumbled, "Thank the five realms solstice has only one night remaining."

Asp and Ryan exchanged grins and followed.

Once inside his rooms, Haven pointed to the far side of the room. "On the lounge."

Asp and Ryan dropped their burden and stood back to make room for the healer who had arrived.

"You may return to the beach." Haven watched the healer work.

"Advisor Haven, perhaps Pagan could return with us?" Ryan asked.

"Pagan could benefit from new surroundings. He left for PAC HQ at sunrise."

Ryan would have responded, but Asp shook his head slightly. While he didn't trust Asp, he was willing to concede that any fae better understood their rules of conduct. They bowed and left.

The duo walked past the guards and were on the path to the beach before Asp explained, "As punishments go, PAC HQ is a reward. It is well known that Pagan desired a post there. Most will think his brother removed him from Lady Faun's sight because they are so young. Many will wonder if Lord Elros approved of Pagan's actions and recommended the assignment." As they moved closer to the revelers, Asp said, "As Lady Faun will be displeased to hear of Pagan's assignment, perhaps you could tell Lady Dawn. She can inform her sister."

Ryan nodded, "I had the same thought, but I think we're doomed." He pointed to where Lady Faun, followed by Phoenix, rushed toward them.

Lady Faun came to an abrupt stop in front of the duo. "Where is Pagan?"

"Don't you mean how is Odell?" Lady Dawn murmured.

Lady Faun shrugged, "I don't care about Odell." She glared at Asp, "Where is Pagan? You would have taken Odell to Haven, and surely one of you thought to ask."

"They are male." Amusement from the gathered crowd greeted Lady Windy's wry response. "Perhaps they were thinking of their empty stomachs."

Asp grinned, and said, "Ryan asked. Pagan left for the Seen this morning. He finally received approval to work at PAC HQ. I return there myself tomorrow. If you desire, Lady Faun, I can deliver a message to Pagan."

She turned and stomped away.

"I'll go after my sister. There is no reason for you to bestir yourself, Phoenix. Lady Sara, it would please me if you made sure those three ate."

"Will do," Sara grabbed Asp's arm and walked toward the tables, ignoring Ryan and Phoenix.

"Hey, why did Sara just grab Asp's arm?" Shawn approached the group, unconcerned that Lady Snowbell held his arm in the same manner. He glared at Ryan, "And why aren't you doing anything about it?"

"Asp's not so bad, and I tire of taking fools to the Southern Realm advisor. Don't start anything." Ryan followed Sara and Asp. Food was sounding pretty good.

Phoenix clapped Shawn on the shoulder and followed Ryan.

Chapter 42

"Where are your guards?" Joey frowned. He and Sage had finished a planning session, and she prepared to leave for a meeting, wearing full battle gear.

Sage crossed her arms, "I don't need guards to meet with one prif."

"Does Tempe or Kyan know where you're going and who you're meeting with?" Joey planted his feet in a wide stance, blocking Sage from leaving the room. It was a symbolic gesture. If she wanted him out of the way, she could move him easily enough.

"If I say yes, will you move? Or do I need to move you?"

Joey shook his head in irritation, "Dimitriy is not someone you should see alone. I think it's a trap."

"Not a trap, a challenge. I need to stop the speculation. As long as Tempe and Kyan stand in front of me, the prifs will not trust me."

"Then call Ryan. Take someone with power with you." He cringed. That was the worst thing he could have said.

"Speak to no one about this. I don't need anyone else's power, I have my own," Sage snarled. Using wind, she pushed Joey out of the way and left.

Joey picked himself up off the floor, dropped into one of the chairs, and sighed. How could he get around that order?

*****

"She'll be here any minute." Dimitriy reminded the others. He didn't care if they were ready or not. Though they didn't know it, they were here to die by the sovereign's hand while he carried

224

out his plan. If she didn't kill them, he would do it himself. There could be no witnesses to this deception. The two other prifs were hiding and would join the fight once it started. Three prifs against the young sovereign would be enough. Rafael turned down the invitation, but he would still play a part. The sovereign would die in Rafael's territory. The alphas would look to him as the killer.

A gate opened, and Sage walked out, in full battle gear. Dimitriy smiled. The child wasn't as big a fool as he had believed. He bowed, "Sovereign, thank you for coming."

Sage planted her feet in a wide stance with her hands on her hips. "Let's get this over with. Say the words."

Dimitriy straightened his back. "I, Dimitriy, Prif of the Saint Petersburg Clan, challenge you, Sovereign of all shifters, to a duel to the death in the shifter tradition. No seconds, no weapons, except the elements and magic you possess. The winner becomes, or remains, the sovereign."

"I accept." As soon as the words were out of Sage's mouth, Dimitriy threw a fireball. She blocked with water and used wind to toss him into a tree. While he staggered to his feet, a tire iron rushed toward her head. She caught the attack out of the corner of her eye and blocked it with wind. Then she swept up the wielder of the tire iron and tossed him to the ground with the power of tropical storm winds, crushing his body. Her first kill. At least her first as sovereign. She turned back to face Dimitriy with her shield in place against another round of fireballs.

Stanislav walked out of the woods firing an automatic weapon. The bullets bounced off her shield, and he had to duck behind a boulder for safety. Sage turned back to Dimitriy, "Three against one? This isn't an honorable duel in the shifter tradition."

"You are too young to lead. You must be removed. Your family isn't up to the task, but I am." Dimitriy walked steadily toward her.

Stanislav left the safety of the boulder once the bullets stopped ricocheting but stopped his approach to watch a motorcycle top the hill. The bike became airborne for a few seconds, crashed to the ground, and slid across the field without a rider. The rider had jumped and landed on Stanislav, taking him down and breaking his neck. After he bashed in Stanislav's head and heart to prevent recovery, Rafael removed his helmet. He tossed his helmet toward his bike and bowed. "Sovereign, if this is a duel in the shifter tradition, I await your victory. If it's an ambush, I await your orders."

Sage didn't respond but turned back to Dimitriy, "You miscalculated." She pulled wind and surrounded Dimitriy, once again slamming her opponent into the ground with enough force to crush bones. She looked at the two men she had killed and then at Rafael's kill, in total, three dead prifs. "Such a waste."

"I disagree, Sovereign." Rafael approached with a smooth stride and bowed again. "Today you have become blood proven, a distasteful, yet necessary, step to secure your reign. These three were your major detractors and their deaths, especially when it becomes known they did not follow shifter tradition in the challenge, will ease tension... as strange as that may sound."

"There are those who say you are my biggest detractor."

"Like many, I did not think a young adult could successfully lead a clan, much less all shifters. You proved me wrong."

Serenity and Kyan ran out of a gate, prepared for battle. They slowed to a walk, took in the scene, and realized they had missed the fight. Kyan held out his hand to Rafael, "Thank you for notifying Serenity of Dimitriy's plans and for being here to protect the sovereign."

Accepting the proffered hand, Rafael shook his head. "The sovereign needed my protection not at all. Neither does she need yours to deal with shifters. I simply removed a minor irritant, but she won the challenge on her own. Dimitriy attempted to deceive the sovereign with lies. His challenge was not in the shifter tradition. I will attest to that."

Serenity eyed the three dead, walked up to Rafael, and kissed him with a single-mindedness that was impressive. Rafael responded in kind.

Kyan raised an eyebrow but didn't speak.

Sage snorted. "Get a room."

Serenity broke contact and looked over at her sister, her eyes twinkling in the moonlight. "Excellent suggestion, Sovereign. Raf, is your motorcycle road worthy?"

He chuckled and walked over to his bike, grabbing his helmet along the way. Rafael pulled the bike upright. There were cosmetic scratches and dents, but the engine started. He handed Serenity his helmet. While she placed it on her head, and got comfortable on the bike, Rafael looked at Kyan, "I expected Tempest."

"She's playing charades with the Sovereign's Squire," Kyan retorted.

Rafael didn't understand, but he didn't care. He laughed, started the bike, and drove off after Serenity put her arms around his waist. She was finally right where he wanted her, almost.

"Charades?" Sage asked.

"Next time you give Joey an order to not speak of something, you might want to rethink your wording. He's pretty good at charades, but Tempest was just about to enter his mind to figure out what was going on. Serenity ran into the room with the info from Rafael."

Yes, she would most definitely work on that. Sage opened a gate and led the way home.

Since both Sage and Serenity had opened their gates under the shield of elementals, the AIB's newly formed TAC (Tactical Aberrant Containment) team didn't know they had missed a gate event until the rumors of a shifter insurrection were whispered around the world.

Sage soon found that Rafael was right. Shifters, and other preternaturals, calmed down about Sage's age once news of the fight and her kills were circulated. It saddened her that she had to kill to be accepted as the leader of her people. Sage had assumed the 21st century was more enlightened than that.

*****

Last night of solstice revelry, Ryan sighed and watched the activity. Lady Dawn was, once again, rushing around doing whatever tasks she was expected to do. Jarvious was again singing songs for those who wished to listen. Ryan was no longer interested in hearing songs of a bard's interpretation of his actions after the previous evening when Jarvious sang *The Ode to Decorum* (the official title), although the fae asked for it under the title *Shifter Courts the Lady*. No names were used, but the players in the ballad were easily identified. No wonder Tempe didn't like to hear the songs sung about her. If the songs sung about him were any indication, they were less than accurate. It was embarrassing that the fae assumed he had planned the entire evening, using Faun to attain Dawn. While that had been the result, it wasn't a planned action like the song depicted. Ryan's goal had been to not make a fool of himself in front of Dawn.

Ryan's eyes settled on Victoria. The geeks were with Victoria, discussing stuff he was sure he had never studied, and Ryan was thankful for that. At least Fred was happy, relaxing next to Victoria, secure in the knowledge that the other males and females around her wanted to talk science, not revelry.

Next, Ryan watched Lady Snowbell lead Shawn away from the crowd around Jarvious. Obviously, so Shawn wouldn't see Sara and Asp approaching from the tents. Perhaps he should warn Shawn that Lady Snowbell and Sara had become friends, or at least friendly in their shared desire to enjoy revelry. Ryan nodded to Murdoch. Without discussing it, they had divided up the area and were watching everyone from the Seen. Lady Windy approached Murdoch, and Ryan hid his grin. The two of them fell into a relaxed conversation. Ryan glanced up at Montore, who was once again feigning sleep on the hill.

"Still guarding everyone?" Lady Dawn offered him a cup of the drink that reminded him of lemonade with some type of berry added.

He took a sip and smiled, "It's what I do. I guard, and you see to everyone's comfort."

"Yes, but my duties are mostly done for the night. Are yours?"

Ryan shook his head, "No. Perhaps we could sit on the hill overlooking the beach and enjoy a snack."

"I was thinking the same thing," Lady Dawn smiled coyly and showed him what was in the basket.

The next day the revelers departed back to their realms or the Seen. It was odd to exchange polite and formal goodbyes with the fae, but that was the way of things. Only during solstice revelry could the single fae behave as anyone could in the Seen.

Ryan pressed a kiss to Lady Dawn's hand and joined the others from the Seen on the platform. He opened a way, and they were gone.

228

Chapter 43

"Ryan, pay attention to my signals or your spell will hit me. I'm sure it is unnecessary to tell you that if you spell me, I shall become angry." Kulvir glared at Ryan. "As to the elements, fire will never harm me, though impacting my body will change the trajectory of the fire. Wind and air could impact my flight pattern. Water, unless you send a lot, will have no impact on me. Pay attention."

"Sorry," Ryan sighed. Riding a dragon and casting spells required concentration. There was a lot to consider. Not the least of which was the art of casting a spell in the correct direction when someone else controlled the direction and speed of the motion.

They made another pass at the poor, unfortunate tree Kulvir had chosen as Ryan's target today. Although, in an honest appraisal, it appeared that the tree fared better than the surrounding foliage. Ryan's aim could have been better. Ryan leaned to the side for a better angle and promptly fell from Kulvir's back.

Ryan shifted into his eagle form before he hit the ground and flew back toward Kulvir. The dragon hovered in the sky and sported the same expression Tempe did when he failed during practice. Landing on Kulvir's back, Ryan shifted and settled again. "Yeah, I know. Remain seated during battle."

"At least you know what you did wrong." Kulvir prepared for another run at the tree.

*****

"See you guys in two weeks," Victoria smiled as the fae filed out of the Northern Realm's training facility. Training the fae was gratifying. They were prepared, and rarely did she have to repeat herself. It turned out Salix was right. He and the other fae in the training program were conversant in the hard sciences, and they had no trouble keeping up with her instruction. Sometimes their questions even required her to research the answers, just to make sure she was right. All in all, it was enjoyable to teach such dedicated students. Ryan had inspected the facility, and as long as Montore was with her, she didn't need a host of guards. Better still, in an unexpected – according to Tempe – show of cooperation, the five realms agreed that they would attend studies together in the Northern Realm, cutting down the amount of travel Victoria had to do.

During breaks, Montore would fly her, and sometimes Fred, over the Farseen landscape, and Victoria had nearly completed her map. Soon she would be able to track gates in the Farseen, with or without Destin's cooperation.

In the Farseen, only Fred and Montore guarded her. Ryan was around, but he frequently dropped her off with a waiting Montore and left to take care of some other business. It was interesting because Ryan typically returned with cuts and bruises he refused to discuss.

Fred stuck his head in the door, "Come on, Ryan's waiting at the gate platform."

"Don't the fae still called it a way?" Victoria said as she grabbed her tablet.

"They admitted defeat. As have we all. Everyone calls it a gate now."

She smiled, grabbed his arm, and headed for the gate platform. As was his custom, Montore walked with them.

Chapter 44

"Back to the Farseen already?" Ryan groused since he was alone with Tempe. "I'm clocking more time there than at PAC HQ."

"It's time for Star's next visit to the Northern Realm." Tempest leaned back and smiled, "You can stay here if you wish. I'll be there, but it will be advantageous if you are a frequent visitor. A few members from the other realms will be visiting at least part of the time, including Lady Dawn. Apparently, the open exchange of science in the Northern Realm has opened up the borders, and there's a lot more visiting among the unmated members of the court."

"I'm in." Ryan watched Tempe chew her bottom lip and asked, "What are you concerned about?"

"Lord Ellwood has shown great humility of late, especially with you and Joey. I suspect he's up to something."

Ryan nodded. He had thought the same thing. "Do you suspect or know?"

"I can't read Father, even if I try. I've never been able to."

"Okay, we shall be ever vigilant," he said, borrowing the phrase used by warriors in the Farseen.

*****

Two days later, Star's personal guards – Landon, Phoenix, and Brandi – formed a semi-circle around her, as once again Lord Ellwood welcomed them to the Northern Realm for two weeks of parties and posturing.

After greeting his daughter and granddaughter, Ellwood turned to Ryan, "I have been informed you command both the Patron's Sword and Kulvir now."

"The Patron's Sword chose me, and I believe it would be more accurate to say Kulvir is training me. I don't command him."

Laughing, Ellwood turned to walk down the hallway, saying, "Lady Saffron, escort the shifters to their rooms."

Saffron's bohemian skirt swished as she walked down the hallway, discussing the events scheduled for this visit. Eventually, she said, "Lady Yunnan is currently residing in the family tree houses as a long-term guest of the Forest Lord. I didn't think you would mind."

"Why?" It was unusual for any realm lord to house a guest long term. Star noticed movement down the hallway. Yunnan came into view. She walked by a window and the light shined on her face, Star exclaimed, "What happened?"

"I'll let Lady Yunnan explain." Saffron bowed and added, "As always, the green star on your itinerary is mandatory."

Lady Yunnan bowed to the shifters in a blatant attempt to hide her black eye.

Ryan stepped forward. "Permit me to carry your basket, Lady Yunnan."

Yunnan stepped back, clutching it tightly. "There is no need. Excuse me." She hurried past them and entered her rooms.

"Stay here." Star ignored her guards' protests and knocked on Yunnan's door. There was no answer, so she opened the door and barged into the room.

Brandi followed Star in and shut the door. She gave both ladies an apologetic shrug and stayed by the door.

"Lady Star, there's no reason for you to concern yourself," Yunnan said, emptying her basket of fruit.

"No need! You're bruised. Who did this?"

"It matters not. Lord Ellwood has offered me a place of safety.

"Yunnan, what happened? I'm not leaving until you explain." Star sat down and selected a fruit from the basket. She took a bite and focused on her fruit. Hiding behind court manners was a standard way to keep another fae out of one's business. They

232

were better friends than that. Star finished chewing and looked up at her friend. "Are you going to sit or not?"

Yunnan looked over at Brandi who crossed her arms in front of her chest.

"Enough. You know Brandi keeps our secrets. What happened?"

"Unhappy with the results of the havoc he caused, Spruce blamed me for not doing as Father ordered. He met me in the woods as I returned from a visit with Styrax's grandmother. I think he would have killed me if Acer and Salix hadn't come upon us." She dropped into a chair and hid her face with her hands, and admitted, "I don't know what to do. I can never return home. Ascan invited me to his home, but he has enough problems with his enemies questioning everything he does now."

"What about Styrax' grandmother? You've stayed with her before."

"I sent Styrax away. I can't bring my family's shame into his."

"This is ridiculous. Everyone knows you and Ascan had nothing to do with stealing the sword or using it to try and trick me."

"Perhaps, but it's an excellent way to detract someone. I won't do that to Styrax's family. Lord Ellwood and Lady Saffron have been kind, more so than I deserve, but I need to leave the Northern Realm. I just don't know where to go. No other realm would allow me to visit now."

"Do you know that no other realm will have you or are you assuming?" Brandi asked, speaking for the first time. Both ladies looked at the guard. Brandi's lips turned up into a smile. "Legitimate question. I spent years running from my family, certain my half-vampire status would cause them harm. Don't see any reason for you to do that. Your brother might need to hide in shame, you don't."

"Well said." Star turned back to Yunnan, "Stay for the two weeks I'm here. And then maybe you could visit me in the Seen for a while.

"I will not allow my family's shame to harm my friends."

"Quit being so morally superior. It's irritating." As Star stood to leave, she added, "You will attend tonight's repast and sit at my table."

"Is that a command? Are you ordering me to the feasting hall tonight?"

"If it has to be, yes." Star marched out of her friend's room.

*****

Star finished dressing and tracked Yunnan down. Star, along with her consort, her guards, and her friend, walked toward the feasting hall. Yunnan was unhappy, and Star was irritated. They reached the public area of the residence to find Styrax's grandmother, Lady Lindera, in front of the hall of battles. An unusually high number of fae, and not just the unmated ones, milled around the pillars depicting battles fought by the lords of the Northern Realm.

Yunnan turned to Star, "Did you plan this?"

"No."

Yunnan's voice dropped to a whisper. "Why is she here? She never comes to court."

Star shrugged.

The grandmother of Salix and Styrax moved to stand before them. Lady Lindera eyed the new arrivals. "Lady Yunnan, why have you sent Styrax away? Is he no longer acceptable to you? When last you visited my home, the two of you seemed to enjoy each other very much indeed. What did my grandson do?"

"He did nothing, Lady Lindera." Yunnan curtsied to hide her blush.

"He must have done something. Come, you will stay with me, and I am sure we can work this out." The females, who had giggled when Lindera first spoke, grew quiet when the invite was extended.

"No, Lady Lindera, I cannot impose."

Lady Saffron and Salix joined them in the hall. Salix had Styrax by the arm and pushed him to his left so that Styrax would be closest to Yunnan.

"Are you saying you prefer life in the court to the amusement of my holdings?" Lindera stared in surprise. Turning to Saffron, she asked, "Have you ever heard of such a thing?"

"No, Lady Lindera. Your holdings are by far the more enjoyable, much less pomp with a lot more amusement to be had, especially if your grandsons are in attendance. However, it occurs to me that Lady Yunnan is attempting to spare you any hurt her visit might cause." Saffron lowered her voice and still managed to make it carry as she added, "Perhaps she is concerned by her family's current stain."

Lindera turned a confused face to Yunnan. "Is this true?" Yunnan, red-faced, nodded. Lindera went off into a peal of laughter. "Oh, my dear, if only those who had no fools in their family were allowed in my house, I would never have visitors. My own brother thought to mate Lady Tempest or Lady Temperance – I don't remember which – and I can assure you, he never managed to secure so much as a dance with either. Come to think of it, I was never sure who trounced him so badly that he moved to the Western Realm. 'Tis a lovely thing someone did. He spoke vows with a lady who is far too good for him, and they are happy together. Males are ever doing foolishness for some female, but most eventually grow past such silliness."

"But, my brother…"

"Lady Yunnan, your brother is a fool, but he has yet to see one hundred years. Perhaps he will grow out of it. Is this the only reason you rejected Styrax?"

"Of course, why else would I?" Yunnan asked in surprise.

"Then, my dear, Styrax will remain at the court's pleasure for the next two weeks. When Lady Star returns to the Seen, Styrax will escort you to my home for an extended visit. Now that that's settled, I suspect Styrax will wish to join you at Lady Star's table." Lindera walked toward the feasting hall.

Those who had waited throughout the columns followed, most disappointed that the meeting had not been more entertaining.

Styrax placed a hand on Yunnan's chin and raised her head to look at her black eye. "Who did this to you?"

Yunnan lowered her eyes. "It matters not."

"Aye, it matters. I will…"

"No," Joey laid a hand on Styrax's shoulder. "No blood feud. Much better to run into the offender away from court."

"Excellent advice," Ridge murmured as he walked by. "It distresses me to observe that male shifters are becoming better at court maneuvering than the males born and raised in this court."

Liron watched from the obscurity of the shadows, pleased that things worked out for Yunnan and Styrax. He was also delighted that Ridge's comment would make an excellent song.

Chapter 45

During Star's visit, while most of the court slept, Ryan left his quarters every morning before the sun rose to continue training with Kulvir. Kulvir seemed pleased with their progress, but Ryan was unsure casting spells while riding. His command of the elements came naturally astride the dragon, and he no longer feared he would fall off when Kulvir dipped and rolled through the sky. This day's training had been better than most and Ryan sported a satisfied smile. He and Kulvir had created a saddle and, to check it out, they were on a test flight. As Kulvir flew near the Northern Realm residence, Ryan said, "We're getting awful close."

"Yes, it's time we confirm what the fae already know. You and I are partners and will fight together."

"I sort of hoped no one had to know," Ryan muttered.

"They already know. Why not let the courts see?"

Ryan sighed. He had enjoyed training with Kulvir in private. No one, fae or shifter, watched to see if he failed or had a weakness to be exploited.

Kulvir turned his neck to look at Ryan, "I too have enjoyed our private training sessions, but to better protect those who need us, we have to show ourselves. I can drop you off at the floating stairs of the Northern Realm. It's where I dropped Valiant the Bold so that the guards didn't think they were under attack."

Ryan nodded. As they crossed the river from the wastelands into the Forest Lord's home woods, he saw a fight next to the river. When he recognized Styrax and Spruce going at it, he said, "I guess we should stop that."

"No, but we'll land and take the wounded to a healer." Kulvir glided down to the ground and landed.

Ryan jumped from the dragon's back and landed beside the watching fae. "Well met. I find myself curious as to the purpose of this gathering."

"Nothing curious about it," Liron retorted. "We were walking with Styrax, attempting to convince him that forcing a fight with Spruce would be worse for him than Spruce, as Lord Ellwood might revoke his permission to be with Lady Yunnan to stop a blood feud."

"That's the moment my idiot brother jumped Styrax and started beating him," Ascan added.

"Since they exchanged punches before we could intervene, we await the outcome. We shall explain this as a simple fight between two foolish young males," Salix offered. "Since Ascan is Spruce's eldest brother and I hold that title for Styrax, we will explain that there is no blood feud, only one male who doesn't think another male is worthy of his sister."

Ryan scoffed, "Who's going to believe that?"

"No one," Salix admitted, "But with both of us saying it's so, no one will contradict us in court. How could they?"

"Well, that will give us a new conversation for the feasting hall," Ryan mused.

"Since you rode Kulvir here, you will be the main topic tonight. I will remember the timing of your reveal, as it might save my family some irritation this evening." Salix bowed before turning to Kulvir. "Kulvir, defender of the worthy, well met. 'Tis pleasant to see you again. Your absence has been noticed with regret by many."

Kulvir inclined his head but didn't speak.

Ascan pointed toward the fight, "I don't think Spruce has much fight left."

"Neither does Styrax. Ouch! That will leave a mark," Salix commented. Styrax landed a perfect right cross to Spruce's left eye.

"And Spruce is down," Ascan sounded unconcerned as he ambled over to check on his foolish brother.

Salix grabbed Styrax before he could jump on Spruce's unconscious body. "He's done for, and so are you. This will not happen again. You have avenged your lady, and this is at an end."

Styrax looked like he wanted to argue but he remained silent.

"I shall return Spruce to my progenitor." Ascan opened a gate, tossed Spruce over his shoulder, and was gone.

"Progenitor? Why not Father?" Ryan asked.

Salix shrugged, "Ascan split from his father over recent events. He no longer addresses Pinus as Father."

"But he still addressed himself as Spruce's eldest brother?" Ryan raised an eyebrow. Yet something else he didn't know about the courts.

"He only denounced his father."

"I offer my back to fly all of you to the floating stairs." Kulvir lowered his body so that the four men could climb on.

"My first dragon flight," Liron grinned.

"If it pleases you, turn that into song instead of the fight." Salix helped his brother climb onto Kulvir's back.

Ryan grinned and hopped onto the saddle once the others were settled. "He'll write both."

"Today has given me three new songs, my friends." Liron laughed as they flew into the air.

Chapter 46

"Are you serious?" Victoria's voice carried down the corridor.

Ryan swallowed his unprofessional retort and explained again, in more detail. "In the Farseen, all red dragons will protect you, not just Montore. In the Farseen, the fae understand exactly what the dragons are willing to do to protect you. Here, in the Seen, dragon protection is not part of the picture and even if it were, humans – and a lot of the Seen preternaturals – don't understand what dragon protection means. You may not go anywhere in the Seen without guards."

Victoria glared at him. "Who's going to track me in the mountains? I want to go on a day hike with Fred. I know a nice mountain trail that opens into a lovely field about six miles in. We'll be fine, just the two of us."

"Un-huh? What did Fred say?" Ryan leaned back on the wall, outside her quarters, and crossed his arms.

"He thinks I need guards," she snarled.

"Then why are we having this conversation?"

"Because, mister powerful alpha, defender of the masses, you were supposed to agree with me." Victoria wrinkled her nose and snarled, "If you said yes, Fred would agree. It's just a hike. How many human kidnappers do you think would follow us six miles into the mountains?"

"It only takes one."

"So, I'm to spend the rest of my life in Calabozo? How about Father's Day? Do I get to go home to see my Dad or will he be brought here under cover of darkness and magic for a visitation?" She had been embarrassed that, on Mother's Day, her mom and dad had met her at Eli's. The entire shifter clan, plus a host of alphas, supervised the visit. It was kind of the shifter to open up his house, but it wasn't the same as being back home with her entire family.

"If we're voting, I like option two," Fred quipped as he joined them. Ryan rolled his eyes and Victoria lit into him, punctuating words like overbearing, idiot, and knuckle-dragging Neanderthal. She finished her tirade, and he tried for understanding, "I know it's hard…"

"You know nothing! I will not be kept here like some weak little female in the shifter knowledge protection program."

"It's not the female they worry about so much, as the human in your genetics." Destin approached the trio. "It's not my place to tell you where to bandy your words about, but we can hear you in the break room. Bets are currently being placed on who'll get punched first, Ryan or Fred."

Ryan rubbed his forehead, "Seriously?"

"Oh yes, I put money on Fred."

Ryan noticed Tempe's approach and stretched his neck in a vain attempt to reduce the tension. "You know, if the dual full moons hadn't happened, I would be in college right now, perhaps dating a cute girl and worrying about finals."

"But it did happen. No reason to dwell on what might have been. That road is full of regrets and serves no useful purpose. Destin, you may leave. Victoria, let's go into your quarters and finish this discussion. I've already received five texts from concerned shifters who think a human female is going to kill Fred, Ryan, or both. And in this case, they are more concerned about the female genetics, than the human ones."

Destin laughed and walked away. Victoria snarled but opened her door. Tempe, as the last one in shut the door and leaned on it. "If you want to argue, do so where the entire facility can't hear you."

"Sorry," all three muttered. Victoria added, "I've been cooped up here for weeks. I want to get out, see the sun, get back to nature."

"What precautions do you think are appropriate? Keep in mind the humans are still unhappy over your refusal to talk to any of their representatives. They feel that you are unjustly penalizing them for one person's actions."

Victoria eyed the powerful shifter, "Is there a suggestion in there?"

"What do you think?"

"It sounds like you're saying if I meet with them again, it could reduce their interest in kidnapping me and I might get some freedom."

"No," Fred blurted out. "I mean, it might reduce interest for some but not for all. There would still be danger."

"It's everywhere," Tempe shrugged. "The goal is to minimize danger and maximize defense."

Fred nodded and asked, "Can I see a map of the shield around Calabozo?"

Tempe tapped the screen a few times and handed over her tablet. Fred angled the screen, so Victoria couldn't see it. She harrumphed, leaned back in the chair, and crossed her arms.

After a few minutes of staring at the tablet, Fred asked, "How about a compromise?"

"What compromise?" Victoria glared at him.

"We could take a walk through the woods inside the shield of Calabozo. There are a couple of nice places to picnic on the property. For Father's Day, you could go to your folks, but there would be guards, less visible perhaps, but they would be there."

"I like the walk inside the shield," Ryan leaned forward, "And I think we could make the trip to her parents work, but I'm not sold on the idea."

"I want more freedom in the Seen, but I'll take it by inches. After all, enough inches and you get a mile."

"Ryan, provide a detailed inches-to-freedom plan for review in forty-eight hours." Tempe left.

*****

Fred helped Victoria across a small stream, and said, "I thought you would be happier out here on the trail."

"Yeah, me too." Victoria wasn't sure what was wrong. She was thrilled with the homemade bug spray Sara had given her. Sara had assured her that magic wasn't involved, just essential oils, but

242

Victoria wasn't so sure. The bugs weren't biting at all, and normally she was a magnet for biting critters. Suddenly she looked up and snarled at an eagle, "Is that Ryan?"

"Not every bird in the sky, or predator on the ground, is a shifter." Fred adjusted the backpack that held the picnic supplies.

"That's not an answer."

"Fine. That's a young bald eagle. Ryan takes the form of a golden eagle. Therefore, that is not Ryan."

"You don't have to be so snarky," Victoria said. She wouldn't admit it out loud, but Victoria felt like she was being watched, and she probably was. She was willing to bet all of her undergraduate degrees that shifters were trailing them. The woods were lovely, but she couldn't relax. Victoria walked to relieve stress or to think. Now she was busy looking for her guards. She suspected this would be her life now. Guarded, never a moment alone. Victoria glanced over at Fred, "Do you know anyone who takes a bald eagle form?"

"Contrary to popular belief, we do not have a database of shifter forms." He held up a hand for silence, "I know you're asking if anyone in Calabozo takes that form. Serenity and Loane are the only two I know with a bald eagle form that frequents our facility. Both shift to adult bald eagles. Don't know if either is local at the moment. And I don't know the form of every shifter in the local area."

A squirrel crossed the path and raced up a tree. Fred grinned, "I know of no shifter anywhere who had chosen a squirrel form."

Turkeys gobbled from somewhere on their left. Victoria huffed and asked, "Wild turkeys?"

"Again, I know of none." He pointed off in the distance at horses. "No horses either."

Victoria pulled out her binoculars and stared at the horses. "How about deer? I see a doe and faun in the horse pasture."

"Not a chance. Unless it's a slip at first shift, we usually take predator forms." Fred's smile disappeared. "Come on, we're near the ledge."

"Ledge? I thought we were heading for an open field." Victoria frowned. She had thought the horse pasture was their destination. It looked lovely.

"This is better, trust me."

Fred cut up a small trail that grew smaller and more vertical with each step. A few minutes later, hanging onto a kudzu vine for stability, Victoria asked, "Just how upset will the sovereign be with you if I fall to my death?"

Fred chuckled without slowing down. "Shifters with a flying form have flown here to get away from everyone for a while now. Recently, others have made a trail up here."

"I'm not sure I'd call this a trail." She used her scarf to wipe the sweat dripping off her face and continued to climb. "I repeat, how upset? I'm a valuable resource and..." Victoria stopped speaking and stared. She had arrived at a rock outcropping, with trees above, below, and to either side. Someone had carefully trimmed the trees below so that the outcropping was somewhat hidden but anyone on the rock could see out. Below them was a beautiful, lush valley, including the horse pasture, she had thought was their destination. The Smokey Mountains surrounded them. It was breathtaking.

"Okay, props to you. This is a much better place for a picnic than an open field." Victoria joined him on the blanket he had laid down. He produced wine glasses and a leather flask of what had to be wine. She grinned. "Not sure I can drink wine and walk down the trail we just came up."

"That's okay, the flask doesn't hold much, so we only get one glass each, and we have the afternoon." Fred grinned and pulled out bread, cheese, fruit, raw veggies, and fried chicken.

Victoria looked over the valley and back at the spread. Nice.

*****

"We need to head back before the sun dips behind the mountain."

"Going down is going to be tricky." Victoria handed him the leftovers as he loaded the backpack for the return trip. There wasn't much. Shifters ate everything in sight. Must be nice to have that type of metabolism.

Fred grinned his little boy smile, and Victoria sighed. She had learned that the cute little boy smile usually meant he wasn't sure she would be happy with whatever he had done. "What?"

"Well, I sort of wanted you to take the trail up. It's the best way to get that first awe inspiring view."

"You mean there's another way to access this view?"

"Yep. Most shifters know about this place now, and even some of the kids have snuck up here a time or two. They're bored with all the restrictions. Tempe was concerned that someone would get hurt, so she built a rope ladder and net system." He moved her toward the other side of the outcropping and showed her the system. No more than ten feet between each net platform the rope ladders connected in a crisscross pattern.

Turning to face Fred, she commented, "That looks a lot easier than the trail we took."

"It's fun, too. Once you're comfortable with it, you can jump from net platform to net platform. Just be sure to aim for the center of the net." To prove his point, he jumped and bounced on the highest platform.

"No. I will not jump. I don't have a flying form as backup. I will climb down, thank-you-very-much." She grabbed the rope ladder and slowly lowered herself. The rope swayed, just as she thought it would, but she enjoyed the ladder and landing net much more than hanging onto kudzu on the side of the cliff, with no safety net. Just as she started down the next to last rope ladder, she let go, and dropped to the net, bouncing until it stabilized.

"Victoria!" Fred, already on the ground, climbed back up, and moved quickly across the net to check on her.

Victoria grinned, "You're right, that's fun."

He forced a laugh, narrowing his eyes on her "You could have told me you were going to drop for fun and not because you lost your grip."

She was amazed he was able to speak considering how clenched his teeth were. How sweet, he worried about her. She leaned up and kissed him. "Sorry, just wanted to try it."

Once they were on the trail through the woods, Fred asked, "Have you completed testing on tracking gates to specific locations in the Farseen?"

Biting the inside of her lip, she stared at the location of the shield, even though she couldn't see it. She didn't want to look into Fred's eyes. "How did you know?"

"Every spare moment in the Farseen, you had Montore fly you around. I assumed you had video going to map everything."

"You told everyone, didn't you?" She couldn't stop the blush that crept up her cheek. "What else could I do? Destin obviously knows how to track gates in the Farseen. He wasn't interested in the project at all."

"If you knew it was already done, why work on it?" Fred stopped walking as his voice trailed off.

She waved her arms around. "Why do you think? You guys keep stuff from me. There's so much to learn."

"Do you have any idea how valuable you are? Every group wants you working in their facilities. Everyone. The fae and other preternaturals are playing nice right now, but if the opportunity presents itself, they will secure you. And you know the humans aren't above kidnapping. The more you know, the more valuable you become." Fred ran his fingers through his hair. "We've managed to keep the humans in the dark about the Farseen, to prevent them from planning an attack on the fae. The fact that iron is deadly to the fae and the Farseen is a known fact. Do you want the fae's homeland, their entire dimension, destroyed just to satisfy your curiosity?"

Both angry and embarrassed, Victoria stomped down the trail. Knowing Fred was right only increased her anger. "I know the way back. You don't have to stay with me."

Fred ran to catch up, "Actually, I do. The only way Ryan would agree to this outing is if I promised to stay by your side. You only have one guard today, me. Don't make this harder than it already is."

"You did not just go caveman on me. I'm an adult. No guard needed." Victoria ran down the trail and took the right fork, knowing full well the left fork would take her to the entrance. Not that it mattered. She could hear Fred closing in.

"Victoria, wait!"

She picked up speed and ran full out. Oh sure, Fred would catch her, but he would have to work for it. Friggin' shifters. So confident in their knowledge. Especially this one. Although, Victoria conceded, the know-it-all attitude might be because he's a male.

246

"Stop, there's danger ahead." Fred's order did nothing to slow down or soothe Victoria.

Yeah right. Surrounded by a powerful shield that no one without the proper genetics could get through, the worst that could happen to Victoria would be a strong shock when she ran into the shield. Too bad humans like her couldn't see it with the naked eye. It was the last straw. She had been kidnapped, beaten, and hounded by the AIB. She just wanted to learn. Learning should be rewarded, not penalized.

Sweat ran into Victoria's eyes, and her breathing became labored. She would have to stop soon, just to catch her breath. Fred probably wasn't even breathing hard. A pocket of fresh air hit her face. Victoria slowed down and was grabbed.

"Got her."

The voice didn't belong to Fred or anyone she recognized. Before she could fight, her eyes were drawn in the direction of a gunshot, she saw Fred on the ground, blood pouring from his chest. He reached for her, and they put another bullet in him. A blow to her head knocked her out.

Chapter 47

Victoria woke to a pounding headache. She slowly opened her eyes and saw a cell that was clean enough to be an operating room. Along with a plate of raw fruits and vegetables, a carafe of water and a glass sat on the table. How civilized. Her eyes darted around the room. Based on the visible technology, the style of the room, and the lack of red dragons attacking, Victoria was still in the Seen.

This was all her fault. Fred had been shot following her while she had a temper tantrum, and somehow, they had left the shield. Maybe the humans attacked the shifter stronghold and the shield over Calabozo was down. This was bad. If the shifters were fighting for their lives, there might not be anyone to rescue her this time. Maybe she used up her allotment of saves, especially since she had been whiney of late.

Victoria heard footsteps outside the room, she grabbed a weapon and waited. Even in this grim situation, she couldn't stop the smirk. Her captors had at least one gun, and Victoria held a fork. Oh yeah, this would go well for her.

The cell door opened, and a man said, "Toss her in with the other."

Victoria watched helplessly as another woman landed on the floor. She had been severely beaten and they dumped her with no regard for her wellbeing. The door shut, and Victoria dropped down beside her new roommate. The unknown woman wore a military uniform with the name Monroe stitched onto it, and rank sewed on the upper part of the sleeve, but Victoria didn't know military grades, except that stars on the top of the shoulder meant general. This rank consisted of stripes and a star. Using the cloth napkin, dipped in water from the carafe, Victoria carefully cleaned Monroe's wounds and waited.

In a surprisingly short amount of time, Monroe groaned.

"Stay where you are. No obvious breaks, but you've been beaten pretty bad."

Monroe opened the one eye that would open and looked around. She faced Victoria, and her good working eye widened, "Aren't you that super smart chick who knows how to track magic?"

Victoria huffed. "I'm Victoria, and I am a chick. As far as super smart goes, this is the third time I've been kidnapped since I discovered how to track dimensional gates. I think it's safe to say I've been bleeding IQ points for a while. And what infuriates me most is that if I had listened to Tempe, Ryan, and Fred, I wouldn't have been kidnapped the last two times. Seriously, does that sound super smart to you?"

"Not particularly, but at least you're smart enough to not get beaten."

"Based on previous experience, I think they haven't gotten around to it yet."

Monroe chuckled, and her split lip cut open again. "Ugh, that hurts. I'm Amy Monroe."

"Nice to meet you. So, who are our captors? I was knocked on the back of the head before they introduced themselves."

"The AIB, or at least people that used to be in the AIB." Amy touched her front teeth like they were loose. "I think I know who Tempe and Ryan are, but who's Fred?"

"He's an overbearing, knuckle-dragging Neanderthal of a shifter who thinks he knows what's best for me." Her voice dropped to a whisper, "They shot him twice when they took me."

Amy continued to look for broken bones. "Shifters heal fast. I'm sure he'll be okay." In an attempt to lift Victoria's spirits, Amy grinned and said, "So your boyfriend's a shifter, and he's been trying to protect you from danger. And now you're mad because he was right."

"If you're going to throw facts around instead of joining in my rant, I'm not sure we can be friends."

"I apologize. You're right of course." Monroe attempted to stand and decided it would be prudent to remain on the ground before she passed out again. She moved around trying to find a position that didn't hurt and put her hands in her pockets. "Why are you here?"

"They haven't told me yet, but I suspect they want to pick my brain. How about you?"

"I arrived at my grandparents' home for a few days of leave, and some of their neighbors had gone missing. I didn't even have time to change. I tracked two of the teenagers, only to end up kidnapped, like you. Because it's well known that I worked with Tempest once during the dual full moons, these AIB goons tried to beat me for information." She raised her voice in case anyone was listening, "I haven't seen Tempest for months, and I only met her one time. I don't know anything."

Victoria patted her right shoulder, as it seemed to be the only place Amy wasn't wounded. Victoria said, "Based on the last time the AIB kidnapped me, they don't care if we know anything or not. They just like to beat people."

The door opened. Dave Roberts followed two guards into the room. "Staff Sergeant Monroe, we know you tried to save Tempest's son at the Salt Lake mega gate. Tempest would have given you a way to contact her."

"She thanked me, but she didn't give me a phone number or email address."

"She gave you something, though. Didn't she? Some way to contact her if you're in trouble. You are now in trouble and need to call her. If not for yourself, for the shifter teenagers you were tracking."

"Those kids aren't shifters! I used to babysit them when I spent summers with my grandparents."

Dave leaned down and smiled, "We have an informant who says they're shifters. We'll test them and discover the truth."

Victoria glared at him, "You don't care if they're shifters. You kidnapped them thinking the Sergeant would track them, allowing you to grab her. She's bait! Your way to Tempest. Well, I will be more than happy to call her. I know a number that will get to her, and I feel quite certain she'll come when I call." Her eyes narrowed on the guards, "And, not that she'll need the help, but I'll bet she'll bring some friends with her. Probably friends of the guy you shot when you kidnapped me."

"We didn't kidnap you! We saved you." One of the guards growled.

"You saved me? From what? I work with the shifters. They respect me. They don't lock me in a cell or beat me." Aside to Amy, she added, "At one time, I wanted a corner office in a prestigious university. Now I just want to work somewhere safe. My standards have lowered." Tapping her foot, Victoria held out her hand, "Give me a phone and I'll call."

"No. I don't want you to dial a number we already know. I want Monroe to contact Tempest. The fae are sure the medic who tried to save her son received some sort of bracelet from the half breed, and I want to see it."

Amy rolled up both sleeves to expose her wrists. "Aside from a bracelet being non-regulation, you can see that I have no bracelet on at this time." She bit back her irritation. She had removed the bracelet and dropped it in her pocket, but maybe she shouldn't have. Amy didn't want Tempest to show up to a trap.

*****

"What's the verdict?" Ryan adjusted his gear and waited for the report. Kenley had been fast with the tricorder, and Ryan had assumed everyone could use it quickly.

"Still working on it," Phoenix growled. "Maybe we should have brought Destin with us."

Ryan sighed, apparently not.

"Yeah, we need more humans in the field." Gerbold held out his hand. "Give the electronic toy to the shifter who manipulates electronics."

"Fine." Phoenix tossed Gerbold the tricorder.

Gerbold barely glanced at the device. "Three cells in the basement with a total of five humans inside. Another room, heavy on technology, is where Victoria and the woman wearing Tempe's bracelet are being kept."

Phoenix's mouth dropped open. "How did you do that so fast?"

"Later," Ryan held up his hand for silence. "Pat, take Phoenix and Kaleb, check out the cells and rescue anyone you can. Gerbold, you're with me."

Pat reviewed the schematics and teleported the three of them inside the facility.

Ryan turned to Gerbold, "Tell me about the heavy technology."

*****

The alarms sounded off as soon as Ryan opened a gate into the hallway near where the girls were held. Cloaked under his invisibility shield, Ryan and Gerbold were able to hug the wall as guards ran past them to the open gate.

"I feel like a hobbit with the one ring on my finger," Gerbold whispered.

Ryan ignored the comment and moved down the hall.

Gerbold used the tricorder to point toward a heavily guarded room. The guards had iron weapons and an iron net. This had been a trap for Tempe. "That's the room we're looking for."

"Of course, it is," Ryan sighed. He checked his phone and nodded to himself after Pat and the others were gone. "Okay, follow the plan."

Gerbold nodded, and Ryan dropped his shield. Gerbold short-circuited the power, and the facility was engulfed in darkness. Before the backup power kicked in, he short-circuited that as well.

Wearing night-vision goggles, both men ran for the door knocking people out of the way. It wasn't difficult since most people were hugging the walls, unable to see in the total darkness of the underground facility.

The two guards in front of the door were well trained. As soon as the lights had gone out, they had closed ranks and, shoulder-to-shoulder, were prepared to fight. Even in the confusion, no one approached the guards, as if everyone understood going near that guarded door would get them killed. Ryan held out his hand and used wind to move both guards out of his way. A few unfortunate wall huggers were blown down the hall as well.

Ryan guarded the door, while Gerbold rushed in to grab the girls. Without goggles, the girls couldn't see, and Amy kicked out when she was grabbed.

Gerbold groaned and fell to one knee as the kick made contact with his groin. "Shifter here. We're rescuing you."

"He's with us," Victoria yelled, hands out, searching for Amy in the dark. "He's one of my guards."

"Sorry," Amy said.

Gerbold clenched his teeth and stood up. She didn't sound sorry. "I have to guide you. Ryan opened a gate." He grabbed Victoria again and turned to grab Amy. She had moved in closer, and he elbowed her in the stomach, "Sorry." He didn't sound sorry either.

He moved them toward the gate. A bullet whizzed past Ryan and embedded in Gerbold's shoulder. He pushed the girls through the gate and followed them. In the light of the PAC HQ pad, he got a good look at Amy. "Why didn't you say you were injured?" He provided his designation and passcode, lifted Amy, and ran through the checkpoint, yelling "Victoria, keep up." Shifter guards circled around Victoria, and they followed Gerbold.

The rescue had been planned, and the wizards on guard duty were expecting them. Everyone got out of his way as he ran for the clinic. Gerbold laid her on the cot. "You should have told me you were beaten."

"You're shot. Of the two of us, you're in the worst shape."

"Shot? One bullet. It's nothing."

"Let Lea remove the bullet and clean the area before it closes." Jeff pointed Gerbold toward the only chair in the room where he could get treatment. To Amy, he added, "Gerbold is right. You were badly beaten. He should have carried you instead of you risking more injury."

"I'm fine," she retorted, sitting up. "We have to go back and get the two teenagers those fools thought were shifters."

Jeff gently pushed her back down on the cot. "Counting you and Victoria, seven people were rescued from the facility. I'll have someone verify the two you're worried about are with them."

A guard stepped out of the room and returned a short time later with two boys.

"Amy, you alright? They said you were injured trying to help us. You look bad." A teenage boy winced.

"Tyler! Where's Hunter?"

"I'm here," Hunter stuck his head in the doorway of the crowded room. "Did they do this to you because you tried to rescue us?"

"No, they beat her because of me." Tempe walked into the room. "I need to adjust the spell on the bracelet. No preternatural would have beaten you with a Bracelet of Honor revealed. I'll have to do something to keep humans away."

Amy frowned, "Hmm, Tempest, I've used the bracelet. You said it could be used only once."

"I'll reset it. I think you need protection still."

"Yes, she does. I'll guard her for a few days until it's reset," Gerbold said.

"I don't need a guard. I'm a soldier."

"You're a medic. You need to be guarded." Gerbold's tone brooked no opposition.

Amy sputtered. Tempe laid a calming hand on the sergeant's shoulder. "Gerbold's right. You need a guard, and he's offered. Would you prefer someone else?"

"No, if I have to be guarded by an overbearing male, it might as well be him." Amy looked over at Victoria, "You're right. Shifter males are overbearing, knuckle-dragging Neanderthals."

Tempe chuckled and checked a text before asking, "Have you boys been cleared by medical? Your mom is here."

"Yes, Ma'am." Tyler nodded. "Um, Amy, since the AIB will probably hold a press conference, you should know."

"Know what?"

"We're preternaturals. Not powerful, like Tempest –"

"Nowhere near as powerful," Hunter cut in to add. "We're just witches. I'm pretty good at lighting candles and starting bonfires. Tyler's got a real gift for electronics. We can both work a couple of minor spells, but otherwise, we're not powerful."

"Yeah, if we were, the AIB wouldn't have gotten us," Tyler added.

Amy peered closely at the boys. "They didn't beat you?"

"No, took blood for the test and tossed us in a cell. The AIB mentioned something about using us. I think they only took us to trap you. Bonus for them, they chose well and know we're witches now."

"Not your fault," Tempe said. "If you go with Joey, he'll take you to your mom."

Fred walked in as the boys left. Victoria squealed and jumped into his arms. He staggered back into the wall. "Take it easy. The healer and doctors did a great job patching me up, but I'm still weak."

"Sorry, I'm just so glad to see you alive." Victoria snuggled into his arms.

"I'm glad to see you too." With his arms still around Victoria, Fred looked over her head at Tempe, "The gate closed. Ryan didn't return."

Chapter 48

Ryan heaved a sigh of relief. Fred and the humans were through the gate. He turned to follow, and something pierced his skin. Ryan reached up and pulled out a dart. Dizzy from the dart, he watched Dave order two soldiers to enter the portal. Ryan's "No!" came out as a slur. He pulled the dart out and fell to the ground. He fell unconscious and the gate closed.

Ryan woke up on a hospital cot, raised as high as it would go, in a clean room, with a mesh of iron covering all four sides, as well as the floor and ceiling. At least he wasn't in those magic stopping cuffs again. Ryan smirked. The iron wouldn't hurt him, but if a fae were in this room, they wouldn't survive long. The humans believed iron harmed all preternaturals. If he left, they would know the truth, so he'd wait and look for a better opportunity.

His hand touched the hilt of the Patron's Sword, and it vibrated. Ryan looked down and verified that the sword was still there. Why would the humans leave him a weapon? Tempe said they wouldn't see it, but he hadn't really believe that.

A screen on the wall flickered and turned on. Dave Roberts, Sr., smiled. "The fae we put in this room died in under thirty-six hours. Wonder how long a shifter can last?"

"Guess we'll find out." Ryan swung his legs over the side of the cot that was locked in place higher than a normal bed, letting his feet dangle. "Have you heard from the men you sent through my gate?"

"No, I'm waiting for the sovereign to call and offer an exchange. My men for you."

"Don't hold your breath," Ryan muttered. Louder he added, "Anyone inside a gate when it closes simply disappears. We don't know where they go or if they simply cease to exist when the gate does. The only thing we know is they are never seen again."

"You lie!"

"No reason to. It's a fact. Preternaturals don't enter a gate opened by someone who's injured and might pass out. It's not worth the risk."

Dave cut the feed into the room.

Ryan leaned back on the bed, stretched his arms, and tried to contact Sage, mind-to-mind. Nothing. He took a deep breath, centered himself, and tried again. Still nothing. Was a preternatural helping the humans by dampening telepathy? If he opened a gate and left, the secret would be out that only the fae were affected by iron. Unsure what to do, he pretended to sleep with his hands behind his back. With any luck, the humans would think he was weakening from the cold iron. His hand closed on a chain with some type of pendant. He fingered it but didn't look at it. No reason to let the AIB know what he had found.

Within a few minutes, the door opened. Ryan sat up and dropped the necklace in his pocket, prepared to fight. Two fae were tossed on the floor, and the door slammed shut. He jumped down and picked up Lady Faun, the nearest to him, and placed her on the cot. Then he grabbed Lady Dawn and placed her beside her sister. There was only one cot, and it was the only thing in the room that wasn't covered with iron. "How did they kidnap you from the Farseen?"

Neither spoke.

Ryan balled his hands into fists and glared at Dawn. "Don't tell me you let your sister talk you into bringing her to the Seen to see her boyfriend. You're smarter than that." He cut his eyes to Faun, "You both are."

"Apparently not." Dawn sighed.

"Does anyone know you guys are here?"

Faun winced, "No. Don't blame –"

"No names," Ryan ordered.

Faun nodded her understanding. And pointed to Dawn. "Her. It's my fault."

"For you always win our fights? I don't think so." Dawn faced Ryan and explained, "I agreed to bring her here. I opened a gate outside of PAC HQ, planning to contact... him."

"Oh?" Ryan crossed his arms. "As soon as you approached PAC HQ, all four realms would have contacted your father. Heck, the shifters, wizards, and even the vampires would have contacted him."

"We thought of that when we saw the check-in line," Dawn agreed.

"Okay, we're leaving." Ryan raised his hand to open a gate, but nothing happened. He tried again. Still nothing. He raised an eyebrow and turned to throw fire at the door. Nothing. He turned back to his friends, "We're in trouble."

The screen clicked on again. Dave's elated smile covered his face. "This is much better than I'd hoped. Your magic is completely contained. Now we can run some real tests."

Ryan snarled. Hopefully, they would have to open the door to run the tests. Otherwise, they were screwed.

*****

"Got 'em," Sage's excited grin turned into a frown, "Nope, gone again." She pounded the desk with her fist, "Why can't I contact him?"

Tempest leaned back in her chair. "Obviously, he's in some type of enclosure that prevents telepathy, and the seal flickered for a moment. I should have gone after the Sergeant. Playing decoy at PAC HQ did not work."

"No. They were waiting for you with iron nets and weapons. You wouldn't have survived that," Sage said. Gerbold, Destin, Fred, and Victoria walked in. "Got anything?"

"It's more than just a telepathy block." Victoria nodded to Tempe and plopped down into a chair. "Geoffrey Watson, my old boss, created a shield that no magic can get through. When I left, he must have had a flash drive of my early designs. He built on my rough design to block magic." She put her elbows on the table and her head in her hands. "It's all my fault. I thought the design had merit as a secure location where no one would be able to use powers, a safe place to meet. It didn't occur to me that it could be used to trap preternaturals. I'm a fool."

Fred patted her on the back.

"It's not new. We have something similar for negotiations during wartime," Sage admitted.

"But you didn't give the knowledge to the AIB, did you?"

Tempe shook her head. "No, but at the time you thought you were working for your government. You trusted them to do the right thing."

"Like I said, I'm a fool." Victoria cut her eyes to Fred, "How did we end up outside of the shield?"

Fred looked at Sage, who shrugged. He took that as permission. "To keep the shields permanent we've had to make some adjustments. It takes a lot of power to keep them going. Those who can set shields were getting weak from the strain."

"So?" Victoria looked between Tempe, Sage, and Fred.

"So," Fred cleared his throat. "Most shields only keep people out now. Anyone can leave a shield once they are inside."

"And you didn't think to tell us?" Victoria's eyes flashed.

Fred's expression tightened. "You ran for the shield thinking you couldn't get through and would be hurt in the attempt. How much sooner would you have left if you had known?"

She opened and shut her mouth a couple of times, before she whispered, "I'm sorry."

"Blaming yourself accomplishes nothing," Gerbold leaned back and asked Sage, "Were you able to find Ryan?"

"No." Sage crossed her arms in front of her.

Gerbold turned back to Victoria, "That device has to use some serious power. Any chance you can find that power signature?"

Victoria gave him a look that screamed duh. "Why didn't I think of that?"

*****

Ryan had never felt so helpless. He looked up at the cameras. The screens were blank, but he bet they were recording everything. If the door opened, Ryan could fight his way out, but it appeared the humans weren't taking chances. Dawn and Faun grew weaker by the hour. They lay together on the cot, but the nearness of the cold iron ate away at their strength. At this rate, he estimated the sisters wouldn't live another twenty-four hours. At least his watch worked in the room.

"If you get the chance, take… her… and run." Faun's voice was barely a whisper. "It's my fault we're here. Save her if you can."

"No," Dawn's voice was even weaker.

"I'm getting all of us out of here." Ryan's voice was firm, though he had no idea how to make that happen. His hand once again touched the hilt of the Patron's Sword, the vibration of the sword soothed him. How? He was careful to not look. How could the sword still have the magic to vibrate? Hmm, it was dragon made, and dragons had strong magic, perhaps, like sea serpents, they didn't fall to cold iron, or maybe nothing could stop a dragon made sword. He looked at the door again. One shot. If it didn't work, Ryan would be forced to hand over the sword. Still, the AIB would have to open the door to get the sword, and his magic would flow. Win-win from Ryan's point of view. Looking back at Faun and Dawn there was no choice. Soon the sisters would be too drained to stand. In fact, they might already be too weak.

"Sit up," Ryan demanded.

"Huh?" Both ladies looked at him in confusion.

"Sit up. I want to see how much strength you have left."

The sisters looked at him, and Ryan placed his hand on the sword. They moved to sitting positions without taking their eyes off the sword. Trusting the sisters were ready to jump and run, Ryan turned and faced the door. In one smooth move, he pulled the sword and swung it in a high arc, slicing through the door. Instead of the wood he expected, it was made of some type of fiberglass. As soon as the sword sliced an opening, he felt his magic returning.

Keeping the sword gripped in his right hand, he used his left to open a gate to Beryl Lane, Tempe's home. "Go." Dawn and Faun entered the gate holding each other upright. They had to take a step on the iron mesh before reaching the gate. Both stumbled from the effort but made it through. Ryan created fire and let it consume the room as he followed them.

The unplanned gate opened in Tempe's yard. The two ladies of the Southern Realm walked through and immediately passed out. The shifters were immediately on high alert, manning defensive positions in case the humans attacked. Bryce stood over the girls talking into a phone. Truman, Tempe's human grandson, checked their injuries.

Ryan walked through and closed the gate.

"Ryan just arrived," Bryce said into the phone. He turned the phone on speaker and faced it toward Ryan.

Assuming Sage or Tempe were on the other end, he said, "Tell the Southern Realm, the ladies Dawn and Faun are here. They were stuck in a room of cold iron for nearly twelve hours and are weak."

"Set them up in the house. Jeff and Lea are on the way."

Following Tempe's instructions, Bryce picked up Lady Faun, and Ryan picked up Lady Dawn. They headed for the house with the girls.

*****

"Welcome to my home, Lady Ivy. Your daughters are this way." Tempe greeted her at the door. At Lady Ivy's signal, her sentinels remained outside the house. The fae healer accompanied them.

The fae passed the kitchen bar, where Ryan sat eating a large sub. Ivy paused. "You have once again pleased me, Ryan. Should you ever desire assistance from the Southern Realm, contact me. My patronage is assured."

Ryan swallowed and looked up in confusion. Tempe, standing behind Lady Ivy, gave him a get-with-the-program stare. He stood and bowed. "I was privileged to be in a position to be of service." He wasn't sure it was the right thing to say, but he heard Ridge make a similar comment once, and it seemed like a proper reply. He raised his eyes to see Lady Ivy smile and Tempe nod her head ever so slightly. Even the healer seemed to think the response was appropriate. The women turned and continued to the recovery room. Crisis averted, Ryan sat down and took another bite of sub. Joey gave him two thumbs up, and they both grinned.

Lady Ivy and Tempe returned down the hallway. Ryan and Joey were sitting on the couch that gave them a view of the hallway. Both pretended to look at their phones.

"Joey, inform the sovereign that Lady Ivy will be staying at PAC HQ until tomorrow when the girls will be ready to return home. Healer Shepry will remain here with the ladies Dawn and Faun."

"Yes, Lady Tempest." Joey bowed and left the room.

After Ivy left, Tempest motioned for Ryan, and he followed her into the office. She opened a safe, one Ryan didn't know about, and pulled out the translated journal, and tossed it to him. "It occurs to me you haven't had time to read this. It will give you more information on the sword and its capabilities." Tempe sat down in her chair and asked, "How did you learn the sword could break through the magic block?"

"I touched it, wondering why they didn't take it from me when I was unconscious, and it vibrated."

"The humans would not have been able to see it. Unless someone knows you have the sword, and they truly believe you have it, they can't see it until you wield it. Even if they heard you had a new sword, humans trust their eyes and wouldn't expect to see it, so they didn't."

"Handy magic, that. It also explains why everyone tried to goad me into unsheathing it."

"Yes, well, I'm sure the humans now know you have a magic sword, although I'll bet they don't have a clue why it worked."

"So, you knew my magic was blocked?"

"We figured it out, eventually. It seems Geoffrey had a flash drive with some of Victoria's early designs on it."

"We need to get it."

"No reason. You can bet Dave Roberts, Sr., has already had the drive backed up to multiple locations."

Ryan sighed. He should have thought of that. "I woke up in the magic shielding room, Dave Roberts said a fae had died in that room in less than thirty-six hours. No name, but I found this in the room. Writing looks like ancient fae to me." He dropped the necklace on the table.

Tempe picked it up. "Hmm, Central Realm, of Queen Ceridwin's line." She pursed her lips and handed the necklace back. "You need to return this to the senior rep of Central Realm at PAC HQ. They deserve to hear your report from your lips. It belonged to Kamden. His father, a healer, is frequently on duty there."

262

"Kamden," Ryan repeated. That death hit just a little too close to home. They were about the same age. If he hadn't been there, wearing the Patron's Sword, the same could have happened to Dawn and Faun. He glanced at Tempe. If she had responded to the bracelet, she would have died in that room. "We have to keep them from building more of these enclosures."

"Yes, but for now, you need to contact the Central Realm. My fae sisters and I have a task that cannot wait," Tempe said.

Chapter 49

Ryan approached the Central Realm's wing of PAC HQ. He stopped before the guards and waited.

Evin, in the full ambassador gear the fae senior reps wore, moved down the hallway and stopped in front of Ryan. "You have something for the Central Realm?"

"Yes," Ryan pulled the necklace out of his pocket and let the pendant dangle. "I regret to inform you this was found in an AIB stronghold, inside a room that blocked magic and was covered with a mesh of cold iron. I was told a fae had died there."

Evin reached out, took the necklace, and read the inscription. "The same room that held you, and the ladies Dawn and Faun from the Southern Realm?"

"The same." Ryan schooled his features into a mask, but he was surprised that story was already out. He expected it to take a bit longer to make the rounds.

"Come, I will take you to Healer Iason, Kamden's father. He will hear your words." Evin turned and walked into the Central Realm wing.

The guards parted and bowed, allowing Ryan to follow.

It was a short walk to the healer's workspace. He stood over a microscope, reminding Ryan of his own father.

Healer Iason looked up at Evin and smiled. The smile turned to a frown. The alpha Ryan stood behind Evin. A shifter in the Central Realm wing of PAC HQ was not a good sign. And Ryan was the protégé of Lady Tempest, the shifter assassin.

Evin nodded to Ryan who held out the necklace and repeated his earlier words.

Iason sat down on a stool without taking his eyes off Ryan. "Aside from the necklace, have you proof it was my son?"

"Lady Tempest, Lady Temperance, and Lady Saffron are investigating now." Ryan looked down at his feet and admitted, "I believe there is a protocol I'm unaware of. When I told Lady Tempest, she called her sisters, and the three of them left immediately. I was sent to inform you what had transpired."

"Understandable. They want the guilty found before Mother decides to attack the Seen."

"Mother?"

"Queen Ceridwin."

Ryan gulped but didn't speak. Freakin' AIB, killing the grandson of a fae queen. He had expected Kamden to be some great-great-great-something, not a close relative.

Lady Windy rushed into the room. "Envoy Cloud has requested all of you in the control room. He said Ryan, Wielder of the Patron's Sword, is invited."

Before he could respond, Ryan received a text. "Sorry, I must go." He ran from the Central Realm wing and to the gate platform.

Liron, of the Northern Realm, greeted him. "Good, you're here. Lady Tempest is holding a gate open, awaiting you."

Ryan nodded. He hopped on the platform and walked out of the gate. Looking around to get his bearings he saw one of the farms he had searched while looking for the Sword of Veracity.

Saffron pulled him down into the bushes. "Let's not announce ourselves."

"Are you nuts?" He glared at his aunts. "Iron will kill all three of you. You know this is an AIB TAC stronghold, right?"

"Of course, we know," Tempe said. "We can't get near the place. They've planted iron throughout this area. It's a landmine that only kills fae. Kyan is on the north end of the house with Phoenix and Landon. Murdoch is with them. You make sure that the humans are taken into custody, except for Dave Roberts, Sr. He must be turned over to the fae queens, or we'll have a war on our hands."

Ryan's mouth dropped opened.

Saffron pushed him toward the house. "Don't stand there. Go, lead the shifters."

Ryan shifted to his wildcat form and ran around the side of the house. As he shifted back to human and approached the men, Ryan reviewed various ways to give Kyan, the oldest male shifter still living, orders.

"Additional orders?"

Kyan's simple question eased Ryan. He should have known his uncle would do everything possible to make this easy for him.

"Contain the humans, alive if possible. All will eventually be turned over to the humans for their crimes, except for Dave Roberts, Sr. I'll take him to the fae."

"Understood." Kyan never took his eyes off the farmhouse.

"Murdoch, how about you make one of those impressive holes in the side of the house." Ryan ignored the sword at his waist and pulled his rune baton from his belt and extended it. "We might as well use an entrance they aren't expecting."

Murdoch smirked, pulled his own rune baton, and mumbled a phrase. One section of the wall simply disappeared from the first floor to the second. Phoenix and Ryan shifted to their bird forms and flew through the hole in the second floor. Murdoch and Landon ran in the first floor, throwing spells at whomever they met.

Ryan shifted as soon as he had floor underneath him, landing hits on two humans who fell to the floor while bullets bounced off his shield. Phoenix turned to shadow, and the shots passed through him only to find a home in the humans he was fighting.

"Slumber." Ryan modulated his voice and sent the humans in the room to sleep.

"You could have done that sooner," Phoenix groused.

"Probably," Ryan agreed. He didn't bother to explain that he forgot.

A door opened, and a machine gun peppered the room with bullets. Unfortunately, Ryan's shield repelled the weapon's fire, and they careened around the room, killing more humans.

"You guys should surrender before you kill all of your fellow bigots," Phoenix yelled over the sound of ammo shooting out of the gun. In response, someone tossed a grenade at the

266

shifters. As with the bullets, it bounced on the shield and returned back to the guy who threw it. He caught it before it exploded in his hands. "Okay, these fools are determined to kill themselves."

"Slumber." This time Ryan yelled the enchantment in the hopes of taking out those humans hidden behind doors.

Both shifters stood still and listened for sounds, but the only ones were the sounds of fighting on the first floor. Ryan nodded to Phoenix, "Go help the others. I'll clear this floor."

Phoenix took off running. Room by room, Ryan completed his search and grouped the unconscious humans together. It was pitifully easy to fight humans, and Ryan felt like a bully, picking on the weak. The injured were left where they were while he sent a text for a medic.

He opened the door to the last room he needed to clear. It was empty except for a closet. Not even a window. Thinking it was a storage area, he crossed the room to check the closet. As he opened the closet, he heard the door to the room shut.

"You didn't think we only built one room that swallowed magic, did you?" Dave Roberts, the so-called brains behind the AIB, stood between Ryan and the door as he deliberately clicked the safety off his pistol.

"I had hoped."

"I'll take that sword now."

"No, you won't." Ryan's voice was calm, almost conversational.

"You have no magic in this room, so you can't create a shield. I have a gun. I know you can bleed out, so you've lost."

Ryan pulled the sword, thankful for Kulvir's training. "Yeah, about the no magic thing. You should have read the fine print."

As Ryan marched forward, the sword swallowed the bullets shot at him. Dave looked between his gun, Ryan, and the sword. It was the work of a moment for Ryan to knock Dave out with the hilt of the sword.

*****

Ryan carried Dave Roberts over his shoulder and followed his three aunts through the gate Tempe opened. They exited on the lower level of a two-level platform. On the upper level stood five women. The entire structure hovered above the waves, much like the Central Realm's residence floated high in the sky above the valley.

"This is the Queen's Judgment Court," Saffron whispered in Ryan's ear as he laid down his burden and covered him in a net Temperance handed him.

The five fae queens had each taken a warrior princess guise, including an outfit so skimpy, Ryan blushed. They all looked the same, same hair, same outfit, same stance, same neutral expression on the same face, and the same staff in their right hands. The only difference was their color. Assuming the queens took their color from their realm colors, Niamh, Queen of the Northern Realm was green, from skin tone to hair color, to eye color. Her outfit was also green, nearly matching her skin color. Queen Ceridwin of the Central Realm was a light purple, although her hair and outfit were a darker shade. Queen Eiddwen of the Eastern Realm was beige and gold, her outfit also matched her skin color, while her hair color was the stark white generally associated with the fae. Queen Weindrych of the Western Realm was light blue, offsetting the aqua tint of her outfit. Queen Shreya of the Southern Realm was black as night, while her clothing, hair, and eye color could only be called flaming red. They stood on the platform, waves rolled in the background.

Ryan had seen two of the fae queens before, and they had looked like regular ruling fae at the time, as individual as anyone else. Ryan also noticed that the wind that blew him, Tempe, and her sisters, didn't affect the queens at all. Not even a single hair on their heads moved with the wind. This was some sort of statement.

Tempe walked up to the highest step on the platform, dropped to one knee, and bowed.

"Queen Ceridwin, Lady Temperance, Lady Saffron, Ryan, Wielder of the Patron's Sword, and I bring before you the one who ordered the death of your grandson. His name is Dave Roberts, leader of a band of human outlaws who call themselves the AIB. His crime is ignorance."

"I'm not ignorant. I see you aberrants for what you are. Evil creatures sent from hell."

Tempe, still in a bow, barked a laugh, "He is also foolish, but I know of no dimension where being a fool is a crime." With a whisper, she added, "Although, perhaps it should be."

268

Ryan pressed his lips together to keep from laughing.

Tempe raised her voice and continued, "I said ignorance is his crime because he does not know what a fae queen is. He does not understand that the last time a fae queen lost her temper in the Seen, Atlantis fell into the ocean. He does not understand that if a fae queen declares war on the Seen, it will become as devoid of life as the single moon orbiting it."

Tempe stood to her full height and faced the queens as an equal.

Ryan watched, amazed. Even he knew if the five queens stood together, you didn't make eye contact. It could be seen as a challenge to one or all.

Tempe's voice grew stronger still, "I prefer that not happen. I like the Seen most of the time. To keep the peace between the Farseen and the Seen, I present the AIB leader to you. This is the human who ordered the death of Kamden by trapping him in a room of cold iron as a test to see what would happen. This is the human who attempted the same test with Ryan, a shifter of the Alpha Clan, and two daughters of the Southern Realm. Ryan, Wielder of the Patron's Sword, was able to rescue both ladies without further loss of life.

"This human is yours to do with as you see fit. Those who worked for him will be turned over to the human government, and they can deal with the murderers exercising their laws. If this is acceptable, there will be no war between the Farseen and the Seen. If you require more, I await your demands." Tempe stopped speaking and once again dropped to one knee with her head bowed.

Ryan's brow furrowed. Now she gets submissive? She pressures the fae queens, all five of them, and then drops into a submissive pose. He glanced around, and Temperance and Saffron appeared to be as shocked by her words and actions as Ryan. That was probably a bad sign.

The five lords of the five realms appeared on the bottom platform and walked up the steps, each moving in front of his or her queen and dropping to one knee.

Lord Sky of the Central Realm, the only current female realm lord, spoke. "Lady Tempest has spoken true. We would expect the humans to kill the leader of a fae faction and send the other fae to us, to face our justice. I find no fault with her recommendation."

"I have watched the humans. They have difficulties dealing with crimes involving preternaturals," Queen Niamh said. She used the business end of the staff to reach under Tempe's chin and raise her eyes. "Tell me, why should we trust the humans to take appropriate action with the others? You turned this human over to them not long ago, and they released him. Had you killed him then, we would not be contemplating war with the Seen."

"Humans are still learning about preternaturals. They don't truly understand the fae or the Farseen. They have never seen the power of a fae queen. In fact, they have no clue as to the power of a realm lord. They have seen the enforcement arm of the Tetrad, the Death Squad, in action, but only in a limited capacity. I request you not punish an entire dimension for the actions of a few. Queen Niamh, you are the one who taught me to look for peace, not war." The last sentence Tempe directed at her formidable grandmother.

"If we grant your request, what is offered in return, Lady Tempest?" Queen Ceridwin asked.

Ryan narrowed his eyes on Tempe. The queens wanted something from her, but what? Did she know?

"What can I offer that will appease you?" Tempe asked.

Guess not. Ryan remained still, though he wanted to pace.

"Your homeland in the Seen has an adversarial court that includes a jury by peers. We approve, with the following changes. Any trial in the Seen where a fae is either the plaintive or defendant must have an equal number of representatives from each species, fae and human on the jury. Likewise, the trial will be co-ruled by a human judge and a fae judge. A guilty verdict will result in the immediate execution of the guilty party, regardless of species."

Tempe stood once again and faced the queens. "I have no sway over how the humans conduct their courts. Each government has their own set of laws for dispensing justice."

"You misunderstand. Any dispute between humans and fae will not be held in human courts, but in a new form of an ancient court, the Seelie Court." Queen Shreya smiled. "Like the old Seelie Court, warnings, for accidental offenses where no malice is

270

proven, will be allowed, but death is the response for any guilty verdict."

"We invite the other preternatural species to join the Seelie Court, but that is, of course, up to their leaders," Queen Weindrych added.

"You, Lady Tempest, will be the Queen of the Seelie Court." Queen Ceridwin decreed.

"But –"

"Your leadership is not negotiable. As a child of both worlds, you are our selection for this position. If you say no, the fae will go to war with the humans and the Seen," Queen Eiddwen explained.

Tempe closed her eyes and ground out the words. "I am left with no choice, for I desire peace. If the leaders of the human governments agree, I accept."

Queen Niamh looked past Tempe for the first time, staring directly into the camera that Ryan had not even noticed. Her evil smile filled the screen. "This played simultaneously on every device with a screen in the Seen, even screens without your so-called wireless technology and screens that were turned off. If that is not enough of a show of our power, we offer one additional demonstration. All nuclear, radiological, chemical, and biological devices that were built solely to be used as weapons are gone. You can make more, but it will take time, and we will be watching."

Lady Saffron walked up to the top step and dropped to one knee.

Queen Niamh looked at her youngest granddaughter, "Why have you approached the Queen's Judgment Court?"

"I bring news from the Seen. The U.N. is agreeable to a Seelie Court under the direction of Queen Tempest. The shifter sovereign, the vampire protectorate, the high wizard, and the supreme of the Council of Sorcery are pleased to join the Seelie Court and find Queen Tempest to be an admirable choice of Seelie Queen."

Queen Niamh laughed, "Of her suitability, there is no doubt."

Queen Weindrych smiled kindly, "Excellent. I'm sure the humans know how to get in touch with the Seelie Queen. We are done."

"Indeed," Queen Eiddwen agreed.

Queen Ceridwin looked at Dave Roberts for the first time. "Killing my grandson was a mistake. I find myself hopeful the humans learn from it." Her eyes narrowed, and he caught on fire, turning to ash in mere seconds.

"The Seelie Queen shall return the human remains to his family," Queen Shreya said.

The queens turned and walked off the back end of the platform, disappearing as soon as both feet were off the platform.

Tempe turned to face the camera, her face grim. Lady Temperance gathered up the ashes in an urn and handed it to the Seelie Queen.

*****

Dave Roberts, Jr. walked into PAC HQ. His human military escort, a concession to his mother, had been polite but even his ears picked up the snide remarks all around him. Some preternaturals blamed him for having a father who led the AIB and attacked the preternaturals. Many humans censured him because his father failed to remove the preternaturals from this world. Other humans criticized him because his father furthered distrust between humans and preternaturals. Thanks to Dad, Dave Roberts, Jr., had a whole lot of hate coming his way.

He had wanted to see PAC HQ. But Dave, Jr., never expected to be here for this reason. His mother refused to come. She feared the shifters and all preternaturals. That's how the disowned son of Dave Roberts, Sr. came to be the one to collect his ashes. He still wasn't sure how he felt about his dad. He had yet to reconcile the head of the AIB with the man who taught him to play ball and stand up for what is right. How could his father have forgotten the message he drilled into his son? What happened to his father to make him think killing preternaturals was right?

Dave, Jr., breathed a sigh of relief when he saw Landon and Ryan. He trusted both of them.

"If you come with us, Queen Tempest will see you now," Ryan said.

When the Lieutenant heading the military escort shook his head, Dave said, "It's okay. I know you'll find it hard to believe, but Ryan and Landon are my friends. Queen Tempest introduced us back when we were in college together. Wait here." Landon walked beside him, and they followed Ryan down the hallway to the shifter wing of the building.

They walked into a conference room to find Tempe bent over her laptop. She looked up and smiled sadly at Dave. "I am sorry for your loss, but his death was the only way to keep Queen Ceridwin from laying waste to this world."

He looked at the bejeweled urn on the desk but didn't pick it up. It had to be worth a fortune. "Did you ever find out why he hated preternaturals so much? I looked through all his papers I could get my hands on. I found nothing."

Tempe leaned back and stretched her back. "I know he had a twin who was killed by a bear when they were teenagers."

"I know that, so what?"

"He told numerous people that the bear was a shifter."

"Come on, my grandfather told me that story. Uncle Allen walked into a cave. Dad goaded him into it. The mother bear had cubs, and she defended them."

Tempe raised her hands in surrender. "I'm just telling you what he told others."

Dave picked up the urn and looked at it in disgust.

Tempe stood and placed her hand on Dave's shoulder. "No one knows what will set someone else off. Perhaps it happened as he said, perhaps it happened as your grandfather said. Doesn't matter. Your father developed a hatred for preternaturals, shifters specifically, and he couldn't overcome it. Perhaps he's at peace now."

"He doesn't deserve peace."

"Everyone deserves peace in the end," Tempe said.

"You're a good person," Dave looked at his friend. "I don't think I could forgive him for what he did to that fae, what he tried to do to Ryan and so many others if I were you."

"This isn't my first trip through the compassion quandary."

"Yeah, I guess not." He looked at the urn again. "I promised my mother I would stay with her for at least a month. She refuses to leave that house. I hate it. It represents all the lies my father told me."

"You should try to remember the good." Tempe handed him a bracelet.

"What's this?"

"My way of trying to keep you safe. Put it on your arm and leave it. No one else will see it. If you ever have need of me, take the bracelet off, and it will call to me."

He put the bracelet on and looked at it. "Why?"

"You've been my friend since the day we met at the community college. I have no doubt that someone will try to harm you at some point because of that friendship."

Chapter 50

"The next person who bows and addresses me as the Seelie Queen, Queen Tempest, or any form of address using the word queen, shall be found guilty of stupidity, and I shall behead them." Tempe stormed into the sovereign's office for the Alpha Clan meeting and plopped down into the only empty chair.

Ryan pressed his lips together to hide his smile. She was the last to arrive. In fact, the meeting was nearly over. Tempe had been chronically early before the realm queens changed her life. Joey and Fred bowed their heads for the same reason. Phoenix, Eli, and Quill laughed out loud. The rest of the Alpha Clan covered their mouths with hands, drinks, or tablets.

Sage looked over at Joey and Fred, "You guys are dismissed. I'll expect your reports tomorrow.

Both men beat a hasty retreat.

The door shut, and Tempe glared at Sage, "Have you told them?"

"No, I waited for you."

Tempe sighed and faced the cameras and her family, "I can no longer serve as the sovereign's enforcer. Aside from the fact that my dance card is well and truly full, it will be a conflict for a shifter meeting the Seelie Court under charges by the Sovereign's Enforcer."

No one said anything as they shuffled in their seats and angled to face Ryan. He stared at Tempe with his mouth open, not sure he was ready for the job. He quickly schooled his face into a mask. Things were changing fast, too fast. First, Ryan becomes the wielder of the Patron's Sword, and now he's the sovereign's enforcer? He needed adjustment time.

Tempe removed the large, oval stone ring from her left index finger and handed it to Ryan. "Sorry. It should have been centuries before you had to take this."

The ring that looked so large on Tempe's finger looked small in his hand. Ryan stared at it.

Tempe sighed, "It must be worn on your left index finger. The band will adjust to your size."

Ryan shrugged and put the ring on his finger. His eyes cut to Tempe, "Did the dragons make this ring?"

"Yes. I was a child. You will have to ask Kyan how it happened."

Quill, always willing to point out the elephant in the room, leaned forward. "Um, Tempe, are you still part of the Alpha Clan?"

"Of course, she is!" Sage huffed.

"Just as the judges are still members of their clan, coven, etc., I will continue to be a member of the Alpha Clan unless and until Sage releases all of her siblings from active work. I won't be doing a lot of day-to-day work, but I'm available for emergencies. Since I moved away from the Farseen, my loyalties have been with the shifters. It remains there."

"No one thinks otherwise," Lark exclaimed.

Tempe patted her on the shoulder, "Everyone is thinking it."

"Freakin' telepaths," Phoenix said with no heat. "How about a new family rule, no peeking in siblings' heads."

Tempe shrugged, "So many with the same thought are hard to block."

"Enough, I'll contact you individually to discuss new duties. Tempe and Ryan remain, everyone else, dismissed. Phoenix, send Kyan in," Sage leaned back in her chair and waited for the others to leave.

Ryan looked at the ring again. He was beginning to look like a girl. He had one of the tri-rings (to find Sage and Star) on his right ring finger, and now he had a ring on his left hand. At this rate, Ryan would be jewelry covered in no time. He glanced at the necklace Kyan wore that identified him as the sovereign's personal guard. Ryan had expected to wear the necklace before the assassin's ring, which was what everyone called the enforcer's ring. Another title he didn't want.

Although her eyes flashed with understanding, Tempe kept her features bland. "As soon as that ring is seen on your hand, you will be called the sovereign's assassin. Might as well be prepared for it."

He huffed but otherwise remained silent.

Kyan entered and claimed a seat between the sovereign and the door, as was his habit.

"The ruling of the Queen's Court took everyone by surprise, but relations with the human governments have improved." Sage stood and paced, something she only felt comfortable doing with her three closest advisors. "For now. The humans are still researching how the queens did what they did."

"I wish them luck. No one knows what the real powers of the five queens are." Kyan grinned and added, "Perhaps the dragon matriarchs know."

Sage returned to her seat and opened her tablet, "What about Lady Z? Any sightings lately?"

"No," Kyan leaned back in his chair and sighed. A powerful fae, one who could kick his butt, was nowhere to be found.

"I think she's still here." Tempe shrugged her shoulders. "No clue where, perhaps hanging out with the elementals, but she's still in this dimension."

Sage cleared her throat. "You sound sure of yourself."

Tempe ignored the group, and stared at the wall, carefully wording her response. "Elementals stay away from me if she's nearby. It's rather enjoyable."

"And you're just now mentioning this?" Sage raised an incredulous eyebrow.

"She normally doesn't stay around long enough for it to be a benefit, so I don't count on it."

Sage nodded her understanding and moved on to other business.

*****

After the meeting, Ryan and Kyan grabbed food in the cafeteria and sat in one of the soundproof cafe rooms with no windows. The meeting rooms had only just been completed, providing security for discussions while eating.

Kyan finished chewing a bite of excellently prepared roast and said, "You asked for this meeting. What's up?"

"Something has always bothered me about the spelled jewelry worn by the Alpha Clan."

"Besides the gaudiness and girlishness of the stuff?" Kyan grinned.

"Yeah," Ryan nodded. "You reset the stones every so often, but you aren't a spell caster. Who applies the spells?"

Kyan laid his fork down and placed his elbows on the table, staring Ryan in the eyes. "What do you think?"

"I think a powerful dragon is involved."

"You're right. Tulvir, green dragon supreme matriarch, was a friend of shifters long before Rayna married Lord Ellwood. I started working with her around the time Rayna and Ellwood married."

"How..."

Kyan raised a hand for silence. "That's a story for another day. What you need to know now is that Tulvir, and her son, Kulvir, help us to maintain peace between the dimensions."

"You knew? You knew Kulvir was alive and didn't tell Tempe?" Ryan asked in disbelief.

"She didn't ask. You don't know what Tempest was like after Val died. She blamed everyone. She despised everyone. She was Tempest, not the Tempe you know today. Even the fae bards quit singing songs about her in public. Everyone feared her. I met with Tulvir frequently. She knew but never asked about Kulvir, so I didn't mention him." Kyan leaned back in his chair, "I know you've been training with Kulvir. Val and Kulvir were amazing together. Kulvir is older and more powerful now, and you're at least as strong as Val. The two of you may be unstoppable. The fae will be wary."

"Then how did Lord Ellwood kill Val?"

"Dragons do not intrude on personal vendettas. That fight, between father and son, was extremely personal. Most songs the bards sing now are about Val and Tempe. The songs of Val and Kulvir have not been sung much since his death, but I understand that now, with you wielding the Patron's Sword and training with

Kulvir, those songs are being sung again. Perhaps if you ask Liron, he'll sing some for you." Kyan stood to leave. Bowing to his great-nephew, he said, "Ryan, third in the Alpha Clan, the sovereign's enforcer, wielder of the Patron's Sword, cohort of Kulvir, I bid thee adieu. As the dragons say,

Enter in peace.
Congregate in peace.
Leave in peace.
Or make the blood price so high,
Your enemies will desire peace."

From the Author

Thank you for taking this journey through one of the worlds of my mind. If you enjoyed the book, consider posting a review and telling a friend.

If you would like to get notifications of new releases and special offers on my books, please join my mailing list by going to https://nrtucker.com/contact-form/ and providing your email. Type NRTUCKER BOOKS in the comment section.

Books by N. R. Tucker

Farseen Chronicles

Deceived
Enthralled
Betrayed
Revealed
Destined

Finding Earth

Drifters Rising
The Maiden Voyage of the Okar Lane

More information about the worlds of N. R. Tucker's mind – including flash fiction, character lists, glossaries, and maps – can be found at

NRTucker.com